THE INFINITE GLADE

ALSO BY JAMES DASHNER

The Maze Runner Books

The Maze Runner

The Scorch Trials

The Death Cure

The Kill Order

The Fever Code

Crank Palace

The Maze Cutter Books

The Maze Cutter

The Godhead Complex

The 13th Reality Books

The Journal of Curious Letters

The Hunt for Dark Infinity

The Blade of Shattered Hope

The Void of Mist and Thunder

The Mortality Doctrine Books

The Eye of Minds

The Rule of Thoughts

The Game of Lives

Adult Books

The House of Tongues

#1 *NEW YORK TIMES* BESTSELLING AUTHOR

JAMES DASHNER

THE INFINITE GLADE

This is a work of fiction. Names, characters, places, and incidents either are the product of the author's imagination or are used fictitiously. Any resemblance to actual persons, living or dead, events, or locals is entirely coincidental.

 Published in the United States by Akashic Media Enterprises, also doing business as AME Projects. Visit us on the web at AkashicMediaEnterprises.com. Printed in China by We Think Ink. Interior formatting by Hannah Linder Designs.

Publisher's Cataloging-In-Publication Data
(Prepared by The Donohue Group, Inc.)

Names: Dashner, James, 1972- author.
Title: The infinite glade / James Dashner.
Description: First edition. | [Red Bank, New Jersey] : Akashic Media Enterprises, [2025] | Series: Dashner, James, 1972- Maze runner series. Maze cutter trilogy. | Interest age level: 012-018. | Summary: The Infinite Glade is the final book of The Maze Cutter series, resolving long-unanswered questions of The Maze Runner world ... The group of descendants along with Old Man Frypan are forced to choose between risking their lives to share the painful truth of the evolving maze trials with the world, or escape the chaos with their lives and let the deepest darkest of secrets of the maze stay buried in the glade forever.--Publisher.
Identifiers: ISBN: 9798988421535 (hardback) | 9798988421559 (paperback) | 9798988421542 (ebook)
Subjects: LCSH: Good and evil--Juvenile fiction. | Quests (Expeditions)--Juvenile fiction. | Survival--Juvenile fiction. | Truth--Juvenile fiction. | Secrecy--Juvenile fiction. | CYAC: Good and evil--Fiction. | Quests (Expeditions) | Survival--Fiction. | Truth--Fiction. | Secrets--Fiction. | LCGFT: Dystopian fiction. | Action and adventures fiction. | BISAC: YOUNG ADULT FICTION / Dystopian. | YOUNG ADULT FICTION / Action & Adventure / Survival Stories. | YOUNG ADULT FICTION / Science Fiction / Apocalyptic & Post-Apocalyptic.
Classification: LCC: PZ7.D2587 In 2025 | DDC: [Fic]--dc23

ISBN 9798988421535 (hardback)

First Edition

Akashic Media Enterprises supports the
First Amendment and celebrates the right to read.

This one is for Lynette.
She's the reason we're here.

PROLOGUE

Voice of the Sea

Annie Kletter steered her battered ship through a harsh and unforgiving ocean. An ocean that seemed endless and angry, the devilish sun constantly glinting off its peaks and troughs and slopes, each and every one a piercing of her sight. Of all things, an octopus clung to the hull of the *Maze Cutter* as waves pummeled the starboard side. Kletter had sympathy for the creature. She, too, had tried to escape her home.

This trip was her last chance.

Find the Immunes.

Find the missing pieces. Finally free every last person from the depths of the Flare, that century-old virus that had wreaked havoc across the decades. Madness and death. Death, death, death, so much death. And the virus was changing. Always changing.

"You've got to steer *into* the waves!" Kletter's first mate, Juan, shouted only inches away from her face. Sea spray mixed with his words.

"Haz algo!" the rest of the crew cried.

Kletter gripped the captain's wheel harder. She didn't need their constant opinions and shouts.

A dark storm hovered to the west, approaching quickly, the force of its winds already a great disturbance upon the vast water. Storms in the open ocean were unforgiving, but not as unforgiving as the Villagers. They were watching her every move. Every failure. She only needed them along for the ride to help convince the Immunes of the importance of their mission. The Villagers' desperation for a Cure might be the tipping point, to ensure the elders of the island to give consent, to send their most prized possessions back with her to the Villa. *Tell them of the Village where no babies have been born for decades, and they'll send you their own children happily.*

What an easy thing to say, to speculate, to sound philosophical.

But the truth burned Kletter from the inside out.

The truth of everything ate away at her, as unforgiving as this bastard of a sea.

Another squall of waves crashed upon the *Maze Cutter*; the Village crew had trouble staying on their feet. Kletter's legs were tired, so tired, beyond fatigued from the constantly rocking ship, her arms exhausted from steering into the calm spots of the ocean while increasing speed of the throttle. The storm was picking up its pace and ferocity. Soon, the sun would be swallowed by clouds.

Yes, she steered the ship.

The captain.

But she wasn't the one *in control.*

She never had been and she knew it very well.

No use running from the storm anymore. Kletter finally hit the waves head-on and went toward the darkness, into the beast. Things got worse—gales and roar and spray, constant braying from her companions—and then things got better. The storm wasn't nearly as bad as she'd thought. The winds calmed and the *Maze Cutter* eased back into the natural, soothing, up-and-down rhythms of the ocean instead of being swept away. Kletter's knees steadied under her with more strength as she put the boat in idle, gathering herself. But as soon as the rocking of the boat stilled, the crew grew even more irritated. They'd been low on food for days. Kletter walked over to calm them down: "Tranquilos."

"You keep saying that, but the days go by and we're not seeing any island," a woman named Edita said. Kletter had spent years traveling back and forth from the Villa studying Edita and her daughter Ximena. They were a complete anomaly.

Another crew woman stepped forward holding her belly as if she were pregnant, but no one from their village would ever be pregnant again. "What about us? You've given us hardly any rice these past two days. Tenemos hambre."

"La comida," Kletter said, and pointed to the octopus. "We'll be there soon."

"She's lying." Edita challenged Kletter in a way that only someone who's DNA challenged genetic codes could. Kletter preferred Edita behind a glass pod with her voice muted.

Kletter's joints were weak, her ankles in pain from standing at the captain's wheel for so long, but she stepped forward with confidence. The worst of the darkest clouds were moving on, a sign perhaps. "You'll survive." It wasn't a question or an option. They *had* to make it to the Immunes.

"She's lying," Edita shouted back to the others. "This isn't surviving!"

"You'll be fine!" Kletter raised her voice, walking over to Edita. "We'll *get* to the Immunes!" With one swift motion Kletter lifted her knife, reached over the railing of the boat, and stabbed the poor little octopus clinging to the hull. It wiggled and writhed. Kletter stabbed it again and again until its tentacles loosened and went limp. "There . . . dinner." Kletter flung the sea creature at Edita's feet.

"I couldn't see it until today . . ." Edita lacked any emotion as she spoke to the others, "I have no visions past this boat." The woman lowered her voice but kept speaking. Kletter's shoulders tensed. She absolutely hated it when the Villagers claimed these visions. In the decade or so Annie Kletter had been visiting the Villagers, studying them, testing them, none ever knew the real reasons behind it all. Or why she wanted to help them in the first place. If Edita had any sort of ability, she would have envisioned *that*, surely.

Visions. Nonsense.

"You're all going to be fine. You'll see." Visions were a part of the Villager's faith but only until that faith turned to fear. Kletter motioned to Juan. "Let's divvy some more rice to go with the octopus, eh?"

Juan nodded and let go of the captain's wheel. "How much?" he asked. "There isn't . . ."

He didn't have to finish the thought—Kletter knew the state of rations—but when Juan stepped away from the captain's wheel, she saw it. The truth of why they were lost at sea.

The unmanned wheel pulled *to the left.*

Kletter stared at the salt-crusted circle of metal, moving ever so slightly on its own.

Juan gave the captain a questioning look. Maybe food wasn't their biggest problem anymore. Panic filled every weakness in Annie Kletter's body to fuel her. She ran down the stairs to the lower deck and pulled the captain's log out of her pocket. She flipped to the page with the island's coordinates. Double-checked her calculations.

She knew it.

They should have reached the Immunes days, maybe weeks ago . . .

The wheel had a pull, probably from a damaged rudder. There was no way to calculate how many nautical miles they'd drifted. No way to course correct.

"Hell's bells." Kletter slammed the captain's log shut. The crew couldn't survive much longer without food on the boat, and this news just might topple them over the edge. They were already turning against her . . . and she had no idea how to get back on course. Someone had once told her that desperate times make for desperate measures. She did the only thing she could think of, her instincts telling her that the desperate time had come. Now.

She peeled back a board in the crawl space under the steps. A gun. Her secret gun. She grabbed the weapon and slid it into her back pocket, filled her front pockets with additional ammunition, then threw the now-useless captain's log into the hidey-spot. She snapped the board back into place.

The cabin above shook from the pounding of feet on the deck.

Her instincts had been spot-on.
They were coming for her.
Time for desperate measures.

PART ONE

WICKED is Good

There are things I remember. Good things. Even inside the bad, embedded this whole time . . . good, brilliant, spots of brightness. But I can only see them looking back.

Maybe there is some good in this, too. All this writing of hard, brutal times.

Somewhere in the bad, there is always the good.

—*The Book of Newt*

CHAPTER ONE

Fire and Fuel

I
ISAAC

Brutal, trying to keep up with Ximena. Hot and muggy, too.

As they hiked the tree-lined path leading away from the Villa, Isaac imagined it must be even harder for Old Man Frypan and Jackie —who still looked pale from her run-in with Lil Newt. Isaac tripped over tiny rocks, ridiculous and embarrassing, but his feet couldn't keep up with his brain. Nothing made sense. They walked farther and farther from the Villa, leaving poor Ms. Cowan behind . . . and Isaac didn't have a clue where they were going. He looked at Frypan and Jackie before asking Ximena again, "Hey . . . slow down. What did you mean about the Godhead being its own disease?"

Despite his exhaustion as they headed north, he'd walk a thousand more days if it meant finding Sadina and the others safe. He needed her and everyone else to be safe with the Godhead. He needed that and there was nothing else to think or say.

"You want me to spell it out for you?" Ximena turned around, her hand on her knife. "They're not good people, Isaac." She came to a full stop and Isaac, Jackie, and Frypan finally had a chance to catch up, catch their breath. "The Godhead will do anything in their power to *stay* in power."

Her eyes cut through to Isaac's core. Fire filled his belly and he imagined the inside of his body as a forge. Heat and flame.

She continued. "The Godhead isn't a cure, and they *have* no cure—I told you what happened to my village—it'll be completely wiped off the map in twenty-five years. Your island, too."

"B.S.," Jackie said between a couple of heavy breaths. "How could you say that? Our island is safe, in the middle of nowhere, and plenty of people to defend it, anyway." She turned to Frypan, who placed a well-worn comforting arm around her shoulders.

"Safest Safe Haven there is . . ." the former Glader assured her.

Isaac wanted to protest, but as the heat traveled up his throat he wasn't sure what to say. He wanted to agree with Jackie, insist that it was impossible for anyone to get hurt back home, but he also used to think the same of anyone ever *finding* their island. The impossible kept changing . . . and it made Isaac unsure what to believe.

"It'll be okay, Jackie," was all he could get out.

Isaac didn't have a family back on the island to miss him, but Jackie did. Who knew how many days it had been since the group of islanders left in the middle of the night with Kletter, and how much Jackie's poor family and the others' parents were freaking out.

"Everyone back home is safe and they always will be."

The emptiness of the words almost sucked the oxygen from the air around them.

He imagined how those back on the island were reacting to the missing kids and how the island as a whole was coping with some of their Senators being gone, too. He wanted to make them all proud by helping the Godhead find a Cure and put some good out into the world. He hated to think about Ximena being right—there not being a cure, the Godhead being bad people.

Jackie shook her head..

Trish's parents were probably keeping the council and Senate busy with demands to find their daughter. Dominic's parents were probably sending feathers into the ocean like toy boats, to ask the waves for good luck in bringing him home. And the others . . . probably just re-reading the good *Book of Newt*, hoping things would end much better for their lost children than it did for the famous Glader of the old days . . .

Old Man Frypan nodded as if he knew what Isaac was thinking.

Jackie rubbed sweat from her forehead. "Kletter told us that when we got to the Godhead we'd—"

Isaac touched her shoulder. "I know she did. Don't stress. We'll find the Godhead and the others."

Ximena laughed, firing up his inner forge even hotter.

"What's so funny?" He squinted at Ximena as she stood in front of the setting sun. An outline of soft light surrounded her.

"She thinks we're stupid, Isaac," Jackie said. "Just ignore her."

Ximena huffed. "The Godhead isn't going to help you . . ." She picked up a rock and pitched it to the side with a grunt, sending the thing all the way over the broken cliff. She mumbled something Isaac couldn't understand.

"Huh?" he asked.

"The Villas, the Godhead, it all has to burn to the ground . . ." She could've been talking about a bonfire on the beach, she said it so nonchalantly.

"Alright . . ." Old Man Frypan sat on a tree stump along the trail they'd been walking. "We're far enough from the Villa, and this looks like a good place to camp for the night." He drew a circle in the dirt just in front of him with his walking stick. "Jackie?"

She didn't waste time before gathering kindling for a fire, probably glad for a distraction. "I'll find some beach greens and berries." She completely ignored Ximena.

Ximena definitely noticed. "I'm not saying this to hurt you. I'm just telling you the truth. The Godhead is a big lie they tell themselves and others." But it was clear that everyone had chosen to ignore her negativity for now.

Jackie dropped a pile of sticks, and Isaac started sparking them.

"No, wait." Ximena waved her hands over Isaac and Jackie. "A fire will only bring trouble."

"We've fires every night, no trouble." Isaac blew softly on the kindling to spark a bigger flame. The sticks cracked as they shared the blossoming fire.

"That's the best sound I've heard all day," Frypan said.

Isaac certainly knew what he meant. There were nights back on the island—after Isaac's mom and dad had died—that he clung to the last glowing remnants of a fire. He'd stay awake at night, unable to sleep, and watch the small flickers of light fade until the darkest of nights were over. The forge had been Isaac's saving grace . . . a force to ignite the light back into things by burning them completely. Fire was Isaac's friend. A way to burn up what wasn't needed and make things feel new again.

Jackie fed the small flames with dry brush.

Then Ximena kicked dirt on top of it all, putting it out.

"Hey!" Jackie stood up.

"No. I'm not risking anyone from the Villa finding us." Ximena rested her hand on the knife against her hip, looking crazier than a half-Crank. "I'll never go back with Carlos or the others. Worst of all Professor Morgan." She paced a few steps from the trail, toward the edge of the cliff.

"It's fine. Everything's going to be fine . . ." Isaac whispered to anyone who cared to hear, trying to make his voice sound as calm as possible. Whatever Ximena had been through at the Villa before, it was bad. Very bad. They wouldn't let anyone take her back. "We're far enough from the Villa that no one will find us. We're safe here. They're too busy worrying about all those machines you destroyed, anyway." He tried to especially lighten that last part.

Old Man Frypan, unfazed, extended his walking stick to draw another circle, outline for a new fire spot. "No sense in being paranoid . . . we're here together and they'd have to take all of us if they take you."

Jackie didn't waste any time moving the best pieces of wood to the new circle.

"You don't understand . . ." Ximena looked so frustrated she could bust open. "You may not think they'll come after you, and they probably won't. But they'll be looking for me." Her frustration turned into defeat, shoulders slumping.

"Because of how they studied you?" Isaac asked, trying hard to understand the extent of her fear.

"No . . ." She slowly took off her pack and unzipped the front pocket. "Because of what I took before I left . . ."

"What . . . ?" Jackie looked up from the sticks in her hands.

There remained just enough sunlight for Isaac to see the small object Ximena pulled from her bag. A glass vial, filled with a dark liquid, something handwritten on its label. But she didn't let them stare too long before she shoved it back in her pack.

"What's that?" Jackie asked.

Isaac felt a pang in his gut. "You stole something?"

Frypan just shook his head at the nonsense and tapped his walking stick against his shoe.

"You think I'd be able to get into the master Villa without leverage or something to offer them?" Ximena zipped up her bag with a ferocious swipe. "It's the Cure."

Silence. A very, very long silence.

"I thought you said there was no Cure?" Isaac asked.

Another moment of quiet, except for the buzzing insects.

Jackie reached for some question to make it all make sense. "If that's the Cure then why is Cowan still in a coma?"

Ximena repositioned the bag on her back. "You really don't get it, do you?" She looked directly at Frypan, but apparently *he* didn't get it either. "I shouldn't have shown you." She walked back toward the edge of the cliff.

"Just tell us more. So . . . so we can understand." Isaac walked on Ximena's heels.

"Because Cowan doesn't have the Flare. What about that don't you all understand? She's having some kind of genetic reaction to something they haven't seen before. Probably from all the inbreeding on your island."

Jackie fumed at that nonsense. "We're not inbred!" She dropped her sticks and charged at Ximena before Isaac could get between them. Ximena slipped the bag off her shoulder and shoved it into Isaac's chest.

"Jackie, stop!" Isaac shouted. She pushed Ximena and Ximena pushed back, even harder. Isaac looked down at the pocket that supposedly held the Cure as the women continued to tussle.

Ximena spat her next words. "How are you so stupid to not realize that a fire makes smoke—signals for any doctor, Crank, or degenerate to find where we are? Huh?" This didn't make Jackie feel better. They went at it, another round of pushing and shoving.

"Hey, stop! Stop it!" Isaac cradled the bag with one arm while he put the other in between the two. He'd only seen Jackie fight one person before this, a half-Crank that ended up dead. He didn't want to wait and see what she might do to Ximena.

Frypan sat and spoke calmly as he watched on. "Eh, let them get it all out, Isaac. It's like runners fighting in the Glade . . . they just need to be heard. They need to vent. Who Ximena is truly mad at . . . isn't Jackie, anyhow."

"None of this makes sense!" Jackie took a step back from Ximena but her voice got louder. "There's no Cure, but you *have* the Cure?" She threw her arms into the air. "Which is it?"

Ximena shook her head. "Just because they call it a Cure, doesn't mean it actually is one." She grabbed her bag from Isaac, her eyes accusatory, as if she wasn't the one who just shoved it into his chest. The more time he spent with this girl, the less he understood her. But he wanted to, for all their sakes.

The Cure is what brought the *Maze Cutter* to the islanders and wreaked havoc and mayhem on their lives ever since. Maybe what the Cure meant wasn't the same as they assumed from Kletter. That woman didn't exactly expound on what to expect from the Cure or the Godhead. "I believe you . . ." Isaac said softly.

Ximena looked at him, eyebrows raised. "You do?"

He nodded. "If this isn't a Cure for us, maybe it's a Cure for the Godhead and their people, I don't know. But what's in this vial is obviously more important than life to them, and Professor Morgan would crawl on her hands and knees to get it back. I do know that."

Jackie scoffed and turned away from him, for some reason reminding him of Sadina whenever he'd take Trish's side. But he didn't want to pick sides in all this. He just wanted to be honest and get honesty back.

"Come on . . . Jackie . . ." Isaac needed her to know that he understood her, too. He wanted peace more than anything right then.

"Isaac . . ." Jackie said, but kept her back turned to the group.

He walked up to her and braced himself for anger or tears . . . but Jackie's face didn't show any emotion. It was completely blank.

"What?" Isaac asked. "What's wrong?" But no words came in reply. She only pointed northeast. Isaac looked, then squinted. Just above the tree line floated puffs and whirls of faint smoke, trailing higher and higher into the sky. Someone else, not very far from them at all, had started their own fire for the night.

2
ALEXANDRA

The smell of burnt flesh rose into the Alaskan air along with the ashes of St. Petersburg. Madness. Death. Ashes. One of the only smells that had seared itself into Goddess Alexandra Romanov's permanent memory was the burning of bodies from all those years ago in Crank Palace. A smell she could conjure at any moment in time, although she never wanted to, of course. She tried to focus on the sacred digits, but charred death made it difficult. Death and rebirth. Birth and death. The cycle continued, but now the Goddess had something the Evolution could have only ever dreamed of.

Dearest Sadina, Grandniece of Newt.

"I'm sorry about your city, Goddess," dear Sadina said. So sweet. So innocent. So simple. So easily converted.

"Oh, the city will be rebuilt." Alexandra looked over her shoulder at the charnel as they walked south with the rest of the group. "You will help with that." She lifted Sadina's small hand into her own and patted the top of it three times.

The girl named Trish spoke. Sadina's girlfriend. "We came to help, but I don't know if we can rebuild a whole city. There's a special group on our island who do the building, and let's just say we didn't qualify."

"I meant metaphorically . . ." The Goddess paused, trying to think of how she could possibly explain everything that needed to be explained. "You'll help more than you know."

She faked a smile at Trish. The world would soon return to its rightful Evolution. Sometimes moving forward meant needing to first take a few steps back. That was all the war was. A death before a fiery rebirth of sacred Evolution more powerful and advanced than even the Godhead knew it could be.

Red flashed in Alexandra's vision so bright that she stumbled and winced.

"Goddess?" the boy without a weapon asked. "Do you need to stop for a minute?" The others turned around.

Sadina grabbed Alexandra's arm, helping her balance. "Thank you," Alexandra said as she looked at Sadina, but a red static covered the girl. Alexandra pinched the bridge of her nose, hard. "I think I'm just a little dizzy from everything."

"We can stop and give you a minute to collect yourself," the one with Orange hair said.

"No, no. On with it. We must go." Alexandra ignored their stares and continued walking. "Yes. On with it." She felt an unrecognizable sadness come over her. No war could ruin the fact that Alaska was home to the Maze, and it would still be the home of the Cure. Her vision of Evolution would continue because it must.

"Are we sure we put down the anchor when we landed?" the older woman asked. "I think it might have floated away . . ."

Alexandra didn't care much for the one they called Roxy. She reminded her of the withered Pilgrim who'd turned on her. Although closer to Alexandra's age than the younger ones, she looked ancient. Not everyone had the Godhead's DNA.

"We're close. It's right up here, around the curve of this coast." The boy with the gun spoke. He wore the same uniform as the soldiers who'd shot arrows at Flint, the ones who'd killed her precious servant. "We're not going to miss it."

Alexandra couldn't rid herself of the scenes of horror from her mind and the taste of crumbling buildings from her throat. She coughed just thinking about the city of Gods turning to dust. "Good. We need to get out of here." And just as the smell of burnt flesh reminded her of the Flare Pits, a squealing noise began to seep into the smoke-filled air and reminded her of the screams in Crank Palace.

The screams of those past The Gone.

"What is that, a war-coyote?" the smaller girl asked.

"Sounds more like a pig," Trish added. The islanders knew nothing of the Alaskan shore or the animals and the death it carried before the war, but as soon as the child said the word *pig*, Alexandra knew exactly where the noise came from. Was it unlikely? Yes. Impossible? No.

She had unfinished business to attend to.

"Go on ahead, I have to take care of something."

Alexandra excused herself, began to turn away. But the group stopped walking and looked at her as if they were capable of doing nothing without her expert guidance and directives. "Go ahead. I need a moment." She waved them off. Very used to dismissing her Evolutionary Guard, she was also used to them *listening* to her. "Go on ahead," she said again more forcefully.

They just stood there looking at each other.

"But you just had a dizzy spell," Sadina said. "I'll go with you."

"No," the soldier snapped. "You stay here, Sadina. I'll go with her." He stepped forward.

The Goddess took a deep breath and tried to relax all the muscles in her face. Time for a little lie. "If you must know, I need to relieve myself."

"Then I'll go with you," the soldier with orange hair said. "I'll just be—"

"Absolutely not." Alexandra used all the power of her training in her voice. She'd sooner trust the old hag they called Roxy than depend on either of the two soldiers with the same clothing as those who killed her guards. Flint may have been a useless tool but he was *her* useless tool. Clearing her throat, she said "Like you mentioned, I'll see it along the coast, can't miss it." She forced a smile. "Please. I just need a private moment to myself. And who knows, maybe I'll get lucky and witness a *Hollowing* from the sounds of it."

"She's a grown Godhead, for crying out loud. She can handle it." Roxy nodded and shooed the children off. "We'll see you at the ship." The ancient hag waved.

"Thank you." Alexandra touched the palms of her hands together. *Too easy.*

The soldiers shrugged but listened to Roxy and continued on. Alexandra watched over her shoulder until the group of teenagers and Roxy disappeared along the bend of the coast. The Goddess continued inland, following the direction of the squeals.

Did it sound like a pig?

Yes. Yes, it did.

The most human pig she'd ever known.

CHAPTER TWO

Second-Sight

I
MINHO

Soldiers decided their trust in two ways:

By someone's character, and their competence.

And Alexandra had already proven to have neither. "I don't trust her." Minho looked over his shoulder to Orange after he watched the shape of Alexandra's cloak disappear into the woods. Minho knew enough to identify a liar in his opponent, and the way she squinted when she said the word *Hollowing* was suspicious. "A Godhead, someone of the highest order, would never walk into a brutal 'carving and gutting of a human' alone. They always had guards. Tons of them. . . ." The Remnant Nation's Orphan soldiers were taught just as much about the Evolutionary Guards and how to circumvent them as they were taught about the Godhead. "I bet she never even saw a Hollowing."

"Claims she did."

"She's lying. She's going to get a weapon or something." Minho adjusted the gun strap on his shoulder.

Dominic scoffed. "She doesn't look like she even feeds herself, let alone ever handled a weapon."

"Funny. I thought the same about you when we first met." Minho lightly punched the kid. "I'll be back in a few." He motioned a hand signal to Orange that meant he'd meet her at the rendezvous—the *Maze Cutter*. Orange kept one hand on her weapon and nodded.

Orphans. Always on the ready.

"No, no, wait a minute here." Roxy held her palm out to Minho. "We should really stick together. There's explosions over there and who knows how many half-Cranks might be left in the woods." She shook her head. "I'm not letting you out of my sight. I can't lose you." Then she looked at the others. "Not any of you."

Minho felt something weigh upon him, heavier than all the steel arm and ankle training-weights from the Remnant Nation put together. He felt the fear in Roxy's eyes. Scared of losing him. He never had someone he wanted to do right by before, but he sure as hell wanted to do right by Roxy. "I've got to go alone. I promise I'll be back. Soldiers promise. I've got to see what it is she's—"

"Why don't you trust her?" Sadina asked, never sounding more naive. "We came here to find the Godhead. Well, she's it."

Minho came for a different reason, unbeknownst to the others: he wanted to *join* the Godhead . . . but not anymore. Definitely not anymore. "A Godhead wearing a Pilgrim's cloak."

"So?" Sadina countered. "It's colder up here, they have cloaks. Big deal."

"So, she's either a Pilgrim who's deceiving *us*, or she's a Godhead who's deceiving her *people*." Minho motioned back to St. Petersburg and the black smoke trailing in the air. "If a Godhead is so powerful, where are the other members and why is she out here trying to escape her city like a coward? Any true Godhead would stand with their people. They would stand with their city." He didn't know how else to say it, but either way, Alexandra Romanov wasn't a good person. He trusted his gut.

Miyoko suddenly spoked up. "What does the cloak matter? You're wearing the clothes of a Remnant Soldier, so maybe we shouldn't trust you!" She pointed at Minho's and Orange's uniform.

Minho had never really felt like he belonged in the Remnant Nation. Even as an orphan, he knew he'd rather die alone than die standing beside them in battle. Every bite of gunfire and explosion echoing in the distance of Alaska, north of where they stood, felt like a hammer in his chest. "It matters," was all he could say. He wouldn't waste time explaining all these things to Miyoko or anyone else. All those years training to be a soldier taught him how to kill, how to fight in battle, how to die honorably . . . but he left the walls of the Remnant Nation so he could learn how to *live*.

"Listen," Orange said, and with that one word Minho knew what would come next. Anytime the Grief Bearers wanted to sell their lies as truth or their disappointment as opportunity, they'd start by saying *listen*. "We left the Remnant Nation because we believe in the Godhead. We didn't want to kill her like the others. We're on your side." Lies, of course. But Orange calmed things down, and Minho could have left it at that. Probably should have.

But he didn't want to lie and manipulate the first friends he ever had. He had to say it . . . "Maybe she's not the Godhead. Maybe she's just some crazy woman who we found living on the outskirts of the city . . ."

Orange gave Minho a cringed look of exhaustion.

Everyone got quiet.

Sadina took a step back and held her heart as if Minho had just pushed a knife right into her chest. Did she really believe this much in the Godhead? Had they been brainwashed?

She proceeded to let Minho have it. "We didn't leave our homes, get kidnapped after watching Kletter's throat get slit, get separated from Isaac, my mom, and Old Man Frypan to listen to you complain about what the Godhead is *wearing*. We left our homes, our loved ones, to come here and try to do what we can to help those we can, and if what you came here for is different—then go do whatever it is you came here for. Go fight the Godhead and the city with the rest of your people and die in those flames for all I care—but don't mess up the good we're trying to do to help find a Cure."

She turned swiftly away and continued walking down the coast toward the *Maze Cutter*. Trish, Miyoko, and Dominic—he with a *whatcha gonna do* shrug—followed in support, but Roxy waited behind for Minho.

As they stormed off to the *Maze Cutter*, it had definitely become clear that something about Sadina had changed from the moment they anchored the ship in Alaska. Desperation and death. With every half-Crank they had killed, their perceptions had changed. Minho knew the human-looking things, chained together, were probably the first real threat the islanders had ever seen, let alone had to kill with their own hands. He brushed off Sadina's dramatic exit. Every time he'd had to kill a trespasser back in the Remnant Nation, he felt like he had to prove something afterward—that he didn't kill for nothing.

"Come on." Roxy waited.

Minho shook his head and looked back to the woods where the Pilgrim cloak disappeared. "I'll catch up to you."

"No, no. I'm not having that." Roxy pleaded, "The only thing in those woods is danger, and I cannot lose you. Who cares about the Godhead, if she's the Godhead or not. Let her go. If she comes back, we'll deal with it all then." She took two steps and then another toward the *Maze Cutter*. "Come on, son."

The Godhead who Minho refused to call a Godhead, or a God, or a Goddess, traveled into the woods alone for a reason . . . and Minho needed to find out why. "I'm sorry." He knew it would disappoint Roxy terribly, but he needed to know.

"I'll come back, soldier's promise."

2
ISAAC

"Come on, we've got to see who it is." Jackie locked eyes with Isaac, and he knew what that look meant. Hope. He couldn't say it out loud but he knew exactly what his friend was thinking. *What if something happened to the Maze Cutter and the others never made it to Alaska?* What if around that fire up ahead sat Minho, Orange, Sadina, Trish, Miyoko, and Dominic? Hope needed every question and every curiosity answered, or hope would only multiply itself before turning into *what ifs*.

Isaac nodded to Jackie. Sometimes hope is what made you take the next step.

The smoke rising up into the sky wasn't far from where they stood. "You both can stay here." Isaac turned to Ximena and Old Man Frypan, still parked on the log. "Jackie and I can reach there before it gets too dark and come back to you."

But Frypan leaned hard on his walking stick and stood up. "Can't sit here just stirring on it. I'll go with you. They were all in agreement . . . except for Ximena.

"You're kidding, right?" Ximena asked, then mumbled something else that Isaac didn't catch.

"What?" Isaac asked.

"La verdad quedará enterrada. Extraños nos enterraran. *The truth will remain buried and strangers will put us in the ground.*" She said it with so much confidence that Isaac felt dumb for wondering what it meant.

"Strangers will put us in the ground?" he repeated.

"Just say what you're trying to say!" Jackie shouted at Ximena. "We don't know every last one of your stupid Village riddles!"

Isaac stood between the two in case another fight broke out.

"Second-sight . . ." Ximena sighed. "Your elders didn't teach you?" She looked to Old Man Frypan as if he were responsible for everything they did and didn't know. And in a way, he was.

"We taught them well . . ." Frypan cleared his throat. "They're good kids."

"Yeah," Isaac said defensively. "We may not have the same history as your Village, and we're not going to know all the same things, but I bet there're things the Gladers of Old taught us that you don't know."

Isaac had heard every legend of the Gladers of Old, how they had their memories wiped and were left to learn everything all over again in the Glade. There were a few times Isaac wished his memory could be erased, but that was before he found the forge. Forging gave him steps to remember, things to learn, a reason to have memories again. He imagined that's what the surviving Gladers who established the island communities went through as well, all those years ago after their nightmare ended. And whether Ximena thought so or not, the islanders knew things—Most important of all, they knew how to survive.

He tried to sound conciliatory. "Look, there's a chance the fire up ahead could be our friends, that maybe they never made it to Alaska. We have to find out."

"You're saying what you want to be true." Ximena shook her head. "You see fire up ahead with your sense of sight, and you want it to be your friends so bad that it's all you're thinking about. Every one of you." Ximena pointed to the islanders. "And me, I see that smoke going up to the sky and I see danger." She looked to Old Man Frypan. "They're looking at what they see—but all things we see, lie."

Isaac didn't think his eyes were lying. "You see the smoke too, right?"

"Yes, but . . ." Ximena sighed at the sky as if to rebuke it. "You need to look beyond what you see at first to what you feel or hear afterward."

"So we're going to head over and pay real close attention to what we see?" Frypan asked, tapping his walking stick against the ground.

Isaac waited for Ximena to agree or disagree, but she just looked frustrated.

"It doesn't matter, come on Isaac." Jackie motioned for him to join her in investigating the smoke.

"No. Wait." Ximena held her hand up. "Please. It's so loud. Give me a minute to explain . . ."

"What's so loud?" Isaac asked. "Can you hear smoke all of a sudden?"

"No." Ximena finally smiled. "The smoke isn't loud, my inner-knowing is. Your senses are all connected to your interpretation of something . . ." She looked up and down the trail, but for what, Isaac didn't know. "Those flour cakes at the Villa . . . I bet you were excited when you first saw them?"

"Yeah, we were starving." He had carried Jackie's limp body half a mile and his muscles had been shaking with hunger and fatigue when they'd reached the Villa.

"The Assistants gave them to you with big smiles. And then you held them in your hands and felt how the flour cakes were rock hard, right?" Ximena asked.

"Sure thing. And then we still *tried* biting into the nasty buggers." Old Man Frypan really emphasized the word *tried*.

"Hard and dry like sand from our beaches." Isaac hoped the workers in the Villa fed Jackie something better while she healed. "Did they give you those, too?" Isaac asked her.

Jackie nodded, barely, as if she didn't want to prove Ximena right. "I could only eat half of one."

Ximena had gained a small—a rather tiny—victory. "So your sense of sight lied to you. At first-sight you thought just because they gave you something to eat with a smile that it would taste delicious. But it wasn't even edible. And if you saw one of those terrible cakes now, you'd know better. Wouldn't you?" Ximena nodded as if she'd just proven the earth was round.

Isaac wouldn't admit it, but he had packed a couple of flour cakes in his bag just in case they didn't have anything else to eat, even though they were barely edible. Still, it seemed a silly argument compared to their circumstances.

"Yeah," Isaac agreed to keep the peace. "So the second time we see something—"

"No. Second-sight isn't about seeing something *again.* It means listening for the truth before you are even able to touch or taste it."

Jackie looked up at the smoke trail in the air and then back to Isaac with a shrug.

"I mean . . . you really believe in this?" Isaac asked. "So, what, second-sight is like the *feeling* of what you actually see?" It seemed very far-fetched.

"True sight." Ximena lowered her voice. "And yes, I do. See the truth without attaching what you'd *hope* the truth to be . . ."

Isaac had never met anyone like Ximena. He couldn't pretend to understand these premonitions she supposedly received, but he wanted to. He really did. Isaac's mom had feelings sometimes, ones he used to think were just a mom being overly protective. But . . . she'd had a bad feeling that morning before the storm rolled in that took her life and the rest of his family. She'd told Isaac more than once, *Don't forget where you come from*, as if she knew there would come a day—soon—when she wouldn't be there to remind him. And cheesy or not, he'd try for the rest of his life to make her proud.

"We want to find the truth," Jackie finally relented, "but we also need to find our friends." She stepped closer to Ximena. "You'll stay here, then, and start a camp for us?" She gave a half-smile. It was a start. At least with Ximena making them a fire they could find their way back to her in the dark.

"No. I'll head farther north." Ximena took wide steps up the trail.

Cure or no Cure, Isaac didn't want to separate from her.

"Wait. We should stick together, right?" He looked to Frypan for support.

"The boy's right. We'd like you to stay with us. It doesn't make a lick of sense for any of us to split up."

But Ximena didn't stop walking. Isaac, Jackie, and Frypan followed.

"Please . . ." Isaac asked quietly, hoping Ximena's second-sight agreed. "When I first saw you back at the Villa, at first-sight or second-sight . . ." Isaac tried to speak her style without sounding like an idiot.

"I thought you could help us—and you did, you helped us escape." He didn't want to lose her now. "Stay with us. Just the night."

Ximena stopped walking and turned around. She squinted at Isaac.

"Fine. But only because you had second-sight at the Villa. And I'm hanging back in case whoever's up ahead aren't your friends . . ."

Isaac smiled, his own tiny little victory. "Good. You'll see, it'll be fine."

He dared let himself hope. They'd get there, and as soon as he saw the others around the fire, he'd run to hug Sadina, and then Trish, and then Dominic, Miyoko, Minho, Orange, and Roxy—in that exact order. He'd have to figure out a way to tell Sadina about her mom stuck back in the Villa, but maybe Ximena could help her understand all that the Professor and the others were doing to help her mom. He'd wait to let Old Man Frypan tell the story of the Griever. Or not. Isaac still needed to process that whole thing. *How big the Griever stood. The noises and clicks it made. How scared Ximena looked when it happened. Jackie's scream when Cowan got stabbed. The Griever recognizing Frypan and trying to break the glass pod to get to him.*

He shuddered, losing that brief flash of hope pretty quickly.

And so they went to check it out, after all. As they walked toward the wispy smoke in the distance, Isaac had a thought. A crazy thought. Maybe he'd experienced this second-sight thing when he'd seen the Griever. There'd been some very confusing thoughts and feelings, and not all of it fear and horror.

He decided to ask Ximena about it when Old Man Frypan wasn't around.

Down the trail they went, brushing past leaves and stepping on bugs.

CHAPTER THREE

Thru the Brush

I
ALEXANDRA

The Goddess followed the piggish sounds of squealing terror.

Not always the smartest thing to do.

She felt far more uncertainty than she'd let on, even to herself. Could it be memories from Crank Palace, bubbling up to the surface of her mind? Were the sounds in fact joining her in this dense reality? The horrific sights of war had shaken her beliefs, momentarily. She'd almost gone mad before the children found her. *But they heard the hog squeal, too.* She focused on what she knew to be true and recited the digits.

1, 2, 3, 5, 8, 13 . . .

Her feet sank into the wet, soft dirt of the inland, a mess not meant for a God. Never in her memory had her feet both burned with pain while feeling so completely frozen. Flaring Discipline be damned she grew so tired of these contradictions. She needed a steady truth. The Principles. The digits.

21, 34, 55, 89 . . .

Although war's flames filled the sky above her with smoke, she felt the red blanket of the aurora creeping in. The Pilgrims would never trust the sky above them again. They'd never believe her now that the aurora had lost its mystery and danger. And so be it, they might as well be dead. Those who denied the Evolution, who feared the future, weren't deserving of its gifts.

In a way, the war was a blessing.

Purging Alaska of those who doubted her and the righteous Evolution. Her feet took her further inland and she moved quickly around bushes of wild rose hips tangled and overtaking what had once been a clearing for fishermen. With every step, she recited the digits. The Goddess couldn't help but laugh to herself, just a little. The army could take away anything on the surface of Alaska that they wanted to. They could even damage the reputation of the aurora in the sky for those Pilgrims who lived to remember it as a precursor to war rather than Evolution . . . but that army could never, ever, touch the Maze below her feet.

No. The Maze would remain sacred.

And she would rebuild her city underground.

Yes. What was old would be new again.

She stepped over swampy puddles and entered a field of thick brush where she saw the gleam of metal. A crashed Berg, all hulking metal and angles and joints. She crept closer to its heavy mass, looked through a dusty window. What she saw inside didn't surprise her, but it amused her in the darkest fashion. The Evolution had brought Sadina and the Cure to her, and here she stood watching Mikhail thrash like a trapped rat. Ah, Mikhail. Strapped inside the Berg. Squealing like the mad animal he had always been. She almost laughed at the absurdity of the sound.

"SQUUUUEEEE . . ." Mikhail's body flailed and thrashed. Alexandra moved closer to see the extent of damage the incompetent fool had done to himself this time. *Where was he hurt, besides the depths of his mind?* She knocked on the glass of the Berg three times.

Mikhail's eyes remained closed, squeezed shut in what looked to be utter agony. But she saw no blood on his face or broken bones jutting from his skin. She opened the door to the Berg and lifted the bottom of her Pilgrim's cloak as she stepped inside. "Mikhail." A putrid smell assaulted her nostrils. "Mikhail!" She slapped him hard across the face; his eyes opened—wide, searching, terrified. Stuck inside the Berg and stuck inside his own mind, his pupils were dilated. Unfocused. Mad.

"Dorogaya." He whispered nonsense.

Alexandra finally recognized the smell. Turmeric and urine. She looked down at Mikhail's lap and he had indeed pissed himself. "You've done well, Mikhail." She said it with the usual sarcasm reserved for the inferior mind. He never understood the simple confines of speech after The Gone. Simple words, idioms, figures of speech passed through him without sense or meaning.

Mikhail sputtered out more words as he wiggled back and forth, his right arm still blindly searching for the latch of the belt to release his body. "I did it. It took decades, but I did it."

Alexandra could easily have leaned over and clicked it open, but she didn't. No. She wouldn't. Not until he explained more about what he did or didn't do.

"You did it," she repeated. Nicholas had taught her long ago that the best way to get someone else to admit everything they'd never planned on telling you was to repeat their last three words. Mikhail's past-the-Gone mind was far too simple to understand such manipulation. Even Nicholas—who taught her that very trick—was too simple to know when she practiced it on him. It had been the only way she could safely have a conversation with him. The only way she knew how to keep him from reading her own mind—to repeat what he wanted to hear.

"I did it," Mikhail said again. "The Golden Room of Grief held me as I told the Remnant Nation how to build their army and how to weaken ours." He laughed, his eyes now closed. "I stood in the middle of blood-red walls and with a hooded cloak and told them all your secrets. All it took to take the Godhead down." He laughed again with those eyes squeezed shut. "Nicholas' plan was never going to stop. *You* were never going to stop . . ."

It took all of Alexandra's energy to not react. Scream. Kill him right there.

Mikhail was a damn fool.

She slowly inhaled a deep breath, reciting the digits in backward order. Starting with the largest in her mind and counting down. Mikhail was just stupid enough to tell her more if she asked. "Never going to stop?" she repeated. He was right about that. No one could stop her.

No one and nothing could stop the Evolution.

"The lies would never stop . . ." Mikhail murmured and his voice faded. She slapped him back to consciousness. "Lies!" he shouted.

Mikhail's life was the lie. Nicholas should have never brought him back from The Gone.

"You never stopped being weak," Alexandra seethed through her teeth. "You never understood what was needed for humanity to rise with the winds." She leaned in close and whispered her breath against his cheek. "So weak the very air around you threatened to bring you down."

She slapped him again, hard, stinging her own hand. His eyes shot open and saw her for just a moment before they closed again. Stupid, muttering fool. She looked around the Berg. How inept did Mikhail have to be to land it so poorly? Nicholas would shake his head in shame —if he had a head to roll.

"To take *you* down," Mikhail muttered, his eyes fluttering. St. Petersburg burned in the distance; the land would be scarred for eternity. She winced, but knew well enough not to scream out all the obscenities she wanted to hurl at Mikhail—the islanders might hear and would surely come running.

The space between Alexandra's eyebrows burned. She pinched it. It took all she had to hold back a deep, visceral string of words. She instead whispered to him, quiet and calm.

"Dear Mikhail, you have not taken me down." Her mind's eye blossomed red with anger, her vision static again, but her words floated with incredible force, as if someone else had taken over her body. She held this man hostage with her hatred. The red aurora completely blanketed her mind. "I am standing here. And I am alive. The city and the people will suffer, but the Evolution will live on forever. You are a failure." She couldn't help but smile, feeling a bit mad herself—but the Cure waited for her along the coast. She would travel to the Villa, and all of this would be but a blip in history. A small, meaningless, bump in the road to Evolution.

Those who don't evolve, die.

"No . . ." Mikhail groaned.

"Yes. You couldn't do what you needed to, so you trained an entire army to kill me—but they are failures, too." For just a moment, she was flattered for what Mikhail had gone through, sneaking off every other month for years to gather an army. She felt certain his absences and the Hollowings were intertwined. That he initiated the Hollowings to kill others in order to satiate his own need for madness, just enough to focus on his main task at hand. And what an opulent plan it was. What an absurd waste of time to train hundreds of soldiers to rise up and kill her, while he couldn't find his way out of a crashed Berg.

The Evolution took care of itself, as it always did.

Flaring justice. Flaring justice.

"It wasn't you . . ." Mikhail's head dropped to his shoulder. Confusion. Madness.

She slapped him awake again. "Speak!"

Mikhail coughed. "It's not just about you. Your ego . . ." He choked out a laugh. "Your ego is as big as your vision, if you think this war is just about you!" He coughed again. "The Godhead is everything your ideas touched. Every place you put your plan into motion. It's all been a lie. Everything's a lie that had to be destroyed so the truth . . . the truth could evolve back to it's original form . . ."

Alexandra's stomach burned. *The truth.* Mikhail didn't know his ass from an eyelash. "What do you know about the truth?" she asked, remembering all the ways Mikhail's nightmares had become his reality. All the nightmare images of fire and war that he'd discussed with Nicholas. He had created the very thing he feared most.

"Evolution . . ." He reached for his back as he continued to cough. "True Evolution . . ." He spat a wad of yellow phlegm. A peasant would have had more class. "You've learned nothing from being a part of the Godhead? You think the power you hold is real?" He gagged on his own coughs. "Nothing is real . . ."

The man couldn't be more wrong.

She spoke with measured calm. "You never had any power in the Godhead." He'd always held them back. She'd felt him working against her; she just had no idea the scale of it. "That's how we're different, you and I . . ."

He opened his eyes and his giant pupils met hers. For a moment he stopped his mumbling and his squealing and just looked at her like he used to, before everything—including their names—changed. After Nicholas brought him back from Crank Palace and The Gone, his mind never quite recovered, despite the visions he claimed to see. She wondered how much of Mikhail's reality was purely manufactured by Nicholas—telling him *what* to see and *how* to see it. She'd never forget the week or two in between Alexandra losing Mikhail for good and finding herself, her *true self*, as Nicholas called it. The version of Mikhail after The Gone was never really *him*. That bodied human held the memories of his life inside of it, but that body wasn't Mikhail anymore than Mikhail was a Godhead.

"We're not that different," he whispered. Wrong again. Alexandra leaned into the pilot seat of the Berg and she gently, lovingly, caressed Mikhail's face until the lines etching his pain slowly smoothed themselves out.

"We are different, dear Mikhail." She leaned closer and closer, like she might kiss him, give him one last forgiving moment of affection. Or maybe help him out of the tangled mess of the Berg's safety latch. But when she leaned in close, she whispered, "Because I can easily do what you never could."

She pinched his nose shut.

And nodded her head as if to convince herself that *yes, this needed to happen.*

Yes. It was time.

She pressed herself hard against Mikhail's chest, trapping his arms, and took the corner of her long mustard-colored Pilgrim's cloak with her free hand. She shoved the thick material deep into Mikhail's mouth, pushed it all the way to his throat. His nostrils tried to puff out, but her fingers kept them pinched shut. He tried the usual squealing and wiggling, but like a pig already caught, he wouldn't struggle long. His eyes widened, as if in that exact moment Mikhail escaped his own mind and finally saw Alexandra fully for all that she was and all that she had been. The Berg straps only tightened as he struggled, his muffled noises sounding no different than a dying pig as they faded. She never wavered, never weakened. Finally, the straps that tangled Mikhail loosened themselves from the slack of his lifeless body. *Flaring Justice, Flaring Justice.*

The Flare be damned.

The Remnant Nation be damned.

Mikhail be damned.

At last, there was only One.

2
MINHO

Soldiers were trained for stealth.

To remain unseen while at the same time *seeing* everything.

He watched as Alexandra took a step back from the Berg and smoothed out the wrinkles in her Pilgrim's cloak. Minho ducked down behind a thorn bush. After witnessing the supposed Godhead snuff the life out of someone with her own clothing, he couldn't take chances. His finger rested on the trigger of his gun with the woman in his sights. Kneeling in stealth-mode, he watched through the scope as she walked back in the direction of the coast. Years of training from the Remnant Nation pumped through him as he slowed his breath. Steadied his gun. And exhaled, ready to shoot.

She abruptly stopped walking, and Minho lost her in his scope. *Did she see him?* Every instinct from childhood told him to realign and pull the trigger. She'd be dead before she even knew it. No one in the group would know it, either. He could time any shot with the sounds of war in the background. In half a second Minho could end the Remnant Nations' lifetime fight to kill the Godhead, dispose of her body with the other body in the Berg, and fly everyone the hell out of there.

It sounded like a good idea. The best idea in a long time.

They could all go back to Roxy's house, eating warm stew every night and reading her grandfather's books, living a simple life where the only things they killed were wild animals and feral Cranks. But all this stuff about Evolution had been knocking at his brain. His consciousness. Alexandra wasn't the only one who seemed to believe in this thing. He never cared about disappointing people as a soldier . . . but now Sadina, Dominic, Orange, and Roxy were the voices in the back of his mind. Having people he cared about meant caring about how they felt, too.

Life was easier as an orphan.

Easier when he had no name and no friends.

But those things that made his life more complicated also made life better.

He lowered his gun and stepped out of the brush. "Are you okay, Goddess?" He shouted to purposefully startle Alexandra. He held his gun, ready to fire, just in case.

"Oh . . . yes." She looked over her shoulder to the Berg as she walked closer to Minho.

He looked past her shoulder, too . . . at the Berg in the distance, making sure this fraud of a Goddess in front of him knew that *he knew* what she had just done.

"What are you doing here?" she asked. "I told you I'd be fine; you don't know how many crazed ones might be out here." She shook her head with every word she spoke. "You're just as mad as them. Mad." She wiped her hands against the cloak.

"That's exactly why I came to check on you . . . Goddess." He'd call her whatever she wanted. He could play along even though in his mind, his heart, and in all his bones he knew one thing for sure—she was no Godhead.

Quite possibly the opposite.

Some form of a devil.

"I appreciate you checking on me." She winced a smile.

"A good thing I did. It looks like you ran into some trouble back there . . ." He motioned with his gun. She'd killed that man too easily; the poor guy was injured from a crash and would have died in the Berg anyway. A mercy killing. Minho had surely committed enough of those killings himself. He still wondered some days—the darkest days—if he should have killed young Kit out of pure mercy when he found him in that shaft, all but beaten nearly to death. But a tiny, quiet hope let Minho believe that maybe Kit had survived that beating in the lower levels of the castle. In the place they'd called Hell, deservedly so. Maybe Kit had gone on to begin a strong soldier's life.

"Trouble? No trouble at all." She smiled and lifted the hood of her cloak to rest on her head, draped across half her face. But the wool couldn't cover the lie. Minho once again fought the urge to kill her right there, be done with it. Snap her neck before she even felt his hands touch the hood of her mustard yellow cloak.

But he wouldn't.

He needed to find out what she was trying so hard to cover up. And why. His new friends needed to know that truth before he could do anything too drastic.

The Remnant Nation never gave its soldiers any reason for the war other than *the Godhead was evil* and *the Evolution was bad*, but Minho made it his mission to find out why. What was Alexandra hiding that the Great Master and the Grief Bearers knew, but no one else? One thing, above all, made him feel a tremble of uncertainty.

Who were the good guys?

3
ISAAC

Isaac crept toward the fire.

The bushes stabbed him with tiny prickly, pokey things. Even the berries on the bush looked like they had thorns growing right out of them. He motioned for Old Man Frypan and Ximena to stay back while he and Jackie got closer. "Hey, be careful . . ." he whispered to Jackie as she leaned against the same bush. "It has spikes on it."

"Why does everything on this island double as a weapon?" she whispered with full annoyance. Isaac didn't bother correcting her that the four of them weren't on any island. They might never be on an island again. But as long as he could find his friends, Isaac would be okay.

He leaned into the bush and his ears stretched as far as they could to hear Dominic's laugh or his singing. Dominic's awful, dreadful singing. He reached with his senses, hoping to hear Trish scolding Minho, or Roxy telling one of her tall tales from all those books of hers. But as much as Isaac wanted something—anything—he could only hear the swooshing of his own blood inside his head, followed by the heaviness of his breath as he exhaled. He looked over at Jackie hunched down in the brush next to him. "Can you see anything?"

She shook her head. "No. But it smells like fish."

Isaac smelled the cooked fish, too, but almost thought he was imagining it. He couldn't even remember the last time they ate a proper meal. He leaned in closer to the thorny bush and moved a thick branch from his field of vision so he could see the size of the fire just on the other side of the clearing. Flames sparked high. It was certainly a big enough fire for all of their friends to sleep beside . . . but Isaac only counted two shadows. Two adult-sized shadows. *Ugh.* All his hopes fell to the back of his throat. He swallowed hard and backed himself out of the thorn-trap, but not before getting one of those damn spiky things stuck in his finger.

"Wait . . ." Jackie said. "No way . . ." She pulled at Isaac's elbow.

"What?" he whispered as he pricked the thorn from his finger.

"Doesn't that look like those people . . . the ones who kidnapped you?" She pulled on him harder.

Isaac shook his head without leaning back into the bush. He didn't need to look. There was no way Lettie and Timon had survived and were the two shadows sitting in front of the fire. No way. But *what if?* He couldn't leave any question unanswered. He held his breath and leaned into the gaping hole in the brush to take another look. He prepared himself to see the fire-lit faces of his kidnappers—but the two shadows were gone.

What the heck?

Isaac peered at every corner of the clearing, waiting for them to reappear when Old Man Frypan suddenly cleared his throat right behind him. The exact same way he did at the Villa, every time one of the Assistants approached the glass pod cell, to signal that they were no longer alone. The blood swooshed harder in Isaac's ears. He slowly turned to see two tall strangers, no longer shadows, and definitely not Lettie and Timon. Older than Isaac's two kidnappers, but much more dangerous, as they each held a crossbow, aimed and ready to shoot. Isaac held his hands up to show that he had no weapons, but thought about the knife strapped to his ankle, the one Minho had given him.

"No sudden moves . . ." the one wearing a red scarf said. Very slowly, Isaac looked over at Jackie. They should have listened to Ximena's second-sight. They shouldn't have been so stupid as to think they'd find their friends this soon. He tried to show how sorry he was, and she looked back at him with an emotion in her eyes that he'd only seen once before . . . when Carson and Lacey died.

Sad. Devastated. Helpless.

Something deep inside of him broke.

CHAPTER FOUR

War Games

I
MINHO

Minho walked behind Alexandra, constantly checking for movement in all directions. Neither of them spoke as they made their way back to the coast, and it wasn't until they finally turned the bend to see the *Maze Cutter* that Minho relaxed.

"*That's* the ship?" she asked.

"Yeah." With every step closer he could better see Dominic, Roxy, Trish, everyone already on board.

"It's too big. We'll have trouble in the inlets. There're too many rocks and plenty of places where the water isn't very deep. We need a small fisherman's boat, or a canoe—"

"A canoe?" Minho scoffed. "How do you expect us all to fit in a canoe?"

Alexandra paused, her eye catching Sadina atop the ship. It was clear to Minho that she didn't care about anyone but herself and Sadina. The Orphan named Minho didn't understand the reason she cared so much about Sadina and her family, because he didn't yet completely understand the inner-workings of families. But he understood why she *didn't* care about the others. The Goddess was selfish. Plain and simple.

"Fine, we can use the Berg." He'd been wanting to fly one again anyway.

"You're crazy." She sighed. "That Berg crashed if you couldn't tell. A fuel leak. You didn't smell it? The smoke's already gotten to you then."

No, he didn't smell any fuel back there, and he'd looked at every inch of the Berg through his binoculars. There were no dents, nothing that showed a crash, new or old.

"Okay, if you don't want to use the Berg then we're traveling on the *Maze Cutter*." All the while, he'd led Alexandra to the steps of the plank, ready to board the ship. She hesitated, mumbling random numbers. "Unless you have another chariot somewhere?" He turned to her just in time to see her roll her eyes at him before stepping aboard.

"Hey, you're back!" Roxy greeted Alexandra with an unreturned smile. "Hello, son." Her face showed relief and a slight sternness, as he imagined mother's sometimes did. "Don't do that again." She hugged him.

Miyoko came up to them. "Minho, Alexandra . . ." She sounded surprised. Or worried. Or mad. Minho sometimes couldn't tell the difference between all these islanders' constant emotions.

"Where'd you go?" Dominic asked.

"I wanted to make sure she was okay. There're all sorts of half-Cranks and downed Bergs out here to be wary of." He didn't trust the others enough to tell them what he saw. Except Orange . . . she might believe him.

"You good . . . ?" Orange asked, eyeing Minho's fingers lingering on the trigger of his gun.

Soldiers had an unspoken bond. An unspoken language. He nodded to Orange and the rest of the group, maintaining his hand on the weapon so she'd know from his active stance that he wasn't 'good' . . . especially with the Godhead.

"Wait, did you say Berg?" Dominic's shoulder bumped into Minho's. "You mean we can fly out of here? Why didn't you start with the good news?"

"Bergs? Out here? You're crazy. Absolutely mad." Alexandra quickly smiled and tilted her head enough to look Minho right in the eyes.

He stared back at the lying, murderous, Godhead.

He knew without a doubt that she couldn't be trusted. Not because he watched her suffocate someone with her cloak. Minho had killed dozens of people. But she lied about something that didn't need to be a lie. "Really? You didn't see a Berg in the field?" Minho pressed.

She chuckled. "Oh, perhaps the smoke has gotten to your eyes," the God-less Goddess said. "Would you like my cloak to wipe them?" She offered the same corner of her cloak that she'd used to choke the pilot of the Berg and Minho watched as Trish, Miyoko, and Sadina laughed at the exchange. He certainly didn't yet understand all the emotions of the islanders, especially laughter—but this didn't feel like a very appropriate time to do it.

Minho looked to Orange, his finger still on the trigger of the gun at his side.

She squinted and turned her head just slightly before nodding.

They'd been trained in such slight movements and signals.

The laughter confused Minho—it had to be Alexandra's propaganda tactic. Her ways of manipulation were different from those of the Remnant Nation, but unique all the same. He'd keep studying the so-called Godhead to learn what he could, because he had learned something new . . . laughter had the power to cover a lie.

"Don't let them get to you," Dominic said as he put a hand on Minho's shoulder. "Let's get this ship out of here, shall we?" He stepped through the small cabin door, then up to the captain's wheel. "What do you need me to do?" he shouted back.

Minho appreciated this kid. "Let's check the rudder first. The Goddess said it'll be a smooth trip, deep ocean and all that, but just in case she's wrong, I want to make sure the repairs we did will hold together enough to get us through."

Alexandra might have been well skilled in war games and tiny manipulations.

But so was Minho.

2
ISAAC

He almost wished the two strangers with crossbows aimed at his face were Cranks. Sure, full-blown Cranks were absolutely mad and dangerous, but Isaac didn't feel bad ushering them to their fated death. These two random people could be someone's son, husband, father, and Isaac couldn't hurt anyone's father. He wished Minho and Orange were there to take them both out.

One of the men waved his crossbow back and forth, at Jackie, then at Isaac, and then back again at Jackie. The other guy, the one with the red scarf, was less jittery about threatening Ximena and Old Man Frypan, looking like he'd have no problem killing a defenseless old man and a young girl.

"Whatever it is you want . . . just tell us . . ." Isaac said to his current menace. "We don't have much but—"

"Shut up. Let me think." He held the crossbow only on Isaac, now.

In their silence, Ximena shot Isaac a look, and as if he could hear her thoughts, he remembered her earlier warning and second-sight when she saw the smoke: *Strangers will put them in the ground.* He should have listened to her, but his stupid hope for finding their friends smothered any reasoning. Hope gets in the way of fear. Hope makes everything else useless. He mouthed the words, "I'm sorry," to Ximena, to apologize for not believing her intuition.

"Hey! Stay where you are. Don't move!" Red Scarf waved his crossbow at Isaac, making the current count of crossbows targeted on him at two. He held his hands up higher.

"We're lost. We thought you were our friends—but you're clearly not. We'll get out of here and head back to our camp . . . or up north, far out of your way." He tried to step out of the direct line of both the crossbows, but the strangers kept him in their sights. He realized that for some reason the two strangers must have felt most threatened by him. He'd never thought of himself as a threat before, in any sense. If they only knew that Jackie had killed a Crank with her bare hands, Old Man Frypan had outlived more terror than anyone, and Ximena had a fire inside of her greater than any forge, these two men would've changed their priorities immediately.

"You think they're one of 'em?" Red Scarf whispered to his partner, a frowny, angry man who was a couple of inches shorter.

"We're not one of anybody." Isaac didn't want to know what it felt like to have an arrow pierce his skin. "I mean, seriously, we're not who you must think we are."

"Doesn't seem like they are . . ." the shorter one lowered his crossbow to the side. "They're just lost."

"The boy's right," Frypan finally said. "We didn't mean to bother you, just looking for our friends."

Isaac caught Ximena's fierce eyes flash at him, like she was trying to say something without words. . . . The look reminded him that he had Minho's knife. Before he could think another thought, Ximena pulled out her own knife.

"Get back!" she shouted, waving the weapon in front of the two strangers, but the sheath still covered the knife's blade. She shook the knife until its embroidered covering fell off and tumbled to the ground in front of her.

Red Scarf raised his crossbow back up and pointed it at Ximena.

"No. Don't!" Isaac shouted as he jumped in front of the man.

Frypan bent down directly in front of their arrow-wielding weapons in order to pick up the leather sheath Ximena had dropped. "Just a mistake. The girl thinks she's some sort of invincible force. All youngins do . . ." He handed the sheath with its embroidered eagle on the back to Ximena. "Here. You can put that away now. We're alright."

The embroidery of an eagle wasn't exactly threatening, but Red Scarf practically gasped at the sight of it.

"Kletter. You're with . . . Kletter?"

Ximena looked down at the knife's case, hiding the shock she had to be feeling along with Isaac. They knew Kletter? Ximena nodded, just once.

"Damn," Red Scarf said. "She's with you? Close by?"

They both lowered their weapons. "Sorry about that. We thought you were a group of the Hollowers."

Isaac felt the relief poor into his heart, slowing it down. "We don't know what that is, but we're definitely not that. We're from the island of—"

"Isaac," Jackie cut him off.

"Flare me to hell," Red Scarf said while he looked to the other stranger and then back at Isaac. "You're of the Immunes, aren't ya?" He waited for confirmation but Jackie gave Isaac a *don't-say-anything* look. Red Scarf suddenly started hooting and hollering and picked up his partner in a celebratory hug. Isaac just looked at Jackie. *What the heck?* "Look, we're sorry, come on in and sit by the fire . . ." Red Scarf held his hand in the direction of the smoke they had followed.

"We just cooked fish, more than we can eat," Shorty said.

Isaac glanced at the others, about to speak on behalf of everyone and accept the invitation to dinner when Ximena responded, "No, we're fine. We'd better get going."

"No, please . . . I'm Cian," the taller man said as he untied his scarf. Once he loosened the red material, he instantly looked friendlier without that awful thing around his neck. It reminded Isaac of how Ms. Cowan had tied her scarf to hide her symptoms before they got to the Villa. Thankfully, this guy didn't have a rash. "And this is my brother, Erros."

Isaac started to introduce himself. "Well, I'm—"

"We're leaving," Ximena said forcefully, her eyes just as scared as they'd looked five minutes ago, even though the men had put down their weapons.

"Give me a minute . . ." Isaac said to the one named Cian. He walked over to Ximena, whose trust issues were perfectly understandable, what with Professor Morgan and the others at the Villa. But not everyone they met would end up trapping them in a glass pod.

"Ximena, let's get something to eat. They put down their weapons, right?" He whispered, motioning to the duo. "Give them a chance, they could help us . . . and I know you've got to be starving."

"You're really serious . . . ?" Ximena threw her backpack over her shoulder and gave Isaac the sense that the question she'd asked wasn't about staying or leaving but about believing her premonition. "You'll be buried in the ground." For Isaac, the word *buried* held more guilt than it should have. He couldn't help but think of the burial of Ximena's mom and the others on their island. Maybe one day he'd be able to tell her about it and take her there to her mother's final resting place. It overlooked the ocean and was as peaceful a spot on the island to visit as any.

Isaac kept at it. "I know you're hungry, and all I have are flour cakes in my bag. Let's just join them to eat and then you can decide if you're still going north, okay?"

She shook her head stubbornly. Isaac looked back at Old Man Frypan and the others.

"Come on, Isaac," Jackie said.

Isaac tried to think of the right argument, something he may have used with Sadina in the past. "Maybe your second-sight, your premonition was about—"

"Don't," Ximena interrupted him. "*Don't* tell me how my second-sight works. If you don't believe me, fine. But don't tell me how to interpret *my* own inner-knowing. And just so you know, it's even stronger now than earlier." She whispered the cryptic warning again to Isaac, "*Don't let the truth stay buried. Strangers will put us in the ground.*"

He didn't know how else to tell Ximena that she was wrong. "I know you have a bad feeling. But I have a good feeling." She rolled her eyes at that. "Okay, maybe a good feeling doesn't cancel out a bad feeling, but maybe you're feeling *bad* because it felt . . . *loud* . . ." She had said it was getting louder the closer they got to the fire. "What if it's a warning that something good is about to happen? Maybe these two men can help us *find* the truth?" He reached for her backpack. "Please, at least just stay to eat one bite? One?" He once again turned around to Jackie and Old Man Frypan for support.

"The boy's right, we could use a good meal." Frypan was practically all the way over by Cian and Erros' fire already.

Isaac tilted his head to Jackie, urging her to speak up, too. The fish on the fire smelled like one of their feasts back home. "Yeah . . ." she added half-heartedly. "Be pretty dumb to head out now, in the dark, alone . . ."

Ximena looked over at the men, crossbows at their side, waiting to welcome them.

The shorter one named Erros spoke up. "We're not bad guys, just afraid of the Hollowings is all. If you're friends of Kletter, you're friends of ours."

"What're Hollowings?" Jackie asked.

Cian and Erros looked at each other and shook their heads. "It is . . . unfortunately, exactly as it sounds . . ." Cian said.

Erros explained a little. "Heathens that go around carving up bodies and leaving them lie 'round just for the fun of it. To learn the anatomy of the human body, maybe? Who the hell knows."

"When societies crumble, they break all the way down to the most simple of curiosities. Morbid curiosities." Ximena moved closer to the bushes as she spoke, away from Cian and Erros.

"Ximena . . ." Isaac waited until her eyes finally met his. "Stay. Please. We won't let anything bad happen to you."

She paused, holding her eyes steady on Isaac's plea. *Please*, Isaac said in his mind. She shook her head as she walked toward the smoke of Cian and Erros' fire. "Just for a few minutes. Then I'm gone."

"Atta girl." Old Man Frypan gave Ximena a solid arm around her shoulders like only Old Man Frypan could. Relief rushed over Isaac, mainly to have something to eat other than those awful Villa cakes. He walked to the fire that smelled like all the best things of home.

"I'm Isaac, this is Jackie, Ximena, and Frypan." He was so hungry he'd swallow fish bones whole, but he knew he couldn't eat the flour cakes in his bag. At least he could share them with their new companions. He unpacked two wrapped flour cakes and handed one over to

Cian and one to Erros. "They aren't much, but you can maybe soften them with water." Ximena sat down next to Isaac. Jackie sat on the other side of him.

"Oh, we know these well." Erros knocked his knuckles against the flour cake. They were solid. Too solid. "From the Villa?"

Cian shook his head. "They can splice DNA but they can't make a single bread loaf that doesn't taste like sand."

Isaac felt Ximena tense up. He wouldn't be able to forget the sandy texture of Villa bread anytime soon . . . but *how did the two men in front of him know about flour cakes from the Villa?*

"Don't worry, we've got plenty to eat," Erros said as he tossed the flour cake into the fire. A cloud of flames puffed just once before growing higher.

Ximena set her backpack on her lap, her arms wrapped around it. *Damn.* Isaac had temporarily forgotten the stolen loot. "Are you . . . um . . ." He thought about how to best pose his question while exchanging looks with Ximena. "How do you two know the Villa?"

Cian handed Jackie a whole fish on a small palm leaf. "You know one Villa, you know them all." Then he shrugged as if that were enough of an explanation.

"So, where is ol' Kletter?" Erros asked with expectant eyes as he handed a leaf of fish to Frypan.

Ximena squeezed her backpack tighter. Jackie and Frypan both looked to Isaac. *Should they lie and say Kletter was just behind them, back at the Villa doing work, or tell them the truth—that Kletter was dead?* Isaac's mind went blank. The fire crackled. "She's um . . . she's . . ." He couldn't think of what to say. The truth could risk Cian and Erros raising those crossbows again. He really, *really* didn't want to know what it felt like to have an arrow shot through his body.

Ximena spoke with a strange reverence. "Well . . . the truth of it is . . ." She put her backpack on her shoulders, her eyes heavy with a burden Isaac didn't quite understand, even though he wanted to. "Annie Kletter's dead."

CHAPTER FIVE

Buried Secrets

I
MINHO

Minho kept looking back at the tree line of woods as Dominic inspected the ship's rudder.

"Think this'll hold?" The boy asked.

The sounds of laughter from the ship's deck annoyed Minho. No wonder the Remnant Nation wanted to kill the Godhead for years. She was manipulative. Crazy. "Minho?"

"I need to get back to that Berg." He said it so quietly he wasn't sure if he did in fact say it out loud until Dominic spun around.

"What Berg?"

Minho rubbed the spot between his eyes. "Dominic . . . do you trust me?"

Dominic's eyes widened. "Sure as shuck, as Old Man Frypan would say."

Minho didn't know what *shuck* meant, but Dominic's nod reassured him that he could handle the truth. "When that woman went off, I followed her."

"The Godhead?"

"Yeah . . . she likes calling herself that." Minho looked back over to the tree line. If he learned one thing from his life spent in the Remnant Nation it was that anyone could name themselves anything, if they were brave enough. Or stupid enough.

"You really don't think she's the Godhead we're looking for?" Dominic looked like one of those trespassers to the castle after Minho shot their horse but right before he shot them. "She does seem a little . . ."

"Off," Minho said. "And what are the odds the very first person we ran into in this whole country is the one and only Godhead."

"Yeah." Dominic looked down before looking back at Minho. "I didn't think about that."

Minho needed this kid to trust him. "Don't tell the others yet, but there's a downed Berg not far from here."

Dominic stood up and took a step away from the rudder tools. "Why are we messing with fixing this old thing if she's got a Berg?"

Minho shook his head. "She doesn't want anyone to know there's a Berg out there because I watched as she . . . she walked right up to it and . . ." He'd never had trouble talking about death or murder before. Sometimes he, Orange, and Skinny would talk about all sorts of bloody things while eating their meals in the hall, but Dominic's innocence made Minho more gentle with the truth. "She . . . killed the pilot."

"Oh come on . . ." Dominic shook his head in disbelief. Looked to Minho. Then shook his head again. "You saw all this? You're sure?"

Minho nodded.

"So . . . she's got a weapon? What do we do?" Dominic stood tall, trying his best to be a true soldier.

"She doesn't have any weapons."

"Poison . . . ?" Dominic guessed.

"No, she—"

"Killed someone with her mind?!" Dominic whispered in panic.

Minho waited for the boy to stop guessing. "No. She choked him with her cloak . . . took the corner of it and just shoved it in his mouth." He mimicked what she did with his hands and expressed how quickly it happened.

"Oh klunk . . ." Dominic couldn't stop shaking his head. "Sorry, another Frypan word. I thought we were safe with the Godhead. Our whole trip, everything we've been through . . . was to meet the Godhead! Wasn't it?

"Who knows who she really is . . ." Minho looked off into the woods yet again. "Cover for me if anyone asks."

"Wait, what?" Dominic panicked more by the second. "Where are you going?"

"Stay down here and if anyone comes down, just say the rudder needs a tighter fix and I went off to take a piss, okay?"

"Okay. But just so you know, this right here . . ." Dominic motioned to the rudder and the woods and the space between them where he'd just learned the Godhead is a murderer. "All this is taking the piss right out of me."

"I know," is all Minho could say before heading off the boat.

2

Alexandra lied about the Berg for a reason, and Minho needed to find out why. Back when he guarded the walls of the Remnant Nation, travelers who lied were only ever doing so because the truth was far worse than the lie.

He ran to the tree line as fast as he could on the uneven swampy ground. He only looked back to make sure no one followed him.

If the Godhead had killed a soldier or a Grief Bearer of the Nation that ambushed her with war, then why wouldn't she just admit it? There had to be something inside the Berg she didn't want anyone to see. His lungs burned with the suddenly cold Alaskan air as he turned the corner to where the Berg sat. He took another clear whiff of air, and searched for the smell of fuel, but there was none. He knew she'd lied about a leak. He kept one hand on his gun while he surveyed the outside of the big machine and scanned the landing gear for any other possible failure that would prevent them from flying the machine.

The exterior body of the Berg looked completely fine. He could smell the traveling smoke from war and something musky . . . but still nothing that reeked of gasoline, oil, or any fuel. He'd noticed that musky scent before but couldn't put his finger on it. He walked around and climbed into the Berg, and the smell grew more peppery and pungent with every step closer to the cloaked body in the pilot's seat. Flies swarmed around Minho. It didn't take long for creatures of destruction to find their next meal.

Minho carefully ran his fingers along the dark cloak of the pilot. Darker than a Pilgrim's cloak, it looked more like something the Grief Bearers would wear, only a smoother type of fabric and missing the emblems that the Bearers wore. His fingers traced the gold thread of the black cloak. Another thing the Bearer cloaks didn't have. Minho pounded the shoulder of the dead body and startled more flies. "Who are you?" He searched the items inside the Berg for any clues, but the vehicle itself was practically empty.

The dead body slumped over on to itself.

It didn't matter who the pilot was. Minho had confirmed that the Berg wasn't damaged, and that's all he cared about. He could use it to get everyone out of there once they got what they needed from the Godhead or finally believed that she wasn't anyone but a crazy lady in a Pilgrim's cloak. Minho pulled at the cloth on the pilot's body, wrapping the black cloak around his hands until he had a strong grip.

"Come on . . . let's go . . ." He lifted and pulled at the dead man to get him out of the Berg. Not the heaviest corpse he'd ever dragged, but it was the most awkward. After being freed, it still looked like the dead man was sitting in an invisible chair. Minho dragged the pilot's feet outside and across the underbrush until he toppled the body behind a huge tree. That smell again. Minho couldn't put his finger on it but then it came to him like a bullet.

Turmeric.

That smell haunted soldiers of the Remnant Nation who had a bastardly deep wound but not deep enough for death. The Grief

Bearers would pack fresh wounds with turmeric and pepper. It might have helped soldiers heal, but it was its own form of punishment, both the smell and the pain.

"Who are you . . . ?" Minho asked the dead man again. ". . . and what happened to you?" He pulled at the dark cloak searching for a wound until he found it. A knife stab in the man's back . . . right above his kidney. Packed with turmeric.

"You've got an Orphan wound . . ." Minho whispered to himself, more confused than ever.

Kidney knife-shots were called Orphan wounds because they were the first defensive wounds that the Orphans of Remnant Nation were taught to give. No one above the age of ten used them, and this one wasn't a very skilled blow. It must have been delivered by a young Orphan who didn't have the strength training yet to pierce through all the layers of skin and muscles of the back, what you needed to make the proper impact on the vital kidney organ. "Not deep enough to kill you . . . just deep enough to make you wish you were dead . . ."

Maybe Alexandra had done him a favor. He looked back in the direction of the coast, knowing he needed to get back to Dominic and the others, but he had too many questions now. The turmeric and the Orphan wound meant this pilot had to be from the Remnant Nation, but Minho had never seen that style of cloak before. It was stretchy material, and shiny, almost like royalty. He bent over and traced the golden stitching with his fingers. Only one man would have worn something like this in the entire Remnant Nation.

The Great Master.

A man everyone in the Nation knew of, very few dared to talk about, and *none* had ever seen. The Nation's Bearers took orders directly from a cloaked Great Master in the Golden Room of Grief. A hierarchy that spread down even to the youngest of Orphans. If they didn't behave, the Great Master would deem them unfit and they'd be gone the next day.

Sometimes in their sleep. Where they went, Minho only heard rumors about.

He examined the corpse quickly with an excitement he never imagined having. "The Great Master . . ." He had so many questions—none of which a corpse could answer. He searched the dead man's pockets but they were empty. "Come on . . . something . . ." How could a man so profound, so powerful, have nothing on him when he died? And how could an Orphan wound and a crazed Pilgrim be the cause of his death?

He checked the man's palms for defensive wounds.

None.

Only a small swirl of a symbol tattooed on his inner wrist. The lines Minho knew well, a symbol of strength the Remnant Nation carved on every outpost and doorway.

Minho had to get back.

The Great Master took an Orphan wound?

If Alexandra really was some sort of member of a Godhead, then the one person the Great Master raised an Army to defeat . . . ended up defeating him. Minho hated the Remnant Nation. And all the pain he'd ever felt in his entire life came rising up from the dead corpse lying at his feet.

He should have kicked the Great Master.

He should have spat on his stiff body.

But instead, he leaned over and shut the man's eyelids, hoping the birds wouldn't peck them out. Then he hurried back to the *Maze Cutter* with an old war chant rising up in his mind:

Kill the Godhead.

Kill the Godhead.

Kill the Godhead.

3
XIMENA

What's done is done, but Cian and Erros stared at Ximena with disbelief.

"It's the truth. Annie Kletter's dead." She said it again in case the brothers didn't hear her over the crackling of the flour cake in the fire. It felt good to say it out loud. *Annie Kletter is dead.* Murdered. El Día de los Muertos, the holiday for celebrating the dead, used to be Ximena's favorite time of year—but not anymore. Not with her mother gone to the afterlife. If she ever did make it back to her Village, she promised herself that she'd *never* tell the Villagers Annie Kletter died. Absent-minded Annie didn't deserve to be celebrated. Or mourned. Or ever spoken about again.

"Kletter's dead?" Erros hung his head. "Red Seas and Remnants of Russia, I didn't think Annie Kletter *could* die."

"Of course she can die . . ." Cian stood up and started pacing fireside. "Now we're all dead!" He threw up his hands. Ximena held her annoyance at bay by biting the inside of her cheek.

"I just mean, of all the people, she . . . she . . ." Erros stumbled over his words until Cian gave him an accusatory look.

"Dead is dead," Old Man Frypan chimed in.

Ximena couldn't bite her cheek any longer. No amount of pain could hold back the truth. "Annie Kletter wasn't a hero . . ." she said to Erros unapologetically. "And she shouldn't be mourned. She deserved everything that happened to her."

Erros squinted at Ximena. "How could you say that?"

She had more than one reason to hate Annie Kletter, but she said the one thing that hurt her the most. "Because she killed my mom. Point-blank with a gun. Do you know what kind of worthless human being you have to be to do that to someone?"

Erros looked at her as if she were holding a gun to his head right then, but she only had the knife. Kletter's stupid knife. Cian stopped pacing and looked at Ximena the same way everyone did when they thought they recognized her mother's features in her own face. Confusion. Acceptance. Sadness.

"What? You don't believe me?" She grew more annoyed with every single second she spent around this fireside chat that she never wanted to be a part of in the first place.

"Your mother . . . ?" Erros asked as if there was more to say.

"Erros, don't." Cian walked to put his arm in front of his brother. "Just don't."

Did he want proof Kletter wasn't a good person? Ximena was happy to oblige. "Annie Kletter lied every chance she got. She turned my ancestors' Village into a cemetery, and I'm not going to sit here while you memorialize her and . . . and . . ." She didn't know what else to say. She just needed to leave.

"Ximena, wait." Isaac reached for her arm, but their reaction about Annie Kletter was a sign to move on. These weren't her people. She'd rather travel alone in the darkness than sit with anyone who idolized that ruthless woman.

"Ximena, maybe—" Isaac tried to fix things as if Kletter's existence could be undone.

"No." Ximena shrugged him off. "It's the truth. Annie Kletter *deserved* to die." She said it with righteous anger.

Old Man Frypan nodded and whispered. "Let her go, Isaac . . ."

"Do . . . you want to know *how* she died?" Jackie asked Cian, surprising everyone.

What a stupid question, thought Ximena. As if *how* Kletter died made her a victim and by being a victim she'd be somehow innocent from everything else she'd done to hurt others. That woman was a monster. A murderer. A thief of futures.

Jackie continued. "She died after we were waiting beside this house, and these two—"

"Doesn't matter," Erros said abruptly. "We'll never find it now. The whole thing. Done. Gone." His words went from anxious to erratic. "Going to be long forgotten." He threw his hands up at his brother, a common gesture of these guys.

Ximena glared from just outside the light of the fire. They seemed to care about something else even more than Kletter, but Annie wasn't that important.

"Relax," Cian said. "We'll figure it out."

"How are we going to *figure it out*?" Erros snapped a fish bone in half and threw it into the fire. "All the trials, everything—for it to end like *this*?"

Old Man Frypan leaned forward. "Sorry about your friend . . ."

Cian scoffed, "She wasn't a *friend*. The girl's right. She was a thief, a liar, and a murderer. But we needed her. Everyone in the sequence from the highest to the lowest levels needed her." He started pacing again, throwing those arms up and down, but this time he was practically stomping.

Ximena's face flushed as she stepped back into the light of the fire. "She was a liar for sure." She moved her head with Cian's movements, back and forth. "But I doubt anyone *needed* her."

Erros brushed hair from his forehead. "She did everything she could to protect generations and generations of families . . ."

The heat from Ximena's head flushed down her body and into her gut, the place where Abuela taught her all her power and intuition lives. "She destroyed families. Prevented generations. You obviously didn't know her that well." She couldn't sit or stand still with all the anger she felt moving inside of her, she needed to walk it out. She'd hike up the coast and sleep in the daylight. Anything to get Kletter out of her mind.

"Ximena, please don't leave . . ." Isaac said. He was too soft, too kind, and the world didn't deserve someone like him. He would have been better off back in the safety of the Villa's glass pod or better yet, the island he grew up on. Those islanders should never have believed anything Annie Kletter said, and they of all people should be more upset about how she upended all of their lives.

"Ximena, stay. Please." Isaac was practically begging, but she already stayed longer than she should have. "I'm not going to sit here and listen to these two tell you a story as if *she* were some hero for the world."

"Travel safe . . ." Jackie said with snark. "Might want to have your knife out in case you run into any Cranks . . ."

"Yeah anyway, you're the one with *her* knife," Erros said, insinuating that Ximena was either close with Annie, or killed her. Ximena didn't think the anger inside of her could move any faster, but Erros' comment had her feet marching over to him before she even knew what she was doing.

Within seconds Ximena stood face-to-face with a seated Erros and placed one hand on her holstered knife. Kletter's knife. "I lifted it from her dead, decomposing body, and I'll lift your weapon from yours one day too, if I have to." She took only a moment to look at Erros' crossbow and back at him again to make her point clear. "And saying she protected generations?" She pointed back to Isaac, Frypan, and even Jackie. "Kletter single-handedly messed up their generation and ended *all* future generations in my Village." That righteous anger boiled inside Ximena, and her second-sight grew louder and louder. *La verdad quedará enterrada. Extraños nos enterraran. The truth will remain buried and strangers will put us in the ground.* Ximena was a seed that not even Kletter could bury, and she wouldn't let Cian and Erros put her in the ground either.

"Those people aren't buried . . ." Cian said.

Ximena froze as she turned to leave. *What?* She turned around so fast she could have started a fire with the twigs and leaves under her feet. "Why did you use that word?" She had only ever known her Abuela to perceive what she was thinking, but it was based on her grandmother knowing her so well, knowing the small movements of Ximena's eyebrows when she was excited or how her chin tightened when she was nervous. "Why did you say that? Buried."

"It's not your mind I'm reading. It's your frequency." Erros took a deep breath.

"What're you talking about?" Jackie asked, but Ximena wouldn't waste time explaining things to Jackie who was bent on misunderstanding her. If Abuela were there with her, she would have tried to remind Ximena that not everyone has an inner guidance like she does, and that Isaac, Frypan, and even Jackie would have their own knowing to follow at their own time.

"The thing, her knowing about being buried . . . she said about strangers putting us in the ground . . ." Isaac whispered over to Jackie. "Some kind of curse or something, I think?"

"You're practiced in this?" Ximena demanded of Cian and in that moment in front of the fire, she felt everyone's eyes on her, even the eyes of her ancestors who were long gone.

Erros shrugged. “It’s not a practice. All thoughts have frequency.”

“You’re gonna have to say more than that.” Old Man Frypan leaned forward.

Cian took a deep breath. He motioned for Ximena to come back and sit by the fire, an invitation she only accepted because her legs felt like empanada dough. Also, despite the anger burning inside of her and feeling like she wanted to run far away, her inner-knowing was telling her to hear what Cian and Erros had to say. “The Flares didn’t just affect the earth. For obvious reasons, yes, everything changed. But . . .”

Erros picked up where Cian paused. “Didn’t you ever wonder *why* WICKED had set up such elaborate trials, all about the brains—”

Cian broke in. “Don’t say it like that—their brains. It was their minds. Big difference.”

“Okay.” Erros tried again, “. . . the *minds* . . . of the Gladers?”

The word *Glader* caused Jackie, Isaac, and Ximena to look at Frypan one by one.

Frypan cleared his throat. “Every day.” There was silence among the group, just the fire crackling and popping. Ximena knew more than most what Frypan had been through.

“Sorry . . .” Cian said. “We didn’t realize . . .”

“Hey. I’ve got nothing to hide,” Frypan said. “I may be old, but I’m not senile. Not yet, anyhow.”

Cian tossed more wood onto the fire. “The very first Gladers, some of them had telepathy . . .”

“Thomas.” Frypan nodded. “He had an implant. Never found out for sure, but I think we all did.”

Cian ignored his comment completely. “WICKED took credit when they could, but the truth was, everything WICKED did was to map the changes to the brain, I mean mind, and understand how the Flare changed a person’s thoughts into frequency.”

“Thoughts into frequency?” Ximena couldn’t help but repeat the phrase. It rolled off her tongue without her even trying to speak. It felt truer than an eagle landing on a tree. Solid. Perched. A clear view of everything. Thoughts *were* frequency. Why had she never realized that before? A snake-shape of truth-shivers slithered down her back.

"Frequency?" Jackie repeated the word as if it were new to her language.

"Sound. Vibration. Feeling." Ximena humored Jackie. "It actually makes sense." She had no sooner just learned of it herself, but the time spent with the thought in her mind didn't equate to her understanding of it. Her ability to see it. Defend it. Her inner-knowing identified it.

The fire crackled its own frequency.

Understanding was a frequency.

Anger, another.

Erros spoke next. "The ones from WICKED, they thought the Flare had changed thoughts into frequency, but the Flare didn't change it . . . thoughts have always *been* frequency."

"The Flare only made the frequency easier to receive," Cian added. "To understand."

Ximena looked down. The hairs on her left arm stood straight, the kind of truth-antenna confirmation that her inner-knowing did when something proved true. But despite that, she didn't want to believe what they were saying about WICKED. She didn't trust the tales of WICKED any more than she trusted Annie Kletter or anyone at the Villa. The two strangers around the fire seemed desperate, and Ximena knew that desperate people would say anything to get what they wanted. She just didn't know what it was that Cian and Erros wanted. Not yet.

"How do you know so much about WICKED?" Old Man Frypan asked the question they all should have been thinking. Her whole life, all the adults from Annie to her Abuela talked about WICKED often. But most of it was a mystery.

"We know . . ." Cian lifted the fish pan to wipe it clean. "Because we helped destroy the World in Catastrophe, Killzone Experiment Department."

He paused. The fire crackled and hissed. Darkness hung in the sky like a storm.

"Yep. We destroyed WICKED."

CHAPTER SIX

Coyote's Curse

I
MINHO

Commitment to the mission was a soldier's duty.

Minho boarded the *Maze Cutter* and joined the others on deck.

"So we're good?" Dominic practically stepped on the heels of Minho's boots.

The soldier ignored Dominic and nodded just once to Orange as he passed, a greeting only used in the Remnant Nation among Orphans if they were alerting others of danger ahead. Orange pulled her gun in front of her and signaled her eyes quickly to Alexandra and back.

"Good?" she asked.

Minho nodded. "Yeah. The rudder's fine. Not great, but it'll get us there."

"Really?" Dominic whispered to Minho. "But what about the Ber—"

Minho cut him off. "We're ready." He needed to know whatever

Alexandra knew about the Great Master. Then, and once everyone was ready to ditch their mission, Minho could fly everyone out. He couldn't tell Dominic what he found in the Berg. It was too much to explain, and Minho wasn't even sure if Orange would believe him if he told her the so-called Godhead had killed a man. A man who appeared to be the Master of the Golden Room of Grief, the leader of the Remnant Nation. At the same time, he fought the urge to tell her everything right there, out in the open and in front of the islanders.

"Good, we'll be on our way then." Alexandra turned around on the deck to face Minho as effortlessly as she turned around after killing the Great Master.

"The sooner the better," Roxy added, pointing over the bend where the fires from the city looked like they were spreading farther. The smell of the apocalyptic scene reminded Minho of the incinerator at the south end of the Remnant Nation. They never buried bodies of trespassers, not like Isaac talked about doing on the island with Kletter's crew. The Remnant Nation *burned* the dead and their belongings . . . at least the belongings that weren't of any value. Minho had dragged so many bodies into the south incinerator during his time in the Nation that the smell of burnt flesh felt stronger than a memory. It was like a permanent taste in his mouth. Despite the distance and time that had passed since Minho last stepped foot in the Nation and its mighty fortress, he was still trying to escape.

"Let's get out of here," he said to Dominic. "Pull up anchor?"

"Yessir." The boy saluted like an idiot.

2
ALEXANDRA

Alexandra coughed and coughed until phlegm came up the back of her throat. She must have breathed in more smoke from the fires than she thought. She swallowed the phlegm back down, not the most pleasant thing in the world.

"Oh no, dear, you've got to spit that right out," Roxy said.

"Excuse me?" No one told the Godhead what to do. Alexandra lifted her chin up enough to look down her nose at Roxy.

"The smoke, you probably breathed in quite a bit of it when you were fleeing." Roxy finished helping the other boy with the anchor. "You've got to spit that right out or it'll clog up your system."

"I will not." Alexandra couldn't believe she actually had to mutter those words. If Flint were there he would have gotten her hot tea to soothe her cough hours ago. He would have handed her a napkin or the shirt off his back to cough into before he'd suggest she do something so common as spit like a Pilgrim.

"Suit yourself."

"Here I'll show you . . ." Dominic walked up to Alexandra, scrunched his nose, elongated his neck, and sounded like he was calling in the wild hogs from the fields. "You just pull it from the back of your throat like that, then—out." He spat, and a white foamy pile of DNA landed right beside Alexandra's muddy shoe. Disgust curled around her lips. She looked over to Sadina, who watched the exchange with a smile. The Goddess recited the digits and reminded herself why she needed these ignorant children. The loud, stupid, messy children would be the key to the Evolution. Nothing could stop that now. Not Nicholas, not Mikhail, and not a pile of spit.

"Fetch me some tea," Alexandra said to no one in particular, never having missed Flint more.

Roxy ran her tongue in front of her teeth. "We don't have tea. It's not exactly fit for a Goddess on this ship." She looked around. "I can get you water and I can put a drop of lard in it to soothe your throat?"

The Goddess nearly gagged in her mouth. Lard, in water. "No, thank you. I'll just wait until we get to the Villa." Every need inside Alexandra revolved around the Villa. Safe from war. Safe with the Cure. The scientists would know exactly what to do with Sadina and the Immunes. Nicholas always said, *things fell into place as they should.* A shame he wasn't there to see it. The ship pushed off the shore and she looked back in the direction of the woods with even more disgust.

Mikhail and Nicholas would have never even believed the Evolution, even if they'd lived to see it.

Nicholas believed the dead could see.

But he could barely see when he lived. He used people's own thoughts to manipulate them. Alexandra doubted that Nicholas ever held a bigger picture of the Evolution. He only knew how to control people. Pilgrims were easy to manipulate if you know where to pull the strings. For some, it was heartstrings. For others it was the strings of their pockets, financial rewards. For the remaining group of people, they were only influenced by the strings of power. And for the hardest people to manipulate—you had to use all three. That became Alexandra's plan for dealing with Minho. She needed to know more about Mikhail's Golden Room of Grief and the Great Master. She would pull the strings that mattered most to Minho to get what she wanted.

Roxy threw the chains of the anchor on top of each other and wiped her hands on her side.

"The Nation you come from, what's it like there?" Alexandra asked Roxy.

"Oh, I'm not from the Remnant Nation. Just the two kids here are." She pointed at the two soldiers. "I don't think I would have been tough enough for all that mess." She let out a rather pitiful Pilgrim's laugh.

"Sure you would have." Orange tossed a canteen to Roxy which she caught in the air. "See. Natural reflexes."

"Couldn't have killed many people though." Roxy shrugged.

Alexandra once thought the same thing, but now she'd gladly kill someone on the boat for a hot tea. Or even a cold tea.

"Some must die so that others can thrive," Alexandra said aloud. Every advancement of humankind since the beginning of time had required sacrifice of lives in order for the population as a whole to advance. *It's the ebb and flow, the give and take of the world.*

The Godhead had no time for empathy or sentimental nonsense.

She needed to be ruthless.

3
ISAAC

“What? Why destroy WICKED?” Jackie practically screamed at Cian. “I thought the decades had taught us that WICKED is good? Misunderstood. Frypan?”

The old man grunted, as if he didn’t quite know what he believed.

Ximena sat back down, but didn’t look at Isaac. Instead, she stared at the bushes like she was ready to run at the very next mention of WICKED. Isaac had never joined a Senate meeting back on the island, but even he knew from the most basic of politics on their island that without WICKED, none of them would even exist.

Cian wasn’t having it. “WICKED is *bad*. The very word ‘wicked’ means bad, terrible, no good . . .” He laughed across the fire at Jackie. “How people ever thought *WICKED was good* . . . is evil in itself.”

Isaac felt stupid. *WICKED had ended up being good, right?* He looked to Old Man Frypan who had just thrown his fish bones into the fire.

“WICKED is *good*. They saved your ancestors.” The fire sparked, and Old Man Frypan said it again, the same way that some of the elders on the Island of Immunes still mumbled it during feast days. “WICKED is good enough, I reckon. Although as boys, we certainly didn’t think so. They did what they had to do.”

Cian and Erros looked at each other with wide-eyed expressions, like how Dominic feigned surprise when he let out a burp.

Isaac couldn’t stand the uncertainty, now inserted into his beliefs. “WICKED saved the whole human race when they made a Safe Haven for Frypan and those other Gladers. All the *bad* stuff they did was because they were desperate to find a cure for the Flare.”

“Oh . . . wow.” Cian suddenly got very serious.

“No crap?” Erros asked his brother.

“What?” Jackie practically pushed Cian. “What?”

“Look, if you really are a Glader . . .” Erros shook his head at Cian as if he were pleading with his brother about something.

Cian nodded.

"He is," Isaac said. "Frypan, himself." *What were they getting at?*

He looked at Ximena but she still had her gaze set on the bushes beyond the fire with the pokey prickly things on it. Cian took a deep breath. "WICKED's biggest lie was that it was good. . . . Their second biggest lie was Ava Paige justifying the deaths of a *few* to save thousands." Cian opened his arms up wide. "Look around. Do you see any other humans out here? There's not even half-Cranks wandering about. It was never about saving the human race."

"Never," Erros said so surely that his earnest belief annoyed Isaac.

"They tried," Jackie snapped at him. The teachers must've been more diligent in their defense of WICKED over on the west side of the island. "It didn't work. Not everything works out." Jackie threw her hands in the air to mimic Cian's arm waving. "At least they got the Immunes to a safe place so that our ancestors could rebuild. . . . And we're here to help the Godhead with a Cure *now*."

Isaac couldn't tell if it was the word *Godhead* or the word *Cure* that made Erros laugh.

Maybe both.

"You guys sound crazy," Isaac said.

"I told you. The Godhead's a joke." Ximena shook her head and looked at Isaac. "Believe me, now?" The moonlight above was just enough to see Ximena's utter lack of faith. In anything.

"Say what you're trying to say already," Jackie said to Cian as she twisted the palm bracelet around her wrist—the one Trish made her before the rest of the group went to Alaska.

Old Man Frypan stood up with his walking stick. "Let it out, we deserve to know."

Erros nodded, and the fire crackled. "WICKED convinced people it was good, and the deaths of a few were needed to save the entire human race, and all that baloney." He tore tiny leaves from a branch and put one of them in his mouth. "The same way the Godhead convinced its people that the Cure is needed for Evolution . . ." He chewed like a cow.

Cian leaned forward onto his knees and put his head in his hands.

"Look, wanting to find a Cure . . . and the trials were all true, Kletter showing up on your island for you to help is true. But who the Cure is for . . ." Cian paused. "Just leave it at that. It doesn't matter, Kletter's dead, it's done."

"Exactly!" Erros shot up to his feet and little leaves of something fell from his lap. "It doesn't matter anymore! We can tell whoever we want because we're not bound by the Villa or the Sequencers . . . we'll never get back to them!"

Sequencers? *Whatever that meant.*

"Snap out of it!" Jackie yelled at Ximena, her eyes still fixated on the bushes.

"Ximena . . . ?" Isaac asked

"There's someone over there . . ." Ximena replied in almost a whisper. "Someone's coming." She spoke louder and this got Cian's attention.

"Crap." Cian lifted his bow and motioned to Erros to stay put. "I got it."

Isaac sat quietly wondering if WICKED was good or bad and what either of those really meant. Frypan just shook his head. "We ought to—"

Cian's bow discharged with a loud SMACK. Everyone quieted. It was too dark for Isaac to see, but the lack of any sound from the victim —whatever it was—made Isaac think the shot must have been a clean one.

Erros pulled more tiny leaves from a branch. "The people at WICKED—or above them--however you want to say it . . . those people were selfish narcissists. There's no other word for it." The fire sputtered; the wind blew through the branches above them.

"No other word," Cian agreed as he stepped back into the light of the fire, dragging a small animal by its foot. He tossed it to Ximena's feet. "You have good instincts."

"What is that?" Jackie leaned in closer to the dead animal, a single arrow through its neck.

"Coyote?" Erros asked his brother. Cian nodded.

They didn't have anything close to a coyote on the island back home. Most everything from this crazy trip didn't exist back home.

"The trickster spirit . . ." Ximena stood up and backed away from the dead animal. But Isaac realized too late that it wasn't the animal at all. Ximena was backing up from Cian himself and the shadowed half-Crank behind him. A man, wild eyes, shaggy hair, wearing some kind of robe, though mostly hidden by darkness. Isaac tripped over his own two feet shuffling away as he reached for his knife. He fell with all the weight of his whole body on to the knife, stabbing himself in the calf.

"Look out!" Isaac yelled to Cian. Jackie screamed.

"Hollower!" Cian dodged the figure but only for a moment, when the Hollower pulled out a long serrated knife and sliced through Cian's clothing as if it were paper. Isaac could only imagine the time that would go into making that sort of blade on the forge. He gripped the handle of the knife Minho had given him, square in his palm, ready to fight.

"Stains of shitstorms!" Erros had jumped to his feet and grabbed a chunk of wood sticking half out of the fire with his bare hands. He swung it like a crazed lunatic, smashing the fiery part of the wood against the cloaked shadow's head. "Hollowers will get hollowed! You hear me?"

The cloak's top half caught fire, flashing with bright yellow light, and the man screamed a sound, shrill and high-pitched, then ran away, crashing through the woods. Isaac wondered if it had been a half-Crank, after all.

"Don't let me catch you again, you Hollowing heathen!" Erros threw a piece of wood at the bushes where the figure had disappeared.

"What the hell just happened here?" Old Man Frypan asked.

"Hollowers. That one was solo, but some travel in groups." Cian wiped the sweat off his forehead with his red scarf. "We should have killed that one and sent a message, you know." He directed that at his brother.

Erros shrugged. "Eh, I don't kill people on the full moon. It's bad luck."

Jackie and Ximena looked up at the moon. It was pretty full. Isaac took the opportunity to hand Frypan Minho's knife on which he'd fallen.

"Here. Just in case there's another one." He acted like he merely wanted Frypan to be able to protect himself, too. But really, Isaac was frustrated that he'd stabbed himself, and was scared he'd just do it again. A soldier he was not. He felt like a worthless idiot.

"No, you hold on to it." Frypan handed it back to him but Isaac insisted. Cian and Erros were still trying to catch their breath and Ximena looked just as stunned as Jackie about the weird, cloaked figure.

"No, you'll take better care of it." Isaac lifted his pant leg and showed Frypan the gash that the Orphan's knife left him.

"Isaac, you gotta be more careful," Jackie said, just like Sadina would have if she were there.

"I'm fine," he said, but noticed that even Ximena looked worried. "Seriously, I'm fine."

As if realizing she'd shown weakness, Ximena waved him off like she didn't care. "Foolishness. This is all foolishness." She walked right up to Cian with her hand on her knife. "You're the trickster, and your lies end here." She was practically stepping on the man's boots but Isaac doubted Cian felt threatened by her—Ximena only came up to his shoulders.

"Look, believe it or don't. Those Hollowers are everywhere . . ." Cian walked around Ximena as if she were a statue and set his bow down by the fire.

"That's not what I'm talking about and you know it." Her voice grew louder. "We've seen enough Cranks, half-Cranks, and other crazies to last ten lifetimes. The Cure is the real issue. Who is it really for?"

Isaac's heart fell into his gut like a kayak dropping down a waterfall. He didn't like this notion of the Godhead not being real or the Cure not being a cure. For one thing it meant that Sadina could be in real danger. He needed Sadina to be okay.

"What are you saying . . . the Cure's for everyone?" he asked. "Right?" He was embarrassed by his effort to show hope. Looking at

Jackie and Old Man Frypan, he added, "We came here to save everyone . . ."

Cian shook his head at Erros. "You realize what telling them will do . . ." He sat back down and looked at Old Man Frypan. "Look . . ." he started, but then silence floated between the space around the fire for two whole breaths.

In and out. Like the tide moving in and out at Stone Point back home. The caves would fill up, more water in which to swim, depending on the time of day. He used to be afraid to jump off the cliffs back home, always shrinking down to be something less because he felt like less. But right then he'd do anything in the world to make it back there and dive head first into the ocean.

Cian nodded slowly and Erros rubbed his forehead while his brother spoke. "WICKED was good . . . good at thinking of everything." He let out a sigh and walked away from the fire. "You want to tell them, fine. I'm not going to be responsible for it."

Erros followed him into the shadows of the trees.

Isaac could barely hear their argument until Cian shouted something about Frypan's mind getting wiped clean. "But WICKED . . . WICKED did good things in the long run . . ." He stood up, a little wobbly. "Right?" he asked Frypan.

"WICKED is good enough . . ." the Glader of old muttered, and hearing Frypan say it comforted Isaac. Like a piece of home was with him. "And if they did in fact destroy it, whatever that means, then I don't really know what that means, either." He spat next to his seat with disgust, something Isaac had never really seen him do before.

Erros came back and tossed more wood into the flames. "Okay, here's the deal. The formation of people from the Post Flare Coalition who—"

Cian cut his little brother off. "He won't get it."

"I know who created WICKED." Old Man Frypan's jaw tightened as he spoke. "We know about the Post Flare Coalition! What right did you have to destroy anything?"

Isaac had only seen Frypan upset one time, back on the island when a tribute to the Gladers of Old got interrupted by some younger kids goofing off during the ceremony.

"WICKED was good enough," Frypan said again with a stronger voice. "The Island of Immunes. Ava Paige did that . . . she saved everyone she could so that we all could be here now."

"Yeah," Jackie said.

Isaac didn't know what to add. The pain of his calf muscle hurt like hell and made all the voices around him . . . wonky-bonky, as Trish would say.

Erros tried again. "The remnants. The forgotten . . . call them whatever you want, but there are people who were—"

Cian cut him off again. "They don't need to know all that, Erros."

"Yes, they do. Everyone deserves to know the truth, and it feels good to get it all out." Erros spit a fish bone into the fire. The man seemed to have a bottomless stomach. "I don't know. What does it matter?" He held his hands up to his older brother. "Nothing matters anymore."

"Just tell us why you destroyed WICKED," Jackie demanded. "What that even means."

Isaac posed a question. "I thought the Villa was part of WICKED? The Villa wants to find a Cure, right?" He felt stupid asking about the Villa, but if Cian and Erros thought they destroyed WICKED in order to destroy the Cure, then they were plain wrong. Who knew how many Villas were out there, little variations of WICKED, all trying to find a Cure. Ximena shot Isaac a look as she hugged the backpack that held the supposed Cure in her lap. *Crap*. Maybe he'd said too much.

"The Villa is to WICKED now as WICKED was to the Post Flare Coalition back then," Cian said, but Isaac didn't really understand what that meant so he looked to Old Man Frypan to elaborate.

"Do you understand what they're saying?" Jackie whispered to Isaac.

"A little?" Isaac whispered back.

Frypan tossed his own fish bones into the fire; the fat left on the bones sizzled in the night. Frypan usually saved bones—any kind of bones—for a broth.

"Frypan, you alright?" Isaac asked.

"The Post Flare Coalition did their best. They could have done *better*, but it's not like they *caused* the sun flares themselves." Frypan's eyes seemed to stare into the very past. "The worst thing man ever created was the Flare virus and—"

"And the second worst thing man ever created was WICKED." Cian actually laughed, making Isaac cringe.

"No. You're wrong there," Frypan argued. "WICKED had *good* intentions, no matter the terrible things they did to us." He gripped his walking stick and stood up as fast as any old man could stand. "Look, we thank you for the meal, it's much appreciated, but we're not going to sit here and listen to these lies."

He walked past Isaac, Jackie, and Ximena. *Damn.* Sitting around the fire had kept Isaac's mind from racing with questions about Sadina and the others not being safe with the Godhead. He didn't want to leave, and not just because his leg hurt and he didn't want to walk yet. And he wanted to hear whatever Cian and Erros had to say. Even if they *were* spewing lies, he wanted to know what they *thought* they'd destroyed and what Kletter's real mission had been. Even if it all was based on false hopes or information, it was the reason Kletter took everyone off the island.

"Wait . . ." Isaac called after Frypan but the old man had already left the light of the fire. Isaac looked at Jackie, but she quickly shrugged and turned away in a rush to join him.

Isaac begrudgingly limped in the direction they headed, into the dark where the Hollower came from. "C'mon, Ximena . . ." He tried to put as little weight as possible on his right leg, but it hurt like hell.

Cian waved a hand at Isaac. "Fine. Believe whatever you want to believe."

"Wiping your memories and torturing you in that Maze was *good*?" Erros shouted loudly after Frypan. "Separating you from your family was *good*?"

Jackie turned around and shouted back, "They sacrificed a few to save the many. At the heart of their mission—they were good!"

Questioning WICKED meant questioning Isaac's entire life, especially the entire reason for his existence, his parents and grandparents. Of course it was extremely complicated, but the islanders had been taught from the time they could run in the sand a certain phrase.

WICKED is good. WICKED is good. WICKED is good.

"STOP!" Ximena screamed as if she knew what Isaac was thinking. But her voice came from way back by the fire.

"Ximena?" Isaac turned back around to the flickers of Cian's fire, and Ximena's shadow stood the same height as a sitting Erros, the outline of a crossbow at her shoulders. The crossbow itself was practically half the size of Ximena but she held it up high. "We know you're hiding something. Tell us the truth, now." The point of the arrow was only inches from the man's head. "Or I'll shoot your little brother right in the neck. The same artery where you shot that no-good coyote."

"Cian . . ." Erros said in a surprising panicky voice.

"Frypan!" Isaac called ahead. "We need to go back!"

Like it or not, they needed to go back.

CHAPTER SEVEN

Righteous Anger

I
MINHO

The sun was setting, its golden glow spreading across the water.

Minho steered the *Maze Cutter* away from the coast and out as far away from the city and the eyes of the Remnant Nation as he could. In less than an hour they'd be under a blanket of darkness and free from the eyes of all enemies, and safe from the war. These Alaskan mountains, the trees, even the water of the ocean—it was all so different from the flat, barren landscape of the Remnant Nation and its fortress. He wondered how the Nation of soldiers would find out that their Great Master was dead. Maybe they'd never know. After all, no one ever saw his face and they were far from the Golden Room of Grief.

"It's a short trip." Alexandra startled him from behind. "We'll get there before dark." She smiled. Where he'd come from, Minho had rarely seen cheeks raised, teeth gleaming. But he still knew Alexandra's smile was fake.

He would take every opportunity he had to call the phony Goddess out. "Short trip, huh? It would be even shorter with a Berg." He spoke each word as if it were a bullet coming out of a gun—rapid, separate shots.

"Would have been a lot better in a Berg," Dominic chimed in. "A whole lot better."

"Why are you saying it like that?" Trish walked up. "Like there's an inside joke or inside secret or something . . ."

"Yeah, what's your deal with Bergs?" Sadina had joined them on deck.

"Young boys do this, don't they?" Alexandra flashed her fakest smile yet.

The Orphan almost wanted to laugh. "I've taken more lives when I was just a *boy* than most *men*." He turned to face Alexandra squarely. "Have you ever killed a man, Goddess?" This got Sadina's and Trish's attention. And then Miyoko's. Soon enough, everyone on the *Maze Cutter* waited for Alexandra's answer. "Out of mercy or out of spite, for any reason?" Minho added.

"Oh." She feigned surprise for some reason.

Roxy stepped in. "Alright, alright, it's not a pissing competition."

The Goddess stood quietly behind Minho, hovering as he moved the controls. Her itchy wool cloak made her presence all the more known. "Can the captain have a little room?" He was used to life in the Remnant Nation, just him at his spot on the wall—alone.

"Actually, maybe I should steer." She reached for the controls. "You're favoring the right of the wheel too much, and we'll—"

"Don't." Minho stopped her hand from touching the wheel and held her wrist in the air.

"Minho!" Trish snapped. "Stop! Don't hurt her! What're you doing?"

He could have twisted her weak little limb in a single motion, put her into a headlock position, snapping her neck. He could have broken any one of the fingers on the hand coming toward him as a gentle warning, her wrist would swell up larger than her lies. But instead he just threw her wrist down. His eyes searched for Orange.

"I'm favoring the right because the *Maze Cutter* rudder favors the *left*."

Alexandra straightened out her cloak, but Minho couldn't leave it at that.

"Are you surprised that even ships have secrets?" He smirked.

"Minho . . ." Trish scolded Minho again. "Don't be so awkward. We've waited all this time to meet the Godhead, and here we are. We're lucky to—"

"Okay . . ." Dominic cleared his throat. "Let's . . . uh . . . give the man some room."

"Yes . . . here you are." The Goddess smiled in a way that showed too many teeth, a way Minho imagined the Grief Bearers might smile if they ever did such a thing under their hoods.

"And here we *go* . . ." Dominic led the group away from the captain's wheel.

Roxy handed Minho some water but he wasn't thirsty. "I'm good." He steered the boat further right than what it needed to compensate for the rudder pull.

Roxy leaned into him. "Are you good? Because that was quite a back and forth you gave Ms. Godhead. If I didn't know any better I might say you don't respect women in power, but I know that's not it." She shook her head. "Can't be right. Right?" She gave him a stern look.

"No, that's not it." Minho put her fears to rest. *That wasn't it at all.* Some of the toughest soldiers Minho had ever known were women—like Orange. He'd trust Orange with his life if it came down to it. "It's just *that* woman" he said under his breath. "I can't respect *her*."

"This lifetime of training to kill the Godhead . . . is this something I have to worry about?" Roxy let her words hang in the air.

"No," Minho lied. He'd been bred to kill them. Then he'd wanted to join them, discover them from the inside. Now he was right back where he started. What a journey.

"Good. Because these girls are very fond of her." Roxy looked back at Sadina, Trish, and Miyoko, gathering around the Godhead like she was some sort of magical magnet for their attention. The City of Gods burned behind them as the sun faded across the water in front. They sailed farther and farther away from the shore of Alaska. It might've been beautiful to a regular human being.

But Minho barely saw it. He couldn't stop thinking about the Great Master's Orphan wound. The turmeric.

He needed to tell someone, get it off his chest.

Orange.

2
ALEXANDRA

"Careful of these inlets. . . . This boat isn't built for such a narrow passage." Alexandra said as she pointed ahead. As soon as the words left her mouth, she knew what this boat—with the faded lettering on the side that said MAZE CUTTER—was made for. Deep water trials. *The maze trials never ended, they only evolved.* She ran her fingers along the trim of the ship. She wondered what secrets it held. And what else from history had been hidden from her?

Who else besides Nicholas had been so powerful to orchestrate such plans?

It didn't matter. She was the one true God now.

And the Evolution would bring back knowledge to all. The Cure would bring memories back, too. Alexandra looked at the children and the one they called Roxy at the tail end of the deck. They ogled at Alaska's sunset over the mountains beyond the ocean, more than any Pilgrim of the Maze ever did. It was decided. They would be her new faithful followers, and the two soldiers, her Evolutionary Guard. Whether they wanted to or not.

An unearthly sound arose from the bowels of the ship.

Alexandra held on to the railing as the *Maze Cutter*'s bottom scraped Alaskan rocks in the shallow water. There was a terrible squeal, a crunch. She whipped around to Minho. "I told you this is too big! Hold steady and move to the middle of the narrows!" She lifted the bottom of her cloak and stomped over to Minho. Even in the dark, an idiot like Mannus could avoid steering right into sure destruction.

"Do you want to steer?" Minho quipped as he adjusted the boat.

She didn't care if the ship fell apart getting them to the Villa, they just needed to *get there.* Alexandra's plan was simple: hunker down in the Villa. Let the war pigs die down. Get all of the destruction and burning out of their system. The Goddess would focus all of her energy on creating the *new* while they focused on destroying the *old.*

"Would have been a much smoother trip on a Berg." The soldier stared at Alexandra, maybe an attempted threat, but his words were no weapons to a Goddess.

"The Berg?" She shook her head at the stubborn Orphan. "Your eyes only tell you what they *see.* And what you *see* is never the whole truth." The boat steadied again without trouble. "When you use the simplest form of your DNA, sight and stubbornness, you're no better than those at the bottom of the Flare Pits."

"My sight is good enough to know that you're a liar." He sure liked challenging her, but she wouldn't be bothered by him. "Impressive . . . to kill the Great Master, though." He shrugged. "And before you tell me my eyes saw wrong: he *was* dead . . ." The young man paused. "I went back to check."

Alexandra didn't care about the ridiculous title Mikhail gave himself. Titles in themselves were worthless. And Minho could tell anyone on the ship anything he wanted. They wouldn't believe him. She already had control over them. All of them. She was their one true God. She'd seen it happen too many times to doubt, although her subjects hadn't always been quite this easy to manipulate.

"You didn't know about the Great Master, did you?" Minho caught her off guard. "I imagine the Godhead wouldn't know about the Greatest Master of the Remnant Nation."

"Oh, I knew him well." She shrugged. "That man had many names. All of which were false." For years, Alexandra's gut had burned with the belief that Mikhail was undeserving. "What do you know of him as 'The Great Master'?" The Goddess would find out what she could of

Mikhail's bastard nation, even as he walked through the Infinite Glade of Death.

"Only the most powerful leader, Head of the Remnant Nation. Above all the Grief Bearers and armies built to destroy the Godhead." The boy kept his eyes on the waters ahead.

"I'm surprised being as weak as he was, that he influenced such a strong army." The destruction that Mikhail had rained on her city truly did shock her. Damn Mikhail and his maddened, muddy-mind. "No one saw through him to his weakness?"

"No one saw him at all . . ." Minho turned to her. "The Bearers of Grief never saw his face. Only his cloak in the Golden Room of Grief."

What an interesting way to command an army. Through hiding, weakness.

"Coward." She almost wanted to spit after that word, but she wouldn't. "And what a disgusting name for a place." She rolled her eyes. Times like this made her realize how truly far the Evolution had to travel. Her Pilgrims in Alaska would have evolved, but the rest of humankind seemed far too easily fooled to ever dig themselves up out of their ignorance-cloaked existence. She sighed with sadness then looked ahead for the distinctive pine trees signaling the Villa, all while reciting the digits and running new neural pathways in her brain. 1, 1, 2, 3, 5, 8 . . . She kept her eyes focused on the calm waters ahead. "How many hundreds of soldiers took orders from a maddened Crank thinking he was a Master?" She laughed, with as much condescension as she could muster.

"Thousands," Minho answered.

She stopped laughing. The orphan suddenly pulled her Pilgrim's cloak and twisted it tight against her back until Alexandra felt something cold against her skin. "For every hundred you might see there's a thousand you won't see coming," he whispered into her ear. Alexandra looked for the others but they weren't in sight. She tried to step forward but it only tightened the cloak around her neck. "I could kill you right now with just one stab, right here." He flattened the blade of his cold knife against her skin. "Or I could barely pierce your kidney, giving you a slow and painful death." He pivoted the blade so she could feel its point. Minho twisted the cloak even tighter. He pushed the tip of the knife into her skin, the cold of the blade turned to heat.

Her mind instantly went back to the pain she'd felt when Nicholas first brought her to St. Petersburg. The *process to become righteous*, he'd called it. Removing all the toxins that she had knowingly and unknowingly ingested through her mouth, her nose, and skin over the years. Only the pain she'd felt in her kidneys from that removal of the unrighteous could compare to Minho's blade, now. The Goddess reached for the captain's wheel. "The others . . . they'll revolt." She choked the words out. "They've traveled so far to see me, to be a part of the Cure . . ." She struggled for each breath as the cloak squeezed her neck.

The soldier twisted it ever-more tighter and whispered into her ear. "They'd get over it quicker than you'd think."

Alexandra couldn't help but smirk in a way, at how easily the one they called Minho could kill her, but decidedly didn't. Something about him reminded her of a young Mikhail, and instead of being threatened by him, she respected the orphan. Unlike Mikhail, maybe this boy was deserving of his name: Minho. A name that carried a lot of weight, a lot of history.

Perhaps Alexandra finally had an equal.

Someone not so precious and fragile about life and death.

But one who could guard *hers* when needed.

And in time . . . she could train Minho to join her. She hadn't anticipated losing her Evolutionary Guard, the Pilgrims who adored her, and even the ones who feared her. Minho twisted the cloak, the fabric impossibly tighter than before. Maybe he'd slice her head clean off.

She cleared her throat and whispered, "You won't kill me. You're too curious." She reached to pull at the neck of her cloak and free her airways.

"I know all I need to know about you." He didn't give with the chokehold.

"Oh, but I have so much more to teach you about *yourself* . . ." She pushed out each word without being able to take a breath back in.

Minho finally released her with a shove.

The Goddess smirked again. "So, you'll join me . . ." The soldier, the children, even the one they called Roxy, would soon learn the true lessons of the Godhead. The Flaring Discipline be damned, Alexandra would rebuild her followers and save the path of the Evolution.

Follower by follower.

City by city.

Continent by continent.

The world, Evolved, forever.

3
XIMENA

"Tell me the truth." Ximena lifted Cian's crossbow that she had grabbed in a fit of frustration and held it tight against Erros' throat. It was way heavier than it looked but she worked to hold it steady. One flick of her wrist and the arrow would go straight through his neck to the other side. "Tell me!"

Cian stood slowly, defenseless. "Let him go, and we'll leave you alone for good."

"Ximena, hold on now . . ." Frypan walked back into view with Jackie and Isaac behind. "Now just wait a minute, they filled our bellies, and this is no way to treat someone who . . ."

"Who worked with Annie Kletter?" she asked Frypan. *Why wasn't he more upset at what they said?* "They're telling you that your whole life is a lie!" She thought Frypan of all people would empathize with her but he was just like Carlos. When people got older, they got too wise and set in their ways.

"Cian . . ." Erros whispered from behind Ximena's aim of the crossbow. His pupils darted to the corner of his eyes.

"Look . . . Ximena, we know how you feel," Cian pleaded, but knowing how she felt was near impossible. Adults in her Village always said things like that, but how could they know how she felt?

"Were you the only child born in your whole Village? No. Because you have a brother." Ximena's arm muscles burned with the weight of the weapon but she tightened her grip. "I was studied by the Villa my whole life. And Kletter killed one of my only friends when she shot my mom." Saying it all together like that, her life really did sound more like a curse than a miracle.

"Kletter she . . . eh, stuff it. She murdered our mom, too." Cian lowered his arms. Wilted right before her eyes. "We think. We can't prove it, but we're pretty sure. And we owe it to our mom, our whole family . . . to keep trying to finish what Kletter and the others started. Not for Kletter, hell no, but for all the sacrifices made."

La familia, Ximena thought.

"Mi familia es mia fuerza y mi debilidad," Cian said, as if he could read Ximena's thoughts or sense her thoughts' frequencies.

She lowered the crossbow. Her muscles unwound in tension. "My family is my strength and also my weakness . . ." she said reverently. Isaac stepped in and removed the weapon from her hand. She didn't resist.

"There we go . . ." Isaac slowly handed the bow back to Cian.

"Flare me to hell!" Erros ducked away from Ximena and rubbed his neck. "Toss me a coltsfoot!" he shouted to Cian.

"Kletter was the worst. I get it," Cian said before tossing something small over to his brother. "We'll tell you whatever you want to know." He leaned his crossbow against the tree behind him.

The truth.

Ximena just wanted the truth.

It's all that ever mattered to Abuela, and Ximena needed to find the truth before she could return home to her family. Carlos would probably get back before Ximena and tell Abuela all the worst things that happened. But as long as Ximena traveled with the truth, she could go home again.

"The Cure . . ." *She hated using that word*, "I know it's not what these people and the Godhead want everyone to believe it is. I know it's not. Tell me what it's really for." She'd been so tense that she couldn't feel her legs, but she wasn't about to sit back down.

Erros snapped a curt answer. "It's exactly what you think! A cure for people who need it!" He finally stopped rubbing his throat and lit something that looked like one of Annie Kletter's herbal cigars.

"¡Mentira!" Ximena said.

"It's *who* it's for . . ." Cian finally admitted. "It's *who the Cure is for* that you deserve to know . . . you all deserve to know." He pointed a single finger past Ximena. Abuela always made sure Ximena never did things like point fingers; *it was rude*, she'd say.

"Especially you deserve it." Ximena's eyes followed Cian's finger all the way to Frypan, who looked just as surprised as anyone else that Cian was pointing at *him*.

"Why me?" Frypan asked, his voice very hesitant to come out.

Cian nodded, somberly. "It's your family, Mr. Frypan. It's your family who needs the Cure . . ."

4
ISAAC

"Frypan?" Isaac had a terrible feeling, and it wasn't just from his leg, shaking with pain.

"But *we're* your family . . ." Jackie whispered as she looked up at their beloved and cherished Old Man Frypan.

"Of course you are." Frypan wrapped his arm around Jackie. "And whatever these boys say . . . won't change that . . . but hell . . ." He stabbed his walking stick into the ground. "Ximena's near boiling over this, and if she's strong enough to hear whatever these two knuckleheads have to say about the past and Kletter bringing us all over here, then so are we." He looked to Jackie. "Good that?"

Jackie took her time before slowly nodding. "Good that . . ."

Old Man Frypan, Glader of Old, walked back into the full light of Cian and Erros' fire. He and all the rest of them were ready to listen. To learn. To decide what they believed and what they did not.

Isaac sat down next to Ximena, right beside the backpack that held the Cure. Just in case she did anything else crazy. Just in case.

CHAPTER EIGHT

Hidden Truths

I
XIMENA

"How will we know it's the truth—what you tell us?" Jackie asked reasonably.

Hay que sentir el pensamiento y pensar el sentimiento. You have to feel the thought and think the feeling, Abuela would say. An old saying.

"You islanders . . ." Ximena shook her head at Isaac and Jackie. "You went your whole lives without knowing things, and ignoring how bad the rest of the world was because *your* world was perfect. Well, now . . . now, you need to hear it." She felt everyone's eyes on her again as she turned to Cian and Erros. "The truth. All of it." Ximena held eye contact with Erros, the weaker of the two for sure. "*Who* is the Cure for, Erros?"

He looked to Cian as if he needed approval to speak.

Cian rubbed above his eyebrows and winced. "Can't go back, now."

"¿Qué pasa?" Ximena threw her hand in the air. "What truth could hurt you this much that you can't even admit it to a bunch of strangers?" To her, telling the truth was easy. Maybe too easy sometimes. Adults in her Village chided her for being too honest.

"Well . . ." Frypan sat on the other side of Isaac. Ximena waited for Jackie to join, but she lingered in the shadows. "Say it as simply as you can, just out with it." He held his walking stick tightly with both hands, as if it were a sword.

Cian shook his head. "Okay. A hundred years of hidden history is hardly simple . . ." His crossbow slid down the tree it had been leaned against and Jackie finally came close. "Look, I'm sorry we offended you. You're right, there were people within WICKED who were *good.* And there were *other* people who held the responsibility of protecting certain families. Families with special genetics. But they ended up dooming everyone in the long run because they believed in keeping secrets in order to keep power."

Keeping secrets in order to keep power.

Ximena felt the truth in that.

Cian took a deep breath. "The Sequencers held DNA they valued as the future of humankind." He lit his own coltsfoot cigar. "It's messed up, but they decided in all their grand wisdom that people with certain patterns of sequences should be valued higher than others. Those were the people, one from each family . . . that WICKED studied."

"So . . ." Frypan took his time. "You're talking about the Gladers? Each one of us came from a 'special' family?" The old man took in a breath so big that Ximena could hear the air fill his lungs, and again as he exhaled. "Go on . . ."

Erros chimed in. "Families with the best DNA sequences. The ones that the Flare Coalition deemed worthy and in need of protection . . ."

Cian took back the conversation. "Scientists. Doctors. Heads of Political Movements. The top geniuses of the time . . . and their families of course. But because the Coalition included scientists and the outcome of life after the sun flares was unknown, each and every family who participated was forced to agree to a control subject."

"A control subject . . ." Isaac pondered, nudging Jackie. "That's the same thing Cowan said to me. . . . Remember how I wasn't on the list to get on the *Maze Cutter* . . . ?"

Jackie shook her head.

"Frypan and me . . . Cowan said . . ." Isaac paused. "How did she say it?" He paused again. "She said that I wasn't supposed to be on the ship. I wasn't on the original list to go . . ."

"Oh . . . that's right!" Jackie tapped Isaac's arm. "I asked Carson and Lacy where you were because everyone made such a big deal about waiting for you. We went to Stone Point the weekend before and had a great time, but then we were all getting on the *Maze Cutter* without even inviting you . . ." She looked confused. "Sadina begged her mom the whole way to bring you but Ms. Cowan kept saying no, that it wasn't important to bring you and that you'd be better off for the island staying behind."

Isaac turned his whole body toward Jackie. "She told me when I first spotted her rash that it was because I didn't have family on the island."

Ximena couldn't help but feel for Isaac. *Why didn't he have family?* She felt the thought and thought the feeling.

Jackie shook her head. "See! All the more reason for you to go with the only family you've known since they died, right?" Their whispers had distracted Ximena from Cian.

"The important people?" Ximena asked Cian to repeat what she missed.

"Families of top generals, scientists, doctors, engineers, all of the professions and intellectuals a society would need to be born again—they were approached to be part of the Sequencers. They were told about the incoming Flares and WICKED didn't know if the Solar flash would be small or large, or how much of the grid it would take out. There were different contingency plans, but those families who signed up knew only about the most attractive parts of the plan."

"Manipulative language like *hope, survival, interest of the human race* . . ." Erros rubbed his throat again. "They weren't *lies* but . . . it wasn't the whole truth."

"Might as well be a lie . . ." Ximena said.

Jackie tossed a rock into the center of the fire and ash floated up from the flames. "So we were tricked to come here." She was finally getting it. "And Frypan's family was tricked. WICKED is trick-ed." She shook her head in anger.

Cian ignored her. "Frypan, your parents thought you would be protected by the Coalition and eventually what became WICKED . . . they didn't realize until it was too late that you'd become their *property*." It didn't seem to hit Old Man Frypan any less than hearing his family traded his life for theirs. The tattoo on the back of Frypan's neck was hard to read but everyone back at the Villa confirmed that it still said PROPERTY OF WICKED.

Ximena wasn't exactly surprised at what Cian said. She'd been the Villa's property since before her birth. "So . . . study a child from each family, in order to create an individualized protection for those families to have *after* the solar events?" Ximena asked.

Jackie piped in a somber reminder of the past. "Not everyone went so willingly, with so much hope and self-indulgence. We all know the story of Newt, how he was brutally kidnapped and separated from his own sister."

Cian shrugged. "That's most definitely true."

Isaac took a turn. "Wait, based on what you said earlier, you're making it seem like the Post Flare Coalition knew about the sun flares *before* they happened? The virus, too?"

The islanders were so naive.

Of course the government coalition knew.

"Isaac . . ." Ximena tried to tell him. "The truth is always hidden within the lie. . . . The fact that it was called the *Post* Flare Coalition meant they probably had a Flare Coalition too, one that prepared plans in place for any potential devastating Sun Flares." Her ancestors had long known about the coalitions and how they failed to protect her Village.

"She's right." Erros finally acknowledged Ximena as he puffed on whatever coltsfoot was. "Our government—they knew it was coming. It was formed long before the Flares, both solar and virus, hit the Earth. . . . They created WICKED and implementing their plans was just a matter of time. But that very time was against them, and they didn't account for how many people within the organization would disagree. They created the Flare Virus to mitigate the shortage of resources, but they didn't have enough time to test it . . . to know what would happen."

"The worst thing that could have happened, did happen," Cian said.

"Well, what did happen? We weren't there." Jackie huffed as if no one was really coming out and saying anything of substance.

"Yeah," Ximena agreed. She knew her Village's account of what the fallout was but she wanted to hear this history in Cian's own words. "Tell us the whole story."

Cian began again. "The virus was meant to kill the weakest—thin out the herd, so to speak—but it ended up not killing them very quickly. Certainly not quick enough."

"And it spread . . ." Old Man Frypan added. "It spread badly . . ."

Cian nodded. "Look, nothing happened the way it was planned . . . the Sequencers ended up creating their own problems, far worse than the original problem they were all trying to solve."

"I still say, why should we believe you?" Jackie threw another rock into the flames.

"You don't have to believe us at all. In fact, it'd be better if you didn't." Cian threw his red scarf at Erros. "There, are you happy? We told them."

"No. I'm not happy . . ." Erros puffed the coltsfoot cigar and threw Cian's scarf back at him.

"If these special people are so protected, why do they need the Cure?" Jackie asked.

"That's a good question," Frypan said.

Ximena's face flushed with the realization that she still had what Annie Kletter and the Villa considered to be the Cure. Almost like she'd forgotten that she took it, all in a fit of anger, hoping to use it as leverage when the time came.

She glanced at the backpack, then Isaac's eyes did the same before looking back up at her.

She pleaded with him, pleaded with her whole expression.

Please don't say anything. Don't tell them. Please. Please.

Isaac didn't react. Didn't say a word, didn't make a face or offer a nod.

He turned away from her and refocused his attention on their new history teacher.

PART TWO

WICKED is Bad

Writing all of this down . . . will anyone even understand? Will anyone even read this or will this get thrown into the Flare Pits like a body that used to be a person. A mind that used to be its own . . .

The Flare takes things away, but bloody hell is it giving certain things back. Things that feel like I've always known, but I don't remember from where. There's numbers I can see in my mind. So many numbers floating.

—*The Book of Newt*

CHAPTER NINE

Griever Alive

I
ALEXANDRA

The *Maze Cutter* left a wake through Alaska's cold, blue waters. Alexandra closed her eyes and breathed in a lung full of ocean air. The Goddess never imagined, not even in her nightmares, that the very home above Alaska's Maze would catch fire. Never mind it all.

The Evolution would rise from the destruction. Of this, she was certain.

"Stop, knock it off," Sadina's girlfriend was laughing, very gaily.

Alexandra winced. *Why must they laugh at nothing?* Their acts of simplicity were a mark of stupidity. The Goddess tried to crack her neck to release tension, but ever since she'd ordered Nicholas' head removed, her own head felt heavier. A weight that she felt—from pressure behind her eyes all the way to the pounding in her ears. Her vision dispersed to red static again. Her feet shuffled below her. She turned from the railing of the *Maze Cutter* and spotted the cabin steps and door to the lower level. She needed to sit in the Infinite Glade. She hadn't had a single moment to herself since the war started; surely that was the source of all the dizziness. Her thoughts needed a moment to catch up with themselves.

Steps to the cabin creaked, and the cold air from below reminded her just how frigid the waters of Alaska were at this time of year. *Ugh.* The lower level of the ship smelled like a Hollowing. She pulled her cloak over her nose. Her feet on the wooden floor echoed—in her mind—the sound of Flint's knees hitting the ground when he collapsed. Destruction . . . she once thought she was immune to it, but seeing everything happen so quickly and so out of her control infuriated her. She sat underneath a small window in the cabin. She remained the only living Godhead, exactly what she wanted . . . and yet she had never felt more powerless.

She closed her eyes and rubbed the back of her neck with both hands. She inhaled for three seconds, held her breath for three seconds, and exhaled for three seconds. The Goddess concentrated on nothing, nothing except clearing her mind of the way things should have been, forgetting all that ever was, including the war. *Mikhail be damned.* She breathed in for three seconds, held her breath for three seconds, and exhaled for three seconds. A ritual as important as the digits. She . . . entered the realms within her own mind. In the open, empty, vast space of nothingness and everythingness, she floated inside that place in her mind where anything was possible and all was revealed.

The Infinite Glade.

Colors and shapes swirled around her within the Infinite Glade as if to ask her *what would you like to know?*

She needed to know more about the book Sadina held. Nicholas had always hoarded his knowledge from her, but now the Evolution would bring information back to everyone. The sun would illuminate all that stands; knowledge would soon become visible to all.

It starts with the Cure.

It started with Newt.

Her mind spun with images of the Goddess herself holding on to the book. Pages flipped in front of her. A feeling of power rushed over

Alexandra with every glimpse of Newt's book. Greater than any feeling, even more overwhelming than the Cure Nicholas had injected into her at Crank Palace all those years ago. *What is in that book?*

The sound of footsteps descended into the cabin, and Alexandra watched as the *Book of Newt* closed and dropped out of her vision . . .

"Excuse me . . . Mrs. Goddess. I have a question."

Sadina.

Alexandra opened her eyes. Had it not been the girl, the one she needed most, Alexandra might have snapped. But it was Dear Sadina, the one whose very own blood held elements of Newt's blood. "Yes, Dear Sadina, bring me all your questions and I'll give you fitting answers." Alexandra straightened her back as her head pounded with more pressure. The red heat of war warmed her face. The Goddess felt her forehead.

"Are you okay?" Sadina asked.

"Oh my, yes." Alexandra answered. "Was that your question?"

"No . . ." Sadina looked at the Goddess as if she was unsure. "You just seem sick or something."

"The Godhead has evolved past sickness, my dear." She pulled Sadina's hand into her own. "Ask me what you really want to know."

"What'll happen when we get to the Villa? Can they talk to the other Villas?" Sadina moved closer to her, sitting on the edge of her cloak. Alexandra tried not to let it bother her but the Goddess wasn't used to people being so close that they sat on top of her garments. She pulled the cloak from under Sadina's thigh. "Oh, . . . sorry," the sweet girl said.

"Don't you worry. When we arrive at the Villa, there are three women scientists who are at the very top of what they do. And they will, with your permission, draw some of your blood—the bloodline of Sonya and Newt—to help with a Cure and the Evolution." Alexandra couldn't help but smile thinking about this sacred lineage. She kept her smile to a tiny grin.

"But they talk to the other Villas?" Sadina asked quietly.

Other Villas weren't something Alexandra worried about. Or cared about. Her neck tensed at the idea of more Villas, more Remnant

Nations, more Mikhails and Nicholases out in the world somewhere. Heat pulsed behind her eyes and pain traveled at the base of her head.

Sadina looked up at Alexandra expectantly.

The Goddess inhaled for three seconds, held her breath for three seconds, exhaled for three seconds. Such a simple thing; so important and powerful. "Yes, they have a way that they can communicate with others . . . and other Villas."

"But how do you know?"

Explaining to a child the element of knowing was like explaining a Griever to a spider. It just is. "The Infinite Glade, Dear Sadina."

"Oh . . . I think my great uncle Newt wrote about that in his book." Sadina leaned closer. Of all the books in Nicholas' library, he didn't own one written by a Glader of Old. If he had, it would have been the city's most glorious possession, its very pride. Next to the Maze, of course.

"Tell me about Newt's book." It was time.

"Sure. Can you first tell me about the Infinite Glade? I have another question." Of course she did. Children and their incessant questions. Sadina took up more of the Goddess' personal space, but she tried to keep her poise. She needed Evolutionary followers like this child, close to her. Under her influence.

"The Infinite Glade is the place in your mind where a vast field of nothingness and everythingness exists. You can steady your breath and slow down time to reach all the answers of the universe, wherever you are. We believe it evolved from the original Flare virus, after many mutations. It can evolve even more."

"Is it something only Godheads can do?" Sadina asked.

"Yes. Historically. But only because the world has been far too chaotic. Soon, with the Evolution, it's something that everyone will be able to do." The tips of Alexandra's fingers tingled at the thought. Little did they know the Cure was less a cure than it was an *enhancement*.

But they didn't need to know that part. Not for a long time.

Sadina was obviously intrigued. "How do we travel there?"

"No travel needed. The Infinite Glade is always around us . . ." She welcomed the opportunity to teach Sadina as Nicholas had taught her all those years ago. Alaska may have fallen, but the Evolution would rise. "It's the plane of existence where all things are born and all things die. We only have to quiet everything else to see it and hear it. And if you're quiet enough . . . to *feel* it."

"Sounds crazy," Sadina said with an embarrassed chuckle.

Alexandra pulled back. She didn't like that—the insinuation that she might be on the same level as a Crank. "Crazy?" She ran the digits through her mind.

"Crazy as in good!" Sadina smiled.

"Tell us how we do it!" Trish leaned into the open doorway with Dominic and Miyoko behind her. Alexandra's neck tensed and her shoulders tightened. Children took words that used to mean one thing and just redefined them to whatever they wanted? A lack of respect like that could ruin the very Evolution.

Alexandra reminded herself that the other children who'd joined Sadina were also from the island of Immunes and they, too, had elements of the Cure deep within their blood somewhere. The Goddess inhaled for three seconds. The ladies at the Villa would have their work cut out for them. She held her breath for three seconds. She just had to get the islanders there, and she could entertain stupid questions until then. She exhaled for three seconds. So important.

"Tell them what you told me." Sadina pulled on the sleeve of the cloak.

Her mind flashed red. "You must calm yourselves, first. Silence and stillness is the doorway to the Infinite Glade. Your breath, slow and steady, is the path through that doorway." Alexandra focused on her own inner patience.

The non-soldier boy touched all around the doorway of the cabin.

Alexandra shook her head. "The Infinite Doorway. In your *mind*." These children were simple, but they were moldable. They could be taught and guided in any way she wished, like the most faithful of Pilgrims. Her faithful Immunes. "Sit." She motioned to Dominic.

Trish sat next to Sadina but the other two children hovered. "Sit down!" Alexandra said again, this time pointing to the floor. She straightened her back and rolled her shoulders. "You must relax." She reached her fingertips over to Trish's eyelids to close them. "Close your eyes. Inhale for three seconds, hold your breath for three seconds, and exhale for three. Hold nothing in your mind but let everything flow through."

"How do you think something without thinking about it?" Dominic asked.

Stupid boy. *Did she have the same idiotic questions for Nicholas all those years ago?* Probably. "Clear your mind of nothing. Then you will see everything."

"Yeah, I don't get that," Sadina complained.

"Doesn't make sense," Trish agreed.

"I'm not feeling it," Dominic added just to make the resistance complete.

Alexandra tried not to let her annoyance show. "When your mind is clear, you'll enter the Infinite Glade. All things will unravel to you. . . . You simply have to know how to ask for it." She welcomed the silence as the children quieted their minds.

"Can we ask the Infinite any question?" Trish whispered.

"Like . . . if my mom's still alive?" Sadina opened her eyes. The question and her alertness spooked Alexandra. Up until then, she had assumed Roxy was their only guardian.

"Your mother?" Alexandra asked.

"Isaac and the others took her to the Villa along the coast. She had a bad rash and a cough. . . . Do you think it was the Flare?" The dear girl looked at the Goddess expectantly.

Alexandra's own throat itched at the thought. "I'm sure she's fine." The coast wasn't a place for unskilled travelers.

"Can you go into the Infinite Glade and ask?" Sadina leaned in closer to Alexandra. "Please?"

The Goddess nodded. She needed to know if Sadina's mother had the Flare because if she did, it meant Sadina's blood might not be as pure as she'd assumed. Everything Alexandra hoped for could be lost. Gone further than those past The Gone.

Alexandra went into her mind, fought to relax so she could walk through the doorway to the Infinite Glade. But the sounds of the children were distracting. She could hear Dominic mouth-breathing. "Breath through your *nose*," she snapped. The deep mouth-breaths shifted to nose-whistling.

Alexandra inhaled for three seconds, held her breath for three, exhaled for three. Again and again. Then, she asked the Infinite about the girl's mother, and without much effort at all, she saw things expand, her vision spreading toward the southern coast. "They got her to a Villa . . ." She saw a dozen or more workers at this Villa. She fought with her mind to relax, not to question what this Villa did and if Nicholas knew about it. "A Dr. Morgan . . . helped her . . ."

But then, like a jolt of electricity, what flashed into Alexandra's Infinite, she couldn't say out loud. *A Griever walking toward Sadina's mom.* Alexandra's heart raced. *Why was everyone trapped behind glass except her mother?* The Infinite never lied. Alexandra closed her lips tight at the sight as she watched in her mind the Griever attacking Sadina's mother.

It stabbed the woman with a long needle, right in the soft flesh of her shoulder.

Why would they let it stab her?

A pain ricocheted through Alexandra's body as if she'd taken the biting sting.

"Is she okay?" Sadina asked, a bit frantic.

"She's . . . alive." The Goddess didn't have to tell the whole truth. But the girl's mother truly was alive. Stabbed by a Griever, but alive.

"Really?"

"Yes . . . she's alive." *Why must they question the Goddess?* Alexandra searched her mind's eye for what else she might be given in her state. She knew about the Grievers of Old. *Who on Flare's Scorched Earth hadn't?* But she had never seen one. All the countless times she'd gone down into the sight of the sacred Maze, she had never considered the Grievers of Old or if they could still be active. She had assumed not.

She had assumed wrong. Nicholas had assured her there was nothing in the Maze that could harm her. *What else did he lie to her about?* Were there dormant Grievers down there, somewhere?

Her heart pounded ten beats for every breath. She pinched the bridge of her nose to stop the pounding. 13, 21, 34, 55, 89, 144 . . . She recited the digits in her mind to slow the chaos she felt but even the digits were useless. Alexandra opened her eyes. She'd walk further into the Infinite Glade later.

"I'm so glad she's still alive!" Sadina shouted, breaking into tears. "I have to go tell Rox!" Sadina ran up the stairs of the cabin with Newt's book sticking out of her back pocket. The others followed Sadina one by one.

The Goddess sat alone again in the ship's underdeck as the pain in her head grew. Buzzing in her ears carried through her whole body. She quieted her mind, slowed her heartbeat. She rubbed her temples and the back of her skull until the buzzing quieted.

Quiet.

Until the screams.

Wild screams of terror from above. At first it seemed an echo of the Infinite, but then she realized it was all too real, sounding from above like hysteria.

Alexandra rushed up the steps to the screams of the children . . . and to all the beauty of the aurora. Reds, blues, purples, greens—ribbons of light streamed across the sky. Mixing together, like the Immunes joining the Godhead. A comfort to Alexandra. She stood under the beauty with her arms out wide.

"Don't be scared. It's the aurora that has returned." She tried to calm the children's fears, but they were more manic than a maddened Mikhail at his cheery worst.

"*This* is what?" Miyoko questioned.

"The sky is on fire!" Dominic yelled.

Trish's exclamation almost had a squeak to it. "What's happening, is there poison in the air?"

"I've never seen anything like it . . ." Roxy mumbled. "Not a good sign if you ask me."

No. Alexandra had not asked her. The Goddess clasped her hands together and drew all the patience she could from within, then waited until one by one they all calmed down from their ignorant panic and looked to the one true Godhead for her explanation. Now, more than at any point since she'd met them, she needed to say something profound, something they'd never forget. Another manipulation. And so she did.

"My Dear children, that sky is a gift. Everything is going to change." She paused, the oldest oratory trick in the book. Then, with all the solemnity she could summon:

"Welcome to the Evolution."

CHAPTER TEN

Day of the Dead

I
XIMENA

Darkness filled the sky around them, and slowly all her favorite colors of "the day of the dead" filled the sky, too. Green and turquoise hues danced upward. Faintly, the colors were there within the night sky. Ximena had never seen anything like it. Storms had occasionally colored sunsets yellow before a terrible lifting wind, but rarely pink or red, never the teal of Abuela's hand-painted pottery.

"What is all that over there?" Jackie asked. "Some kind of colored smoke signal?"

Ximena didn't like feeling as if she knew less than the islanders. "Yeah. Qué pasa?" she asked.

"Man. It's brighter every day." Erros drew another puff on his cigar.

"Brighter every *night*," Cian corrected Erros.

"Wait, we were out here, along the coast—we never saw this at night before?" Isaac asked before turning to Jackie, ". . . did we?"

There was no point in Ximena's intuition fighting her eyes about what she saw. Something wasn't normal, but she was too in awe to be scared. "It's . . . unreal," is all Ximena could mumble.

"Um . . . Frypan, is this what the sky looked like before that whole solar thing happened?" Jackie stood so close to Old Man Frypan that her shadow from the fire overlapped his. "Is there going to be another Flare?"

"I don't think so. . . . I don't know. I'd like to think I'd remember something like this, but they made sure I didn't remember much of anything." Frypan rubbed his forehead.

Cian packed up some of his other supplies. "It's nothing for you to worry about. It's part of the Sun's evolution. We just happen to be alive to witness it."

"What's that mean?" Isaac asked. "I thought the Evolution everyone talked about was human evolution, not the Sun's?"

"Is the sun going to explode? That would suck." Jackie took a step back.

Ximena wanted to think that was an absurd idea, but her inner-knowing held the word *explode* in her mind, as if that were exactly what caused the colors. "Tiny explosions . . ." she said. "The colors are sparks in the atmosphere from all the tiny solar explosions . . . ?" Jackie was right in a way.

Cian and Erros just looked at each other. Their silence confirmed it. Adults always had trouble telling teenagers when they were right. Why was it so hard to admit?

"How? Why?" Ximena asked.

Erros shrugged. "Doesn't matter."

Jackie seemed distressed. "We're dead, aren't we? This is the end?"

Ximena wanted to grab the girl by the shoulders. She hated how the islanders jumped to the worst possible conclusions.

"Well?" Cian looked to his brother, "you want to tell them everything, go on then . . . tell them . . ."

"I can't . . ." Erros rubbed his fingers over his upper lip. "And if I can't even explain it to a bunch of Immunes"—Eros pointed at Jackie and Isaac—"Then how will I explain it to the Sequencers?"

"You keep saying that word, sequences," Isaac commented.

"Sequence-*ers*," Erros corrected him, but didn't say more until Ximena's and the others' expectant and waiting looks forced him to. "Humanity and its evolution is a sequence, one that grows exponentially, doubling and doubling in size and technology."

Cian snapped a fallen twig in half and drew a circle in the loose dirt directly in front of the fire. A terrible-looking circle that spiraled around itself again and again. "But not just in all the *good* things . . . humanity multiplies in evil, too." Cian looked at his brother. "You don't just have to use words to explain things, pictures help. Remember that, okay?"

Ximena felt that truth vibrate through her bones.

Humanity had multiplied in evil.

If the sky was any clue to what was coming, things would get worse before they got better.

2
MINHO

Trust isn't born with Orphans, it's earned.

Minho didn't like Alexandra guiding their path. "We should have gone out farther around this. It's too shallow." Ocean rocks jutted from the water on both sides. "Rox, can you see anything up ahead?"

No answer.

"Roxy?" Minho said it louder. *Where in Level Hell was everyone?*

"Minho . . . come look! Quick!" Roxy waved at Minho from the back of the ship. Behind the *Maze Cutter*, in the opposite direction of the sky where Minho steered, there were red and pink lights. The Remnant Nation had flare guns for alerts, but nothing in those colors. . . . Minho had spent hundreds of night-watches on the wall, staring up at the night sky, but he'd never seen this before.

"It's weird, I know," Orange said, motioning to the wheel. "Roxy asked me to give you a break so you could go look. I guess it's some phenomenon or something."

Minho looked back at the sky. "It's alright, I got it. The waters are too shallow here and—" Something caught his attention. Commotion from the others. *Sadina waving that damn book around*, the one Alexandra had been eyeing from the moment they found that crazy Pilgrim. The woman held her hand out. "She's going to take Frypan's book." Minho looked at Orange and then back at Sadina and Alexandra at the end of the ship.

"She's obsessed with Sadina and her family."

"Yeah." Minho watched Alexandra as the same exact fingers she'd shoved down a man's throat to kill him grabbed the book from Sadina's hands.

Minho couldn't take it anymore.

Orphans own nothing. Not even what they're given.

"Go . . . I got this," Orange said, taking over the wheel.

Old Man Frypan had given that book to Sadina. It was a part of her family's history. If Minho had the privilege of a family history, he'd have protected it with his life—and he'd do the same for his friends. His hand traced the trigger of his gun as he walked the deck to Alexandra.

"It's simple," Alexandra was saying, gently caressing the book just as she had the Great Master's face before she killed him. "Everything comes back to the digits and the Flaring Discipline." She marveled at the cover and the pages. "I'll hold on to this so it doesn't get lost or damaged."

Alexandra spoke with Sadina as if the girl were stupid, which she wasn't. Naive, yes. Stupid, no. Minho truly despised this woman.

"No," Minho said loudly. "Give her that back." He reached for the book but Alexandra pulled it away from his grasp. *He should have broken her fingers when he had the chance.*

"Hey . . . it's alright . . ." Trish's eyes held a strange panic in them that Minho hadn't seen since Isaac and Old Man Frypan separated with Jackie and Ms. Cowan.

"Steady . . ." Roxy said with an arm held out against Minho. He fell back into a soldier's rest position, which is never a position of *rest* but a less threatening stance. He just wanted to protect their lives and their belongings. Didn't anyone see that?

"That book is *hers*," Minho said with more than a hint of threat in his voice, despite the calm stance. "It's her family's story. Don't take it away from her." He couldn't understand why the islanders were looking at him like he was crazy. Orphans didn't have much, but at least they had respect for each other.

Alexandra was not fazed. "Oh, you see, I wouldn't dream of taking it *away*. I want to do the opposite—to keep it *safe*." She hummed along and turned away from Minho with her killing cloak. Minho stepped forward, wishing he could choke her with her own Pilgrim's wool right there and then. Have her meet the same end as the Great Master.

"It's okay, son." Roxy grabbed Minho's arm. "Let her see what she can find in it and maybe she can help us untangle something with those digits." She patted Minho on the back encouragingly, but it felt like she was trying to pat out flames of war.

He took a deep breath.

"We're safe with the Godhead," Trish insisted. Minho could think of a dozen dangerous things safer than being with the Godhead. That woman had brainwashed these people.

"Precisely. What better way to protect this special artifact than to keep it with the Godhead." Alexandra danced her fingers through the pages and the word *Godhead* sent Grief Bearer–sized lashings down Minho's body.

"Keep it safe with the Godhead?" Minho mocked her and pointed back to the shores that were no longer in sight. "Your city burned to ashes and you've said nothing in retrospect or regret about it. No guilt. No sadness. Just an acceptance of defeat." He turned to the others, everyone staring at him with wide eyes. "The people who once trusted the Godhead—and even those who refused to—they're all dead or dying right now. . . . Because of *you*. Tell me how all your dead Pilgrims were *safe*?"

"Minho!" Roxy pulled him closer to her, but he resisted. He stood tall.

"It's true." Minho straightened his shoulders. "Answer me, how are those dead along your shores considered safe, Goddess?"

"Man . . ." Dominic sighed and covered his face with his hands.

"You guys refuse to acknowledge what's happening right in front of your eyes. She's a terrible person, and a worse leader. She could be leading us right into a place that doesn't even exist right now. Or a place where we'll be held captive and killed!" He pointed toward the icy ocean ahead.

Sadina took a crack at him. "Minho . . . this is the *Godhead* . . . we're in her—"

Minho walked fearlessly up to the supposed Godhead, and no one, including Alexandra, moved. He stood in front of her and made sure to take up as much of her personal space as possible. "Sadina received the book as a gift from a close friend, and she won't be giving it away, not even to the Godhead." He grabbed the top of the book and pulled it, but in a quick snap she pulled it back.

"Don't. Stop!" Sadina yelled. "It's my choice, thank you very much.

"You'll fling it into the ocean, knock it off!" Trish screamed. "Stop!"

Minho thought about knocking the book out of her hands before pushing Alexandra into the cold, icy water below. The only thing he wanted Alexandra to hold right now was her breath . . . underwater.

Roxy pulled him away. "It's alright . . . she's not going to hurt the book by looking at it."

Minho couldn't get them to see what he saw, no matter how hard he tried. He looked to Dominic for something, but Dom just shrugged. Brainwashed, all of them.

"Who gave it to you, again?" Alexandra asked Sadina with a false sweetness. "It must have been someone special . . ."

Damn. Minho shouldn't have said anything. The last thing he wanted was for the Godhead to know about poor Old Man Frypan, not after the way she nearly kidnapped Sadina over her connection to the Immunes.

"It's fine . . . she can hold on to it for now," Roxy said, de-escalating the situation.

And just like that they had given over their most prized possession to the lying, murderous, so-called Godhead. A Goddess of Nothing.

3

The *Book of Newt* was just a book, and Roxy's house was full of books back home. But when Minho had steered the *Maze Cutter* up to Alaska, he'd found Sadina up late one night, reading that thing when everyone else was sleeping—sometimes smiling, sometimes crying.

"It's more than just a book . . ." he said under his breath and tried walking back to the captain's wheel, but his legs and feet wouldn't let him. He turned right back around to Alexandra. If he wasn't able to flat out tell the others what he saw her do in the woods, then he would reveal her fraud in other ways: starting with those damn numbers she claimed did something magical. Minho tucked Kletter's captain's log tighter into his back pocket. He wouldn't let Alexandra see it and get any ideas of adding it to her collection.

"Those numbers," he said. "The ones you mumble to keep yourself from going crazy . . . or should I say crazier . . ." Cornering animals was the best way to hunt. Orphans were taught to corner wild animals, and Alexandra's mind seemed like it had a lot of cracks and more than enough corners. "I don't think it's working for you." He let out what he hoped sounded like a laugh. "Just some stupid numbers . . . 10, 18, 56. . . . Look, I can do it, too."

"Minho!" Trish shook her head. "Sorry, Goddess, he's just someone we found along the way, we don't actually—"

"After all, if your numbers are so magic and powerful, why didn't you use them to save your precious city?" Minho stabbed her with words as the *Maze Cutter*'s starboard side scraped along a chunk of ice.

Everyone except Minho startled at the roaring from the ship's hull.

"What's that?" Miyoko asked Dominic.

"It's alright. We're okay, right, Minho?" Dom asked.

Minho shook his head. "Ask the precious Goddess. She said the waters were deep enough for the *Maze Cutter* out here, that we'd be safe with her. Is she wrong?" He waited for her to call him a liar so he could reveal that she'd wanted to leave the group behind and leave in a damned canoe. He looked up to the sky in frustration, those colors swirling like some haunted dream of a child.

"The digits are sacred, Minho," Sadina said. "What does it hurt to learn more about all of this?"

"Yes, indeed they are . . . they brought me the Immunes." Alexandra squinted at Minho. It would take more for her to crack, so he needed to push her.

"Okay. Listen. Why don't you tell everyone what you were really doing in the woods before we left."

Alexandra shook her head. Her lips pursed tight. "Absolutely nothing."

"Come on, let's get you back to the wheel." Roxy pulled at Minho but he shook her off.

"You killed a man. In the Berg. Tell them." He stared into Alexandra's eyes without blinking.

The Goddess said nothing, but her mouth moved slightly. *Reciting those damn numbers.* Minho counted the times Alexandra blinked. Five times in one second. No one who's stable can blink that many times in a row. Alexandra whispered those stupid numbers under her breath like an Orphan trying to remember the number of steps to the rumored underground bunker. "Even the Orphans of Remnant Nation can count silently in their head . . . you're just a crazy Pilgrim. A desperate, lonely, and crazy Pilgrim that ran from the war. Prove me otherwise."

"Minho, stop . . . please," Sadina begged.

"That's enough! Go!" Trish tried to push him away.

"No! She killed someone back there, and the way she did it . . . I could tell it wasn't the first time she's killed someone. She's crazy. You all trust her, but she only cares about herself, and she's going to get you killed!" He made sure Trish heard every word, but she didn't seem to get it. None of them did.

"That's it . . ." Roxy pulled at Minho again, but Alexandra held up her hand.

“No, he’s right. I did kill that man.” She paused, making eye contact with each of the islanders before continuing. “I’m sorry I didn’t tell you, before. He was a terrible person. The leader of the Remnant Nation. I’m not even sure he was fully human—he’d moved past The Gone years ago . . .” She spoke softly. “You were upset at me earlier for not showing more grief over my city, but a Goddess does not boast. I killed him to avenge all those who perished. My people, my city, would want me to rebuild, and what better way than with Newt’s descendent.” She held out her hand to Sadina.

Sadina glowed with awe and grabbed Alexandra’s hand.

Minho couldn’t believe what was happening. “Horseshit. You don’t give a damn about the city—if you did you wouldn’t be here, running away.”

“Minho, that’s enough!” Roxy scolded him. He shrugged. He wasn’t afraid of Alexandra, and he wasn’t afraid of the others being mad at him for the truth he knew that they didn’t yet understand.

The ship’s hull groaned. “I need help!” Orange yelled from the captain’s wheel. The *Maze Cutter* shuddered a bit.

Dominic and Miyoko ran to the starboard side. “We’re scraping bad here!”

Minho hurried to the captain’s wheel. “See? She sent us on a death trip! There’s only ice ahead. We shouldn’t have come this way. We need to go back to the coast!”

“There’s no room to even turn around!” Roxy yelled.

“You fool, you simple-minded, feral, fool!” Alexandra pushed her way to the captain’s wheel and shoved Minho out of the way.

Stunned, he stepped back. Orange did the same. Sadina, Trish, and Miyoko all looked at him with disappointment, maybe disgust. Dominic and Roxy avoided his gaze.

It was all enough to make him almost miss the old fortress, even the far-bottom level, even the one they called Hell.

4
ALEXANDRA

"I warned you about the inlets!" The Orphan soldiers were about as useless as Flint, in his life and in his death. Alexandra counted on the digits to guide her. 55, 89, 144 . . .

"Everyone, get down to the cabin!" Roxy shouted. "Stay in the center, away from the sides where there might be impact."

"Stupid, stupid fools," Alexandra said under her breath, firmly holding onto the wheel as she recited the principles in her mind. With each digit she felt the boat hit another ice patch. 55, 89, 144 . . . She could smell the pine trees that surrounded the Villa. It was just up ahead, like an X in her mind. 233, 377, 610 . . . The Goddess felt the boat slowing down as if it agreed, as if it knew they had arrived at the Villa's home.

"What's happening?" Orange asked. "We're stopping?"

The boat slowed to a complete halt.

"Minho?" The orange-haired girl grabbed her weapon. These feral, wild, un-Flared children . . . none of them even knew what reverence was. The boat rocked back and forth gently as if to shake its own head at their disrespect.

"It's done." Minho threw his arms up in the air. "We're stuck here. Are you happy now?"

He looked at Alexandra with a point to prove, and she wished she could scream at him. Without the Evolution, nothing mattered. Nothing at all. Heat flushed her body. Her every inch stung with impatience.

"Yes, of course I am." She moved from the wheel and pointed. "It's right up there."

Dominic stepped in. "The ice must have taken off the rudder. We're stalled."

"A sitting target for the Remnant Nation," Orange said, her calm voice somehow more ominous than if she'd yelled it.

"Wait, we're still moving." Dominic looked over the edge.

"It's just the current." Minho leaned over the rail. The natural flow of the inlet moved the ship ever so slightly.

Alexandra paid no mind to the blabber. "The Villa is right there." She walked along the side of the boat. "The water is only a few feet deep here. We can wade though the waters and walk over." She knew this because Mannus had taken every opportunity to complain about it, and they'd been on a boat no bigger than a canoe.

The three others stared at her as if she hadn't spoken a single word. "It's shallow enough to walk through to the shore of the Villa," she repeated herself.

The orange-haired Orphan just looked at her. "But . . . but the water . . . it's . . . Cold."

"Cold? It's freezing. Are you kidding me?" Dominic scoffed. Moments like this really did make Alexandra miss Flint. He was an idiot, but an obedient one.

"Oh, come, now. Are you afraid of a little water?" the Goddess teased. "It's no more than a foot deep a few meters ahead." Their minds would have to evolve through actions. "You said it yourself, we're sitting targets here." She looked for the trees lining the back side of the island. The Villa was well hidden, but as sure as the digits were sacred, it was there. She actually welcomed the idea of the cold water to cool the heat that pulsed inside her. Fires of war had infected her mind and maybe all she needed were these icy waters to reset her nervous system.

Dominic looked to Minho as if he were the one in charge. As if they weren't in the company of the one and only Godhead. Maybe she had lost her momentum.

She didn't care. Things had come to a head.

"Gather the others." She made the order in a voice that commanded respect, filled with the influence of all her training and experience.

They'd obey. What else could they do now that they were stuck?

She repressed the smile aching to burst out.

CHAPTER ELEVEN

Senate of Sequencers

I
ISAAC

Cian drew the seashell shape bigger and bigger until the beginning of the circle resembled the eye of a storm. Maybe it only looked like that to Isaac because everything reminded him of the night his parents and sister died. Especially when he didn't want to be reminded.

"So that's what you're calling these Glader families, sequencers?" Old Man Frypan asked. "But if they're so protected then why do they need the Cure?"

"It's not a Cure . . ." Ximena mumbled.

"The aurora is exactly why they need the Cure." Erros pointed up to the colors in the sky.

"It's bad. I knew it." Jackie kicked up dirt at her feet and grabbed at rocks. The west-siders could be so dramatic sometimes.

"No, actually, the opposite. The sun changes our DNA little by little, natural evolution, and the auroras are small blasts from the sun mixed with our atmosphere that evolve the DNA of everyone on Earth, but the auroras won't touch the sequencers. Not where WICKED buried them."

Ximena gave Isaac that look again. *Strangers will put us in the ground.* She also glanced at his wound and frowned. For some reason she started messing with the material at the bottom of her shirt.

"Erros . . ." Cian shook his head. "Language."

"Sorry. *Buried* is a terrible word. Most cultures bury their dead but WICKED. . . . WICKED buried the living in an underground world built to survive the Flare. They knew it was coming; they orchestrated it years ahead of time. And they were all kept safe from the solar flares and the Flare virus. But if they come out now, they'd never last more than a year. There's too much that their once-precious DNA has missed out on. Even the air is different now; all the coltsfoot in the world couldn't help their lungs." Erros lit another cigar. "They'd die from basic exposure . . . the Cure is for the youngest of their generations to have a fighting chance."

Isaac knew his history, and the world had always been so bonkers that he actually found himself believing Erros. If they could put kids in giant mazes under the ground, why not families, hidden in a different, safer spot?

But exposure for them at this point did seem dangerous. Ever since the islanders arrived to this new land, the environment had threatened to kill them: Lil Newt poisoned Jackie. A rash put Ms. Cowan in a coma. Even that murder hornet that looked like a tiny Griever made Dominic's arm swell up. There were probably things on their island back home that would be extra dangerous to someone who didn't grow up there. Isaac immediately understood the challenges these so-called Sequencers were up against.

"Why didn't they bring them out sooner?" Isaac asked. "Why keep them underground so long?"

Cian answered with one word. "Fear."

"And safety," Erros added. "Familiarity. Comfort. The Senate of Sequencers vote every three years, and every three years they vote to remain. But it's time to shit or get off the pot. For evolution."

"That's why our Village doesn't have a Senate, we have elders . . ." Ximena mumbled as she ripped the bottom of her shirt off and then tied it around Isaac's knife wound. "You need to put pressure on this." She made a knot so tight his whole leg bounced with his pulsing blood. "Plus the Hollowers can probably smell blood and weakness."

"Thanks," Isaac said. It felt like she might have really cared about him there for a second. Until she called him weak.

"So . . ." Jackie turned to Old Man Frypan. "All these fancy people who were once the world's greatest and brightest are now held back from evolving, because they're not experiencing . . . real life? Now that's some irony."

"Sounds like that's what they're saying." Frypan shook his head.

Erros continued. "If the Senate of Scientists would have just studied nature, instead of their human-caused chemistry—they would have understood that in time. . . . Hell, maybe not *their* lifetime, but eventually . . . nature, the earth, the sky, everything would have corrected itself. But they thought they knew better."

"Man always thinks he knows better than nature." Of course this came from Ximena.

"Yeah, well sometimes nature just sucks." Jackie chucked a rock into the darkness.

Isaac understood her frustration. Lacey and Carson died because they came here, all for some Cure to save humankind, and it turns out it was just to try to help a few special families. Isaac couldn't grab all the different questions racing in his mind. "Why didn't Kletter just tell us all this, why didn't she—"

"Would you have believed her?" Erros asked.

No, Isaac thought. But he shrugged. "Maybe."

"Annie Kletter couldn't tell the truth if her life depended on it," Ximena added.

"The truth is always the last thing to be believed. People fight the truth," Cian said. "You," he pointed at Old Man Frypan again. "You couldn't take the truth earlier and left. It's what's expected."

"Well . . . the truth sucks!" Jackie whipped another rock overhead and Isaac waited for the thump of it hitting the earth, maybe a tree, but instead he heard a metal *CLANK*. A sound he missed hearing from the forge back home.

"Watch it, we've got our equipment over there." Cian stood up and looked over into the darkness.

"That Berg's been hit with a lot worse than a pebble," Erros said, but all Isaac really heard was *Berg*.

"Jackie! They have a Berg!" Isaac wanted to scream, to hug her, find his own rock to chuck. Maybe even hug a rock. He turned to Frypan and then to Cian. "Can you take us to Alaska to find our friends? They're with the Godhead. Maybe the Godhead knows how to get to the Sequencers, and—"

Cian cut Isaac off. "Whoa, there, little fella. Bergs aren't cheap to fly. Plus, the Godhead is as power-driven as those in WICKED ever were. The Godhead . . ." Cian looked to where the sound of the rock hitting the Berg came from.

"The Godhead is its own disease," Ximena mumbled.

"But we need to get to our friends. Please." Isaac would get on his knees and beg if he had to. The thought of never finding them or seeing them again had been gutting him since they separated. "Please . . ." He turned to Ximena and the backpack on the ground in between them.

"Isaac, don't even think about it." Ximena shook her head.

"Please." He held his hands together to ask of her the one thing he knew she didn't want to do.

"What's going on?" Jackie whispered to no one in particular.

Isaac kept at it. "We can help them *and* find our friends. Please."

Ximena merely looked at the fire.

Jackie tossed another rock into the center of the flames. Ash kicked up sparks.

"Alaska," Old Man Frypan said. "Huh. Site of the Maze . . . is that where the Sequencers are?"

Please . . . Isaac begged Ximena with his eyes.

Cian shook his head. "Yeah but no. The aurora's gotta be ten times stronger up north in Alaska. I don't know what that will do to the Berg."

Erros didn't add much hope. "And we've already surveyed all of Alaska—no pink or orange lake. We have to save our remaining fuel for finding the mark of the buried." Cian cleared his throat and looked at Erros expectantly. "Sorry, the mark of the Sequencers."

Isaac knew Ximena could convince them. *She had to.* He didn't want to take the Cure from her, but he needed it. "It's bigger than the Villas," he whispered to her. She could destroy as many Villas as she wanted to, but it wouldn't change things. This might.

"Dammit, Isaac," Ximena picked up her backpack.

"Please . . ."

She let out a sigh and stood up. "I can help the Sequencers," she announced to Cian and Erros. "Take the islanders to Alaska to find their friends, and I'll take you to the Cure."

The two brothers said nothing, just stared at her. But it was only a matter of time, now. She'd convince them for sure.

Isaac let out a sigh of relief.

Thank you, he mouthed to Ximena.

2
XIMENA

Ximena had no intention of giving them the Cure. But going to Alaska? Fine.

She'd escape and make her way to the Alaskan Villa, as good a plan as any, but she wasn't dumb enough to give something so valuable away, especially to strangers. She'd make them believe that *she* trusted *them* enough to share the Cure.

Cian didn't seem on board. "It doesn't really matter, anyway. The Cure is useless without finding the Sequencers, and Kletter made sure that the entrance and coordinates were kept secret. We've been looking for . . . well, for longer than I want to even admit." He threw another log on the fire. "You can sleep here; there's plenty of wood."

"Man, I got my hopes up," Jackie said. Isaac just gave her a sad nod.

He certainly seemed to have no intention of giving up. "What if we go up there, and we talk to the Godhead? They've got to know where these people are, right?"

"Wrong."

"The Godhead isn't what you think it is," Cian said while laying down palm branches, apparently for his bed. "Sleep closer to the fire and the bugs won't bother you."

Isaac and Jackie pulled palms over for Old Man Frypan.

Ximena had a strange, nagging feeling that she couldn't shake. Another intuition was coming, and her body was already fighting it before it got to her mind. It physically hurt her to lie, and her intuition always felt like a lie until proven true. The time it took for the pain of the lie to leave her always varied. Sometimes the intuition only felt like a lie for a second or two. Other times it took months, and sometimes years for the truth to be proven. She had a gift, and deep down she knew it was somehow related to the mutations of the Flare virus.

That often made her hate these inner-knowings the most. Her body was all tension and doubt, wondering if she could be going mad. It never got easier, and right now she felt a big hairy lie creeping up in her throat. It got louder inside her head. Then stronger . . .

Until she had to say it.

"I know where the Sequencers are located." Her voice cracked a bit. Then she cleared her throat and raised her voice. "People at our Villa knew all about them, talked about it way more than they should have, obviously. I can guide you to where they are."

Cian looked at her with a focus that felt invasive. Ximena repeated the lie in her head. *I know where the Sequencers are . . .*

"Cian?" Erros asked his brother. "That's what she's been hiding?"

Cian tied the red scarf around his neck and picked up his crossbow. Erros let out what sounded like a chuckle and stepped closer to his own weapon, too. *Had she gone too far, too quickly? Were they about to aim their weapons at her and fire?* All the worst thoughts ran through her head but she stood still, while being sure of nothing but herself.

"Well?" Cian turned to Ximena, kicking the bed of palm branches at his feet. "Since we have absolutely no other leads or hopes, let's get to Alaska and drop these islanders off. Then you can prove yourself and show us where they are. How about that?"

Yep. She'd gone too far, this time.

Ximena tried to slow her heart, prevent the fear from spreading all over her face. Her joints burned with the lie; panic filled her lungs like a million tiny pinpricks. She had no idea what she'd do after they dropped Isaac and the others off. But she needed to figure something out, quick.

They'd called her bluff.

CHAPTER TWELVE

Cold Secrets

I
ALEXANDRA

Ice cold water climbed up Alexandra's calves as the bottom wool of the Pilgrim's coat dragged along the shallow inlet. Like in the ice baths Nicholas had once made her take to strengthen her soul, she welcomed the chilling shivers dancing across her skin. Much better than the fires of war.

"It's freeeeeezing," Trish complained.

"Pretend you're crab-fishing," Miyoko said. That one was calm. Quiet. The Goddess would promote her in time. Those who were quiet, obedient—she liked them best.

"Careful, it's slippery here." Orange focused a tactical light on the water for the others straggling behind. "Let's get there as quick as we can, get it over with."

Alexandra wasn't worried. Never mind the temperature, the three women at the Villa would have a fire lit to warm them up. They'd have tea. And they'd finalize the Cure. Sounded so simple, so close. Maybe even a bit mad.

Every step felt colder as the water rose a few inches in the middle of the inlet, but Alexandra's Evolution was in sight. Even the scent of pine trees harkened that it was near. The war was behind her, the Evolution closer and closer. So close, now. Yes, so close.

"Can the digits warm me up?" Sadina asked sarcastically from behind.

Alexandra had so much to teach her, among the first things: *how to talk to a Goddess.* She hadn't rid herself of Nicholas and Mikhail just to be disrespected by replacements. She was the last remnant of the Godhead and the keeper of the Evolution.

"Numbers can't do squat." Minho lifted his knees with every step, slamming his feet down and splashing the Goddess with icy water.

Alexandra inhaled for three seconds, held her breath for three, exhaled . . .

If she could convince even a Pilgrim like Mannus to bow to her, then she could convince Minho. In time, he would be her faithful Guard.

"Whatever you want to be, see, feel, or find . . . you can shape it with the digits." Alexandra had the urge to run, get to the other side, get warm, but she stood still to let Minho move past her. Then she resumed, close to Sadina. She took her hand.

"Dear Sadina," she said as they waded through the shallow, dark waters. "Reciting them out loud is exactly what gives them power."

"How, though?"

The Goddess needed to start her teachings at the very beginning. There was nothing more basic than the digits. But also nothing in the entire existence of time that could be more complicated.

"Reciting the digits while holding a thought gives those thoughts all the influence of the digits. The intention is entangled into the numbers."

There. She didn't know how to say it more simply than that.

"So the numbers circled in the *Book of Newt*, 1, 2, 3—"

"No. No. No." She said it too quickly and revealed her annoyance.

Sadina pulled her hand back, but the Goddess held on to her. *Blood of Newt's blood.* She needed this girl, needed patience like never before.

"What I mean, Dear Sadina,"—she squeezed her hand— "is that there are two numbers in the sequence before that . . ." No. She would teach her later, by fireside, with tea. "Come, let's climb out and get warm. There'll be plenty of time for lessons later." She let go of Sadina's hand so they both could climb the embankment.

"Here, Miyoko, give me your hand." Dominic helped her and the other young ones scramble up.

Alexandra stood where she was, her feet numb, looking back for Roxy and the orange-haired one, still wading toward them.

Roxy spoke from the darkness. "Go ahead, Ms. Godhead, we're catching up."

"Goddess?" Minho bent over the river's ledge and offered Alexandra his hand. *Finally, reverence.* She put her hand in Minho's and placed her foot on the soft-soiled bank. Had she been able to feel her feet she might have had better footing, but before Minho could yank her up, her foot slipped and the Goddess fell against the bank, then back into the water with an embarrassing splash.

"Minho!" Sadina cried.

"She slipped, it wasn't me," Minho said. "Come on, I got you . . ." The soldier tried again, this time pulling Alexandra from the water by her wrist and her elbow. Her feet finally found solid, stable ground.

"Thank you, soldier." She made to straighten out her cloak and brush off the mud, but Minho held on to her wrist, tightening his grip.

"This marking . . ." Minho clenched her wrist with both hands and twisted.

"Let go. You're hurting me." She tried to pull her hand back to no avail. He was too strong. "Let. Go," she repeated firmly.

"This tattoo . . . it's the same as the Great Master's . . ."

Minho finally looked at Alexandra with God-fearing eyes. He had no idea that his *Great Master* wasn't a master of anything. That he was nothing more than a maddened Crank. She wouldn't address his ignorance on the matter. The symbol of the sequence was sacred, and the Goddess didn't owe Minho or anyone else an explanation.

She pulled against the soldier to free her hand, then hid her wrist within the wet, yellow folds of her cloak.

2
MINHO

Orphans have no names.

No friends. No family.

But in the Remnant Nation, there was one thing they did always have.

Symbols.

Markers.

Minho never learned the meaning of all of them, but in the absence of knowledge, he had made up his own. Mostly something to do with death. "Kill the Godhead" and all that. But despite not knowing the true significance of the etching on Alexandra's wrist, the quickness with which she had covered it up told Minho all he needed to know. She had more to hide than he thought.

"That's a Remnant Nation symbol." He pointed at the so-called Godhead's wrist and called to Orange to see if she recognized it, too. All Orphan soldiers had stared at the same walls their whole lives. Minho had memorized every last molding of an archway and every last scratch in the cement. He saw the walls in his mind as he fell asleep. "This is from the Remnant Nation," he said again, this time louder.

"What is?" Orange asked.

"Her wrist." Minho pointed again. "Dom, you saw it, right?"

Dominic shook his head. "Not really."

"Sadina? Trish?" Minho looked at the others. Someone had to have seen it, too. "She has an etching . . . a tattoo on her wrist that is the *exact* same as the Great Master of the Remnant Nation. I'm telling you. No doubt whatsoever."

Sadina tried to intervene. "Let's just find the Villa, get inside and—"

"I'm not going anywhere until she shows us her wrists." He crossed his arms and planted his feet. He glared at Alexandra, sure she'd try to pass off another lie.

"We can warm up inside and discuss etchings of the Gods later." The Goddess turned her back on Minho, but Dominic held his arms out, blocking her from walking any farther.

"If you don't have anything to hide, why not just show us your wrists?" the boy asked. "Goddess?"

Alexandra turned back to the group. The others didn't scold Dominic for challenging the Godhead the way they did Minho. That was fine. She stood there, looking pathetic until enough eyes were on her, waiting. She sighed and finally pulled up her cloak sleeve. Even in the dark, with only the light of the full moon, Minho could see that it was just a bare wrist. Nothing there.

"What about the other one," Minho said. "Show us your other wrist."

Alexandra whipped her hand around her cloak so quickly that she flashed the material underneath. Thin and shiny, something the Orphan had never seen before. His dullest knife could slice through it, easily. She pushed up her left sleeve on the wool cloak and Minho wondered if her swift motions were supposed to scare him. She turned her bared wrist over to more confused looks. Nothing there.

But Minho knew what he had seen. He stepped up and held both of her wrists until he could see the faint lines of a marking. She raised an eyebrow at him when he finally let go, then rubbed at her own wrist. She rubbed at it until a growing spiral in black ink appeared. Roxy, Orange, and all the rest came closer to look.

"A tattoo? Were you in some kind of trial or ritual?" Sadina asked.

Alexandra let out a laugh. "I'm a Godhead, not an infinite God. The Trials ended long before I was born, child."

"So what's with the tattoo, then?" Trish asked.

"A tattoo? Just like Old Man—" Miyoko said until Dominic elbowed her.

"Old Man who . . . ?" Alexandra looked at them both, but Minho wouldn't let the fake God know about poor Frypan.

"Nothing," Minho said. "What's your etching mean?"

"It's a symbol of the Sequence of Digits. Part of my knowing. A reminder that I am one with the whole. I am a part of everything and everything is a part of me. That is what the digits mean, among other things. . . . The digits are *sacred*. Beyond sacred." She spoke nonsense, as usual.

"If you say so." Minho tried to seem unfazed, uncaring. If he'd learned one thing from the Grief Bearers, this in fact would bother her more.

"The only tattoos we ever saw were from the Gladers of Old," Trish said.

"And on half-Cranks," Roxy added. "I've seen a lot of half-Cranks with markings."

Maybe that explained it. Maybe Alexandra was a true half-Crank.

"Come on. There are many people with inked memories." Alexandra covered her wrist back up with the cloak. "Some of them choose patterns that aren't their own memories but are memories nonetheless." She motioned to a path through the tree. "Can we continue to the warmth now?"

Dominic looked at Minho. "Might be a good idea. We're gonna freeze to death out here."

But Minho couldn't let this opportunity pass. "It doesn't matter where you go, that symbol is a marking of the Remnant Nation. Which means you're not a Godhead at all. You're a Grief Bearer or maybe a part of some other Nation, but you're no Goddess of Alaska."

The group let out a collective groan. He'd lost the chance after all.

"Can we at least argue about this inside? I'm cold." Sadina shivered to prove her point.

Minho shrugged. "Orange?" He needed her to back him up.

Orange shook her head, showed genuine remorse in her expression. Nothing, then.

Minho wished he could forget things from the Remnant Nation as easily as Orange apparently had, but even the smell of the air in the lower level called Hell was something that would never leave his inner senses. Sewage and black mold. "You don't remember seeing that symbol? In the walls? It was a direction marker."

Orange's face went blank.

"There was one by the food hall?" Minho insisted. "Come on. The food hall . . . sometimes after my watch, I'd punch the marker on the wall just outside the hall, and you and Skinny made fun of me for it."

Orange took a deep breath and squinted into a smile. "Yeah, that's why he called you *Happy*."

"Sounds about right," Dominic said.

"Wait . . . you're sure that's the same carving?" Orange asked as the others walked toward the Villa, but Alexandra and her Remnant wrist were already well ahead of them.

"The same." Minho wished he had a wall to punch right then.

Sadina had hung back. "But why would the Remnant Nation have anything to do with the Godhead?" she asked. Alexandra didn't hear or didn't have an answer. She just continued to walk away from them toward the trees like a coward.

Minho caught up to her. The others followed.

Then he shared his thoughts on the matter, clear as day, making sure the woman could hear him. "She's not a God or Goddess or anything close to a Godhead. She's just some lowly Orphan, probably escaped the Nation at a cliff ceremony before coming to Alaska."

Alexandra laughed again, kept walking.

No one else said a word.

CHAPTER THIRTEEN

Nations of Remnants

I
ISAAC

The Berg launched toward the sky, roaring and creaking and shaking. It soon flew smoothly enough, and the inside compartments were a lot cozier than the one in which they'd been handcuffed —that metal beast ultimately crashed. Isaac and Jackie roamed around the cabin as Cian and Erros piloted. "Sort of reminds me of my yurt back home . . ."

"Yeah, they don't clean up after themselves either." Jackie pointed to a scatter of animal hides and piles of weapons in the back corner.

"It's lived in," Isaac suggested, deflecting her subtle jab at his home.

"You trust them?" Jackie whispered. "I still think they're bad news."

Isaac didn't know who or what he trusted anymore. "I trust Ximena," he finally said, looking over his shoulder at the Spanish-speaking spitfire and Old Man Frypan by a window.

"But . . . these guys." Jackie lowered her voice even more. "We know nothing about them other than what they told us. They could be from some other Godhead for all we know. Or Mars. Or criminals." Jackie said the word Godhead as if chewing a piece of fish with too many bones.

Isaac shook his head. He'd seen his family die, had been kidnapped, killed Cranks, stood inches away from a Griever, and he just wanted to reunite with his friends and go back home. He went through his mind and listed the facts he knew to be true. "They fed us. They saved us from the Hollower. And they're going to get us to Alaska to find the others a lot quicker than we could have without them . . . and that's all I care about right now."

Maybe they were terrible people, and maybe they were lying about all the bonkers frequency and sequence stuff. But Isaac just wanted to get back home. Means to an end and all that.

"What about her?" Jackie motioned to Ximena. "I didn't care if she wandered off on her own, but from what we've learned, are you really going to let these guys just . . . take her? After they drop us off?"

Ximena was smarter than Isaac, maybe even stronger than him, too. "I think she'll be okay." And he meant it. He imagined there wasn't much out there that Ximena couldn't survive.

"Well, I think she's hiding a whole bunch of things."

Isaac had found himself believing or wanting to believe every single thing Ximena had said since they met her. She was so sure of herself and pushed for the truth so hard, that he didn't think *she* could possibly lie. But of course that was some serious naivety. He looked over at her and noticed her shoulders were slumped and her head hung down. She no longer appeared confident in the least. "Oh . . ."

"Yeah . . ." Jackie whispered. "And what do you think will happen when Cian and Erros drop us off and find out she lied to them?" Jackie gestured to the pile of weapons. "Those look like weapons they've collected from other people. . . ." *People who are now dead*, her eyes concluded.

"Why can't one thing—just one—be simple? Ever?" He sighed at Jackie then calmly walked over to Ximena. "You really know where the Sequencers are?" he whispered.

She didn't answer.

Which *was* an answer.

Frypan might throw out a *Double shuck* just about then. Jackie had an *I told you so* look plastered on her face.

Isaac's head spun with all he'd learned in the last twenty-four hours. Kletter doing trials on Ximena's Village. Ximena being the last born of her entire town. Sequencers and families hidden underground. There were just too many questions that Isaac needed answers to. And unlike Kletter—who never said more than she needed to—Cian and Erros were willing to tell them things. Maybe Isaac shouldn't leave Ximena alone with them, after all. But that would mean sacrificing himself, and possibly never seeing his friends again. *Any of them.*

"You don't know . . . do you?" Isaac asked to belabor the point.

"I'll figure it out." Ximena lifted her head before lowering it again.

"We've got a stew cooking here, don't we?" Old Man Frypan said. "Let her cook."

"But if she doesn't *know—*" Jackie began but Frypan cut her off.

"She knows a hell of a lot, this young one. She's just simmering is all."

Ximena looked up at Frypan with sad eyes. "*Gracias.* I'll get them to take me to the Master Villa once we drop you off. There'll be something there I can use in my favor—I know it."

"That's your grand plan?" Isaac's worry increased tenfold. "Go to the Master Villa and see what you can find?"

Ximena rolled her eyes. "You should be thanking me. They didn't want to waste their fuel on you."

"Well, yes. Thank you for getting us to Alaska," Jackie said, but Ximena didn't look overly appreciative for the gratitude.

"You should be thanking me for going to the Master Villa to destroy whatever I can, because somewhere in their records is where Annie Kletter got the coordinates to your little island of Immunes." She said each word with increasing ferocity. "And who knows how long it will be before someone else even dumber than Kletter is sent out there to gather *more* of you."

Her words, *gather more of you*, stabbed Isaac in his other calf. His feet felt pulled from under him. He never thought their island could be at risk all over again. Old Man Frypan cleared his throat. Jackie just shook her head. Isaac thought Kletter's journey had been a once-in-a-lifetime lucky shot at finding them, not a coordinated plan with actual coordinates. His eyes stung as he thought of everyone back home. Their lives were at risk.

"You didn't think of that, did you?" Ximena asked him, and that did it. Made his decision for him. He would stick with Ximena and go to the Master Villa, to provide any help she might need. But most importantly, he planned to destroy all records pertaining to their island of Immunes. Especially the coordinates.

2
ALEXANDRA

This time, as Alexandra approached the Villa, she was free from all harm. No traps. No trip wires. No axes. And there it was, hidden in the tall pines. The Villa.

"Come," she called behind her to the others. "It's right here." She couldn't believe the smell of fires hung in the air this far out into the Alaskan islands. The Goddess looked at the skyline, a faint red glow of her city turning to ash with the aurora dancing above it.

"Careful," Orange said. "There's wires along the tree there—they must have alarms set or something." She pulled on one of the wires like an idiot. "Let me go first."

"No. Those have already been spent." Alexandra straightened her oversized cloak and double-checked that the *Book of Newt* remained secure. "Come. Now."

There was no clear path to the Villa. *Create the path by walking*, Nicholas used to say. She hated that all of his quips and phrases and words of wisdom still knocked around her brain, but most of those ideas, thoughts, and beliefs weren't even his. He'd pretended like all the wisdom he shared was his own genius, but most of it was stolen straight out of the books he'd hoarded in his library. He allowed Alexandra to have her innate knowledge, the knowing that came with her evolved virus and her sequencing that she could tap into from the Infinite Glade, but he forbade her from the history and books in his library. A slow smile spread across her face and she realized all of those books, every last one of them, everything Nicholas had once owned and loved, was gone.

Up in flames. Ashes. Dust.

Alexandra had no sadness for the loss of things that were never hers.

She had the one and only thing she cared about.

3

"We'll go in first, make sure everything's clear," Orange said, but the Goddess was accustomed to walking into rooms before her Evolutionary Guards.

"Clear?" Alexandra scoffed. "No need. It's just three little ladies testing combinations of the Cure. If anything, you'll startle them, I'll go in first." This was her city. Her Villa. Her Cure.

"But if there's—"

"I said, I'll go in *first.*" Alexandra walked to the door on the lower level and opened it slowly. She had arrived back to the Villa sooner than the scientists probably expected, but for *good* reason. And with the Orphans and their guns, the Goddess could get the women to give her everything she wanted this time. *Everything she wanted for the Evolution and more.*

"Hello . . ." she called into the empty room. Echoes replied.

Minho and Orange stepped in front of her, their guns drawn to inspect each room. Alexandra recited the digits in her mind. If they insisted on meeting the women first, fine. She walked into the next room with books lining its walls. She would soon be writing new history for all future generations. The fire of St. Petersburg was tragic, the most destructive and stupidest thing Mikhail could have done, but the Goddess would use all his failures to her advantage.

Every last one.

After all, those lowly Pilgrims of the Maze would be dead, all the crum of the city would be wiped clean, and Alexandra could now populate the city with those who *chose* the Cure. No more need to campaign and convince them to join the Evolution. She'd be better off rebuilding from scratch, with better citizens—trusting, moldable inhabitants . . . like the Immunes. Alexandra turned and smiled at Sadina. "Come, they'll want to meet you." She pulled Sadina along with her into the next room.

Empty.

"Hello . . ." Alexandra announced herself louder. Apparently scientists went to bed as soon as the sun set. She'd wake their tired little brains and get them on their feet. "Wake up! Rise to see your Goddess!" She walked through another darkened room.

"They already know about me?" Sadina let go of Trish's hand and clasped Alexandra's.

The child's palm was sweaty and gross, but Alexandra squeezed it and led Newt's great-niece into the Villa. "Are you kidding? Your bloodline is the one they've been waiting for."

"Are you the one who told them about Sadina?" Trish asked.

Alexandra decided she needed to put Sadina's girlfriend into another room, keep her busy while the women tested on Sadina. Inside. Outside. In the basement. Somewhere the Goddess wouldn't be hammered by her incessant questions.

As always, Alexandra tried to hide her annoyance at their ignorance and lack of faith. "These women worked hard to make sure the Cure would come to be." She turned to Sadina and placed her hand against her cheek. "The Evolution was always meant to be, we just needed you for the ultimate and final phase." She squeezed her face gently and smiled. "And here you are."

"Hello?" Alexandra led Sadina down a hall and up a stairway to the lab where Mannus practically got them all killed. Last time, the women greeted her with weapons as soon as her foot reached their soil, and today . . . they weren't anywhere to be found.

"What will they do to her?" Trish asked loudly right on Alexandra's heels. The girl was practically stepping on her cloak.

Alexandra had to force a smile this time. "It's not what they will do to her, it's what they'll be able to do *with her*." There. *That should reassure her.* It didn't matter what they needed to do to Sadina to get the Cure. If the scientists had to break every bone in the girl's body and suck the marrow out with a straw to get what they needed, Alexandra would allow it. Hell, she'd encourage it.

"Hello . . . ?" She called again, stepping foot in the lab.

"It doesn't look like anyone's here." Minho had returned to the group, lowering his weapon.

"Nonsense." Alexandra shook her head. What did a lowly soldier know? "They have to be here."

"Every room's clear," Orange said.

All the younger ones and Roxy filled the room. Alexandra scanned the entire place and her vision went static when she realized nothing had changed since their last visit. "We were just here . . ." She swept the items off the table with one swift motion of her arm. Mannus. He must have scared them so completely that they left.

Mannus be damned.

That idiotic horned-freak.

Alexandra needed a new plan, and quickly. The orange-haired soldier set up guard in the window. "You can see the war fires from here. They probably heard the bombs, panicked, and—"

"Scientists *don't* panic," Alexandra snapped, but it only made her head pound harder. It felt a thousand pounds on top of her shoulders. She recited the digits to herself and started pulling vials out of the cabinets.

"So, what do we do now?" Sadina asked, practically on top of the Goddess.

Alexandra moved around Sadina and looked through the cabinets. She would figure something out—she had Newt's bloodline and that was the most important thing. She'd go mad and jump off a cliff before she wasted this opportunity for the final, ultimate Cure. She looked for needles. "I'll just . . . do it myself . . . 0, 1, 1, 2, 3, 5, 8 . . ." she mumbled to herself, not caring. She said things that hardly needed repeating. Madness. Madness. Madness! But she kept searching, digging, thinking. Talking.

"The Cure. The Evolution will ignite. The code will be complete."

She tore the place apart.

4
MINHO

Orphans have no history, know nothing about where they came from.

And the Orphan named Minho only knew where he was headed.

"Hey, can you take it easy on the Goddess?" Sadina asked softly. That was the problem—Sadina was too soft for her own good. She cared too much about things that didn't matter. Especially people she hardly knew.

Minho leaned in close. "Don't you remember what Frypan said?"

Her face scrunched up. "What are you talking about? When?"

"Back along the coast, when you two would have your late-night fireside talks. He said *Don't trust the trustless.*"

"Exactly, and you don't trust *her*, so maybe I shouldn't trust *you*." She straightened up as if making herself taller would make herself right, but she couldn't be more wrong. Frypan wasted every breath he had left on this girl who didn't understand the simplest thing.

"No, that's not it. He said to trust *yourself* the most." Orange said over the railing of the balcony, on watch.

"Do all orphans eavesdrop on private conversations?" Sadina snapped.

"We can't help that we were trained to have sniper hearing." Orange shrugged before going back to her lookout post. "You two were loud and woke me up."

"Most nights I didn't sleep but laid there on watch, protecting everyone from danger." Minho wasn't just annoyed that Sadina forgot everything Old Man Frypan had taught her, but her weaknesses made it easier for the Godhead to manipulate her. She wouldn't have survived an hour in the Remnant Nation. None of these islanders would have. Weak and malleable, all of them.

Sadina didn't act intimidated. "Well, whatever Frypan told me, I'm sure he didn't mean for you to throw it in my face later."

"We're trying to help you," Orange said.

"Look around. Look where she brought you." Minho pointed out all the shelves of equipment. Devices he had never seen before but he sure as hell didn't want to know how they worked. "She brought you here to do all kinds of tests with your blood and who knows what else. She doesn't care about you!"

"You're crazy! Your whole nation is crazy . . . and you're lucky the Godhead doesn't turn you over to them!" Sadina shouted at Minho before storming away, down the hallway. It was getting harder and harder for Minho to keep his promise to Isaac about protecting her.

"Hey, Happy. You've got to cool down." Orange walked over and kicked the broken glass away from the doorway. Minho ignored her, instead looking behind framed maps hanging on the wall, searching for a hidden safe or a secret room. Nothing was ever hung in the Remnant Nation unless it concealed something else. He knocked against the walls of the room, listening for a hollow sound or any change in sound. Anything that might hide a hidden doorway. He threw framed maps on the floor.

"Seriously, Minho, stop. You're going to scare the others . . ." Orange looked out into the hallway.

"Yeah? Well, they should be scared. We're sitting targets here and the *Maze Cutter* is worthless. The Godhead is worthless!" He tore down another map off the wall, then ripped it to pieces, as many pieces as possible. He was angry at Sadina, but more disgusted in himself that he had ever wanted to join the Godhead. The stupid, useless, evil Godhead that brought them there to an empty Villa with a room full of nothing but black curtains, stationary equipment, and useless maps. "What are we supposed to do now?" Minho asked.

Orange looked around the room and shook her head. "I don't know. Camp here until the war dies down?" She looked back to Minho and adjusted her weapon. "What options do we have?"

He stood and stared at the map of the Americas torn to small bits on the floor. *The map.* He pulled Kletter's captain's log out of his back pocket. He recognized the symbol on Alexandra's wrist from the Remnant Nation, but there was something similar on Kletter's map. He flipped through each page to find it. At first glance, it looked like a pencil drawing of a hurricane or something on the map over an island, but as Minho examined more closely—it was basically the symbol from both the Remnant Nation and the Godhead.

Minho pulled Orange by her wrist to the center of the room, "I need to tell you something . . ." He couldn't let anyone else hear.

"You *need* to get off that fortress wall in your mind." Orange grimaced. "I can see it in your eyes. In your mind, you're right back on that wall and defending. . . . I don't know what you're defending . . ." She let out a breath. "And everyone else is starting to turn against you. I don't think—"

"It's the Godhead—that woman." Every time Minho called her that word, his gut burned. *She wasn't a God.*

Orange softened. "Is it the training? Trust me, I've thought of a hundred ways I could have killed her just from the ship to here. Put your tongue on the roof of your mouth, that's what I'm doing. And pinch your big toe and your little one to the ground while you—"

"I don't need archery tricks to focus, I'm focused." Minho was at least relieved she hadn't lost her soldier instincts. He looked back at the others in the group to make sure no one could hear them before he whispered, "I saw her kill the Great Master and the way she did it . . ."

But Orange just shrugged. "So she wasn't lying about that. What did the Great Master look like?"

"I don't know, an old man."

Orange turned away from Minho, lowering her head. The only other time he saw her so defeated was when Skinny died.

"What? What's wrong?"

"I didn't think The Great Master was real. Thought he was just something they threatened us with. A way to make the lessons and the punishments stick." Orange shrugged and adjusted the gun strap on her shoulder again. "Well . . . I guess it'd be fair that the person a whole army was trained to kill would be trained to kill, too. Wouldn't it?" Despite Orange making sense of it all so quickly, Minho almost didn't want it to. "Look, if you still want to kill her I'm down, but we've got to have a plan because the others will absolutely *freak*." Orange looked over her shoulder at the group.

Yes. Everything inside Minho screamed *yes, kill her before she gets them all killed*, but another smaller voice said, *No, wait. Use her for as long as she's good for.* Like an injured jackrabbit as bait. With Alexandra alive he could find out more about the city of Gods and the Evolution. He still wanted to know if everything he grew up believing was a lie or only some of it. Or maybe none of it. Maybe he should kill her right there in the next room where she stood.

"We can't kill her, at least not in front of the others," Orange said. "Not unless the safety of the group depends on it. Deal?"

"Unless the safety of the group depends on it," Minho repeated and agreed. But their safety already did depend on it. "Orange . . ."

"Yeah?"

"That tattoo on her wrist . . ." Minho's skin itched just thinking about what he was about to say. "The Great Master had the same one."

"The same exact one?" Orange pulled back in surprise.

"Identical." Minho handed her the map and pointed. "And here it is on Kletter's map."

Orange held the map close to her face. "Same swirly thing with lines. What do you think they're hiding here?" She looked up at him.

"Another Remnant Nation . . . ?"

How could it be that the Great Master and the Godhead had anything in common, let alone a marking so distinguishable, tattooed on the same exact spot.

How many Remnant Nations were there?

CHAPTER FOURTEEN

Beautifully Terrifying

I
ISAAC

Cian flew the Berg as if he had been flying one his whole life. "Where did you say you were from again?" Isaac asked, looking at all the buttons and measurements on the pilot dashboard. He needed to know more about the two strangers he'd be stuck with.

Cian and Erros looked at each other before Cian answered. "South of here."

"Do they all have Bergs there?" Jackie walked up and asked, eyeing the controls.

Cian just shook his head. Isaac wanted to ask a million questions, but first he needed to figure out how to tell Jackie and Old Man Frypan that he'd made up his mind to stay with Ximena to find the Master Villa and destroy the island's coordinates from its records. If he left Ximena alone to do it, she might do something crazy and Cian and Erros could get rid of her before she was able to destroy any trace of how to get to their island. It killed Isaac to have to leave the others, and possibly never see any of them again, but he owed it to everyone back on their island. He had nothing left to go home to, but the others . . . they deserved to feel safe and be safe when they got back home. And maybe it was a way that Isaac could finally make his mom proud.

Heavy stuff to think about.

"You're deep-frying something," Frypan said, spooking him. Isaac would miss that old man the most. Somehow Frypan always knew when he was in his thoughts too much.

"Yeah, I am . . ." Isaac looked back at Ximena who had her head in her hands. *Probably trying to use her second-sight somehow.* "It'll be okay though . . ."

"Never another option," Frypan said with a half-smile.

"We're close." Erros pointed ahead, but what he pointed at caused all thought to escape Isaac's mind.

"What the heck is that?" he asked. "More colors?" It was so green but bright, a color he didn't yet have a name for, draped across the deep, deep sky.

"I can't tell if it's beautiful or beyond terrifying," Jackie whispered in awe.

"Feels like both . . ." Frypan added. "This is the aurora?"

The way the colors radiated upward felt unearthly. "Are we . . . are we going to fly into it?" Isaac asked.

Cian and Erros just smiled. "The auroras have fully returned. It's happening. The Evolution. All part of the plan, apparently."

Isaac watched the sky in wonder as they flew right into the mash of flares. Translucent colors and vortex shapes of energy swirled around the Berg. Ximena finally looked up, a bit of wonder lighting up her eyes for once.

"The Borealis is spreading. A tornado of hydrogen and nitrogen in the atmosphere." Cian said all this with great pride, all while he piloted the Berg. "Nothing to worry about."

Isaac knew enough to know that when adults said *not* to worry, it meant there was usually something to worry about. Jackie grabbed Isaac's arm as she looked straight ahead, her eyes fixated on the green swirls in front of them. Faint reds joined in, and they danced together like flames of a fire.

"The Sequencers would love this . . ." Erros said to himself.

A feeling of finality drowned Isaac. He would have given anything for Cian and Erros to fly them all the way back home to their island, but he realized as he looked at the colors moving in the darkness all around them that nothing would ever be the same. He couldn't *unknow* what he knew.

"You okay?" Old Man Frypan asked. "It's something, isn't it . . . ?" He looked ahead with something like glee.

"Yeah . . ." The colors brightened as the Berg drew closer.

"The aurora means . . ." Ximena stepped closer to the window.

"The Evolution." Cian and Erros answered in unison. "Welcome to the site of the Maze, home of the Evolution."

The City of the Godhead. They'd made it. A bright orange glow shone from below, and it grew more solid in the darkness than the other colors floating in the sky. "We should have waited until daylight, how are you going to know where to land?" Isaac asked, looking down. "Wait, there's an aurora on the ground, too?"

Ximena touched the window of the Berg right where Isaac was squinting to see the orange flares of light. "No . . . that's . . . a fire."

Isaac shook his head. "It's glowing. Like the blue aurora we saw but red."

Jackie and Frypan got quiet. The Berg flew closer and closer and the red-orange glow grew bigger. Cian pointed at something that Isaac couldn't yet see. Erros erupted, "Shitstains of Shitstorms. . . . Those are fires of war."

Cian pulled the Berg to the left without another word.

"All these years and now the Remnants strike?" Erros flicked one of the controls.

Cian steered the Berg farther away from the City of the Godhead. The glow of the fire grew small and distant, but the panic inside Isaac exploded in size.

His friends were down there.

“Stop!” he yelled. “What are you doing? We need to get down there to help our friends!”

They didn’t stop.

2
ALEXANDRA

Alexandra pulled out what she could use from the cabinets, letting her inner knowledge guide her. Vials. Liquids. Needles. She had Sadina, *Dear Sadina.* She’d use the digits. The sacred digits. The Flaring Discipline. All of it. The Goddess spread everything she’d pulled out onto the table in the center of the room. *Think, Alexandra, think.* But it was hard to conjure thoughts with noisy children carrying on.

“Stop that!” She turned to their chaos and laughter, and the young ones froze, beakers in their hands. “Take that off,” Alexandra said to Dominic, who had put on one of the women’s lab coats. “Reverence. Please.”

“I don’t know what that means . . .” the boy mumbled.

“Respect!” the Goddess answered. “Don’t you have respect for objects, people, places?”

Roxy set her knife on the table, right in front for Alexandra to see. “All due respect to you, they’re still children.”

“And what’s your excuse?” the Goddess said.

“Excuse me?” Roxy leaned in with her hand on her knife.

Alexandra shook her head. “I’m sorry. You’ll understand that I’ve been grieving. The stress of this . . .” She smoothed out her cloak. “This robe . . . was a gift from my dear friend Flint, who perished from an arrow in his back—from your war-crazed people.” She pointed at Roxy and the other soldiers.

“Yeah, not me. I’m from ya-never-heard-of-it-ville, not that Remnant Nation. But I’ll cut anyone who hurts these children. Any of them . . . they’re all my kids now.” She pulled her knife back from the table. "And they've been through a lot, too. If they want to play dress-up, let 'em."

Alexandra breathed in for three seconds, held her breath for three, exhaled for three. She composed herself. She'd use this to her advantage. She just needed the children's blood. She needed them. "I'm sorry, you're right. Thank you," she gently said to Roxy, who picked her knife off the table with a nod. "I need your help. All of you. Gather close."

"We're not scientists, just so you know," Dominic said. *Of course he wasn't, neither was Alexandra.* But anything was possible with the digits, the Flare, the discipline.

"What can we do?" Sadina asked. Helpful. Sweet. Immune Sadina.

Alexandra didn't have a plan, but she had the tools. "Come closer. Quickly." She lifted the sleeve of her cloak to show them the marking Nicholas had given her when he first taught her about the digits. "This sequence of numbers makes up all life. Makes up all of time. Makes up all of nature . . ."

"And makes up the Cure?" Sadina asked. Alexandra smiled her first true smile since the war had started.

"Yes, Dear Sadina." *It would.*

"Is it magic?" Trish asked in the most imbecilic of voices. Alexandra looked at the girl's face next to Sadina and she couldn't help but touch her cheek. How soft and innocent, yet mind-maddening dumb, children were. She then placed her other hand on Sadina's cheek, a descendant of Newt. *The past could be the future again.* She believed it to be true more than she believed anything. The Goddess pulled Sadina to her.

"Yes. In a way, someone might call it magic . . . yes." Alexandra continued to break Nicholas' rules: to share the secrets of the digits, the Sacred Truths, and the Flaring Discipline with the unanointed . . . because soon enough . . . the whole world would be anointed with the Cure, with the gifts of the Evolution, and she would need a group of Devout Evolutionaries underneath her. To help her usher in the new world.

She traced the lines of her tattoo. "There is a spiral that connects us all. Every piece of nature, every person, every part of history is a part of the spiral." Part of the whole. Every person a digit. Every outcome already set in motion.

"Spiral? Like a pig's tail?" the worthless Dominic asked. Only he would acquaint something so sacred as the digits to an animal's ass. The thought of a squealing pig sent a shiver of death through the crown of Alexandra's head.

The Goddess shook her vision clear. "No. Nothing like that." She scoffed at him. "The Golden spiral. The Sequence. It connects to everything in life and in death, in space and time." She traced her finger around the spiral of the tattoo to show them. They all leaned in to see, and even Minho and Orange came from around the corner to listen.

Minho interrupted her speech. "That's great and all, but we went through the whole place, and there's no food. No water. Pipes aren't working. What's your plan, *Goddess*?" He poked his gun's tip against a hanging medical skeleton in the corner. "We need a plan or this is going to be all of us pretty soon."

"Nonsense," the Goddess replied. "We're safer here than anywhere." But if the soldier was right that the women were gone . . . they'd taken all the supplies with them. She looked through the cabinets for something, anything—she'd know it when she saw it.

"He's right. We can't stay here," Orange joined in.

"How is a wavy line . . . magic?" Dominic followed the Goddess' steps, trying for another glimpse at her wrist as she searched through the cabinets. *Those damn women couldn't have taken everything.* She bumped into Dominic, constantly in her way. *These damn children are impossible.*

"The symbol is *of* the digits." Alexandra motioned for the annoying boy to move aside. She pulled out metal drawers, one by one. Scales. Gloves. More measurement tools. She moved to the cabinets.

"There's nothing." Minho almost taunted her.

"We can drink this." Dominic held up a blue liquid from a fridge unit. Of course, *the units in the corner.* Alexandra made her way over and grabbed it out of Dominic's hand.

"I wouldn't do that if I were you."

3
MINHO

Orphans only had themselves.

Their thoughts. Their sanity.

Alexandra seemed to have lost both of hers.

A thud from the balcony stole Minho's attention. "Orange?" He motioned for her to keep a watch.

"Just some ice falling," she called back. "But the smoke from the city is spreading out here and it's getting hard to see for a good watch. What's the plan?"

Minho looked outside, up at the roof, and out to the waters where the *Maze Cutter* sat stranded. He could barely see the ship through the smoke and the trees. He much preferred the open sights for miles and miles like he'd had on the walls of the Remnant Nation fortress.

"I'll go downstairs to watch for the night. You'll stay here?" Minho asked Orange. They couldn't stay at the Villa without water, but he had to wait until daylight to see just how bad the damage to the *Maze Cutter* was or how to patch any possible holes in the ship. "Check in . . . in a couple hours?"

Orange nodded. "Safe watch."

"Safe watch." He mumbled the old soldier's mantra. It was one of the only things changing guards said to each other—there were no greetings or small talk. Just two words that meant: hello, goodbye, and good luck. He headed downstairs by the light of the gun's scope, his eyes heavy, his stomach cramped from hunger. But it was only a few hours until sunrise and then they'd figure out a plan.

A loud thump from above stopped Minho's descent. He pivoted, ran back upstairs to the balcony, half expecting to see Orange cut in half by a large sheet of ice, his imagination getting the best of him. But she was whole, unharmed.

"Clear?" he asked, trying not to show his immense relief. "What was that noise? It shook the whole damn building. Are Remnant bombs still going off?"

Then he noticed that Orange looked about as broken as Skinny's nose when he died.

"What?" Minho asked.

But Orange just stared at him as if he should already know what happened. He'd never known her to hold back words, regardless of what she thought he should or shouldn't know. She unfroze herself enough to load up her gun with more bullets. "Orange! What's going on, what was that?"

"Minho . . ." Orange's voice shook, another rarity. "Prepare for combat. That was a grenade."

He whipped his head around to look past the tree line from the balcony. Orange had a better eagle-eye view up here than he would have had downstairs. A fire burned in the distance.

"Oh, no." He backed up into the room. "The *Maze Cutter*?"

Orange nodded.

All of Minho's senses came alive, his eyes no longer tired and his stomach no longer hungry—the only sensation that filled every cell in his body was to fight. It was his very instinct, almost his only instinct.

"Airdrop. Maybe they're just doing flyovers." He tried to reassure Orange, and himself, until five gunshots fired off from below, loud cracks that shattered the silence. And then, all at once, he knew it was over before it began. If there was one gunshot there were a dozen to come, but with five shots right at the start. . . . That meant there were fifty soldiers or more. He knew the Nation's tactics all too well.

But as to their response, it changed nothing. "We can hold them off. Fire at the front line and I'll get the back. We can do this."

"Or die trying." Somehow, Orange said the words with a grin. An actual grin. She positioned her gun on the railing of the balcony.

Minho ran downstairs, leaping two steps at a time, yelling at the others. "They're here! It's an attack! Get back from the windows!"

"Wait . . . who?" Dominic asked.

A simple question with a simple answer. In less than two minutes the Remnant Nation, an army of Orphans with nothing to lose and nothing to live for, with chained Cranks or half-Cranks, would attack full-force. Firing ammunition of mixed metals and shrapnel, killing all of them or worse—take them alive.

But Minho couldn't tell Dom that. "Just get back, alright?"

"What do we do?" Dominic asked, "Just hide?"

Minho shook his head. "There's no hiding from these people." Regret pulsed through his blood. *He should have turned the Maze Cutter around as soon as they saw signs of war.* They should have turned tail before ever getting to the coast. He'd failed in controlling Alexandra. He'd failed, utterly. He loaded his gun with as many bullets as it could hold. "If they capture you, don't say a word about anything." Useless advice at that moment, but it was the best Minho had to give.

"Come here, all of you!" Roxy shouted and pulled the islanders close. "Let's stick together."

Minho did a quick count, making sure they were all there. Fear darkened their eyes, wilted their faces. Only one was missing, besides Orange upstairs. And then he noticed a flash of movement, just out of the corner of his eye. Alexandra.

The so-called Godhead opened the back door of the Villa and sprinted away, into the night, into the darkness, soon only a bobbing shadow of yellow. Then nothing at all.

CHAPTER FIFTEEN

Curse of Truth

I
ISAAC

The heat inside Isaac's gut grew, burning like real flames. He pounded the side of the Berg with his fist. "We can't just leave them there! We have to go back!" But he couldn't even see the fires of Alaska through the window anymore. "Please, we can help!" They had crossbows, other weapons, the advantage of a Berg. But then the worthless feeling Isaac had when he accidentally stabbed himself rushed into his mind with doubt. There'd be no helping Sadina and the others. But that only made him feel more anger.

Ximena blocked Isaac's next punch to the Berg's interior. "Let it burn. The site of the Maze was never holy." She always seemed to say the worst things at the worst times.

"This is all your fault!" He let all his frustrations out. Her predictions, her second-sight, jinxing them about the Villas burning. . . . He couldn't take it anymore.

Jackie took a step forward to get between him and Ximena, "Isaac . . ."

"How is this my fault?" Ximena tilted her head and took a step back.

"You're constantly manipulating. You jinxed us, or cursed us, I don't know . . . you . . ." Isaac felt the same way he did whenever Sadina used to say something like, *Don't get stung by a jellyfish today*, and then he did just the thing she warned him about. He turned away from Jackie and Ximena and pleaded for Old Man Frypan to join him in the argument. "We've got to go back there. Please . . ." Frypan could convince Cian to turn around. It wasn't too late. They could still find their friends.

Old Man Frypan knocked his walking stick against his shoes. "I don't think that's a good idea, son."

Isaac couldn't believe his ears. "Sadina . . . Trish . . . Miyoko . . . Dominic . . ." *And Minho, Orange, and Roxy.* "They need our help!"

Frypan shook his head. "I'm sure Minho steered the *Maze Cutter* right out of harm's way. We don't even know if they made it to Alaska. And we're no good to them dead, now are we?"

Isaac turned to Jackie. "We have to go back there." But Jackie had a pitiful, sad acceptance coating her face. "Jackie?"

"Isaac . . . that fire looked like the size of our island. It was huge." She twisted the palm bracelet on her wrist. "I don't want to walk into a war—we'd just get ourselves killed. They're probably not even there, like Frypan said."

The old man put an arm on Isaac's shoulder. "Minho and Orange have that Remnant Nation in their bones, they'll protect the others."

Isaac shrugged Frypan off. "What about the Godhead . . . the Cure?" He pushed against the window, knowing he'd become the biggest fool on the Berg but unable to help himself.

"Is the cure for fire, more gasoline?" Ximena asked, but Isaac didn't have the patience for her riddles any more. "Fire will cleanse the Earth . . ." she said, and then mumbled something else he didn't understand.

Isaac gave up on Ximena, and it didn't matter if Frypan and Jackie were afraid. Only one thing mattered. He focused on Cian and Erros, "Turn around. You said you'd take us to Alaska, and we need to get—"

Cian held a hand up. "Not a chance. It's a guaranteed death trap between the crazed Pilgrims and the Remnant soldiers." He let out something that almost sounded like a laugh. "Look, we're saving you from what you don't understand. There's one hundred years of war and hate unfolding down there."

Cian steered the Berg over open water, but the fire inside Isaac kept burning. He couldn't accept Cian's '*Sorry we can't,*' when he knew that they *could*. They could find a safe spot to land and find their friends . . . and everything would be okay. *It had to be okay.*

Isaac launched his whole body at Cian and the controls. He startled him just enough to wrap his hands around the yolk and pull hard to the right. "We're going back . . ." Isaac said through clenched teeth. "We have to find them . . ." On some level, he knew he'd completely lost his mind.

"Stop! Stop it, you idiot!" Erros yanked on his shirt and everyone dipped to the floor as the Berg leaned hard. Isaac struggled to hold on. His friends. He had to find his friends. He couldn't leave them alone in that horrible fire.

"Isaac!" Jackie screamed as she slid along the Berg's floor, all the way to the weapon pile.

"¡Dios mío!" Ximena held on to a bar below the window.

Frypan held on to Erros as he grappled with Isaac. "Come on, boy, let it go . . ."

"Stop!" Cian shouted, right in Isaac's ear, pulling the controls back. Isaac finally crumpled to the floor of the Berg in defeat. He wanted to scream or cry, but he just covered his head in his hands and did neither. He had made a promise to Sadina to always be there for her from the sea to the sky, and now, flying high above the burning city of Gods, Isaac broke the only promise that had ever mattered to him.

The Berg righted itself and they flew on.

2
MINHO

An army of Orphans was coming at them, hard and fast.

Orange fired shots from the balcony; Minho fired from the first floor. As soldiers fell in the front lines, Minho shot at the next in line, but it was useless and he knew it. No matter how skilled Orange and Minho were, and how well they worked together, the numbers were against them. And the Orphan Army marched closer, with a hunger for war that only the Remnant Nation could have.

In the darkness outside the Villa, shots sailed in both directions, certainly. But the barrage of bullets from the Remnant Nation would never end. Even if every single islander were a trained soldier like him, they wouldn't have stood a chance. It wasn't their war to fight. And winning wasn't an option.

"There's too many of them," he whispered to himself between shots. In between the trees and atop the fallen snow, Orange and Minho had downed at least two dozen soldiers of the Remnant Nation, but twenty more were behind them, and twenty more to the left of them, and a dozen more to the right.

"Orange!" Minho couldn't hear anything from upstairs but the fire of weaponry and incessant thud of bullets. He kept at it, downing one after another of his ex-comrades. Back when he was on the wall, shooting trespassers, he never thought about anything he saw in the scope except the distance between their eyes. But now when he looked through the scope, one by one, even if he didn't recognize them, *and especially if he did*, he felt a twinge of something he never felt when killing anyone before. More than the gun kicking back and bruising his shoulder, he felt something in his chest.

Back on the wall he'd never had a pain in his chest when he shot rounds. He didn't feel this heaviness when he shot the Crank-soldiers chained together on the coast. But with each shot he fired into a fellow Orphan, Minho felt a deep loss there, on the inside.

"Dammit!" He couldn't stop them from advancing no matter how many he shot, but he also couldn't stop himself.

One by one, he took away from each felled Orphan soldier the opportunity to find freedom, or family, or friends. He ushered them to death instead. The pain in his chest amplified, knowing it was all over for him and Orange, the others. The freedom they'd known the last several months, the time away from the clutches of the Remnant Nation—it was all vanishing as the army closed in on them.

Traitors. They'd be treated worse than any enemy that ever existed.

Glass windows blew out in the Villa.

Sadina and Trish screamed.

Minho braced himself to die a traitor's death.

3
ISAAC

Erros pulled Isaac back to his feet and pushed him against the wall of the Berg. His neck flung back and his right leg hung in the air. "You're crazy! You could have killed us!"

Isaac thought about apologizing, but the notion seemed absurd. He wasn't sorry for trying to save his friends. Erros pushed Isaac harder against the Berg's interior. Rivets jammed into his back.

"We're okay." Old Man Frypan tried to step between the two. "The boy's emotions just got out of hand there. He's okay, aren't you boy?"

Isaac nodded. He wasn't okay, not even close, but he didn't want to get thrown out of the Berg in mid-flight. "Please, just land and drop me off, I need—"

"You need your head checked!" Erros let go of him, dropping him to the floor. "Get in the back and stay there."

Isaac crawled across the floor of the Berg until Jackie scooped him up. "Isaac, what the hell? I know you want to get to them, but it'd be great if we were alive, ya know?"

"I know." He fell into Jackie's lap in defeat. "We can't lose everyone

. . ." He didn't have to finish his thought, but he knew that Jackie knew. Being kidnapped. Carson and Lacy dying. And now the fires. Isaac couldn't take any more loss.

She placed her palm against Isaac's chest. "I know. . . . We'll figure it out."

He took a deep breath, fought back the tears.

Cian spoke from the controls. "Look, the fires are spreading to other islands, but we'll find one with enough cleared brush to land—and then we're done with you people. You can find your friends or your death, whichever you come across first."

"Fair enough," Old Man Frypan said in defeat.

"I'm sorry," Isaac whispered to Jackie. He'd never felt so helpless in his life. Jackie's hand over Isaac's chest helped to calm him until Ximena's words pierced through.

"How big was the *Maze Cutter*? Forty feet? Sixty?"

Erros leaned forward over the front controls. "That's a sixty-footer."

Isaac shot to his feet. They'd seen their ship, surely. "They made it to Alaska," he told Jackie and they rushed to the window to look for themselves.

Ximena pointed at some licking flames of fire below the Berg. For a second it looked like the *Maze Cutter*'s outline above it . . . but it couldn't be. Not on fire. "No." Isaac tried to quiet his fears out loud. "There's no way, right?" He spun around to Jackie. "It's not them, right?" He looked back out the window, "It can't be . . ."

Erros noticed Isaac, then grabbed him, pushing him away from the window. "I told you to get in the back! The back!" He pushed him again.

Isaac slowly walked away from Erros' gaze, but he needed Jackie to see it and tell him that Ximena was wrong. "Jackie?" he asked timidly.

"I feel sick . . ." Her words dripped out before she covered her mouth and stepped back from the window.

Frypan shook his head. "They would have swam away if they'd been on that. They're survival-driven." Frypan nodded to Isaac. "And Minho and Orange are protectors. They're okay, somewhere down there."

Ximena seemed determined to keep up the atmosphere of doom. “If they swam in these waters, they’d freeze to death. All the inlets are covered in ice.”

Isaac was one step away from complete insanity. He took a deep breath, one big enough for every single person he loved.

“It’ll be okay, Jackie,” he forced himself to say. Her eyes darted to him in doubt. “Whatever happens, we’ll be okay . . .” He hated saying the same words that others had said to him after his family died. All the *it’ll be okays* felt like such lies, and they were. Because the truth was, nothing would ever be “okay” again. But at the same time, things could never be worse. *Whatever happens, we’ll be okay.* How terrible had his life become, to think things like these?

Jackie looked away. “How are we ever going to tell their families? How can we go back there and pretend like none of this happened . . .”

Isaac felt the Berg start to descend. Cian and Erros seemed plenty happy to drop them off.

“You really want to land in all this?” Frypan asked Isaac.

He nodded. It wasn’t even a question.

Did they really have anything to lose at this point? There was a chance. At the very least, a tiny chance they were down there, alive.

And he’d rather die with his friends than live as a coward.

4
MINHO

It was over.

The Remnant Nation’s Orphan soldiers grabbed Sadina and Trish first. Each one screamed and kicked as if the Orphans needed any encouragement to kill them right there. Minho felt like he was inside one of his nightmares, wishing his body were really just asleep along the coast and that soon he’d wake up from Dominic talking too loudly around the fire. But this was a living nightmare.

“Stay calm, don’t scream!” he shouted at Sadina and Trish just as five or six larger Orphans roughly grabbed Minho. He braced himself, knowing they would beat him, pummel him with punches and kicks on the spot. But instead, they just stripped him of his weapons, twisted his limbs into impossible holds, and carried him away.

His favorite gun fell to the floor. His shoulder blades pinched into each other as they lifted him up, swinging. He twisted then flipped his body, flailing like an Orphan being thrown from a cliff. But it was no good. They had him.

"It really takes half a dozen of you to take me in? They must not train you like they did us." If he couldn't hurt them with weapons, he'd at least annoy them. They carried him out into the cold. "What's your name, soldier?" he asked the Orphan on his right. "You've got a name, I know you do! My name is Minho!" He shouted at all of them, referencing the fact that the Nation didn't let them have names. "You have a name and a brain and don't have to do this!"

"Shut up!" The Orphan on the left punched him in the eye so hard that Minho swore he felt a bone break. His vision blurred, and he knew a traitor's death would only come after much more of the same. As they got him under control and carried him away, he tried lifting his head to look for Roxy and the others. It was still dark, but he saw two soldiers pushing a walking Pilgrim's cloak. At least they had captured the coward of a Godhead. Minho could die happy knowing she would share his fate.

They dragged him to a Berg and Minho twisted his body as much as he could, hoping the soldiers would drop him. If he could break free for even a second, there was a chance he could grab a weapon from the dead on the ground and unload it on them. But they were too strong.

He saw a flash of Roxy, her feet on the ground being pushed and pulled toward the Nation's Berg. And then he saw Orange, three soldiers carrying her. They locked eyes. He didn't know what to say—nothing could make what they were about to go through less . . . *final.* He watched, helpless, as they lined up the islanders and Roxy, one by one. Orange closed her eyes. She was probably thinking about the same thing Minho was trying *not* to think about.

Hell. The lowest level of the fortress. The worst place on Earth.

Two soldiers ripped the back of her uniform as she struggled, revealing the long scars across her back from when she'd been beaten for singing.

They mocked her. "You've betrayed the Nation before, I see," one of them said, and another kicked her in the back where her scars looked like an "X".

"Stay still, Remnant!" one of the six soldiers holding Minho shouted. Clanking metal from inside the Berg made Minho wonder if he'd even make it that far. The soldiers were hungry for death, and they'd take it however they could. He kicked his legs and swung his body again to throw those holding him off balance; he got his right leg free.

"Be still, Remnant!" another one screamed. But Minho was no longer a Remnant *anything*. He kicked his foot out and connected with a soldier, right in the head.

"You piece of shit." The soldier punched him in the same eye again.

His vision went black for a moment, then slowly phased to light and blurry. A warm sensation of blood dripped down his face. But it didn't matter how many times they punched him in the same eye. They could carve out his eye and feed it to him like a grape, and he'd still make his capture as uncomfortable as possible . . . because he knew exactly where they were taking him.

Straight to the fortress. To the depths of Hell.

And even Hell had a special place for traitors.

PART THREE

WICKED is Wicked

WICKED is good. WICKED is good. WICKED is good.
Saving the Immunes will save the human race.
Only runners can survive the maze.
Run to save the others.

—*The Book of Newt*

CHAPTER SIXTEEN

Shoot then Loot

I
MINHO

A large makeshift prison took up most of the interior of the Nation's Berg.

Probably what the Grief Bearers had used to chain up and haul the Crank Army.

The Remnant soldiers tossed Orange into a rusted cage inside the Berg first; her body crumpled into the corner. They carried Minho into the same cage; he stopped kicking once they let him get his feet beneath him again. One quick shove and his face met the floor of the caged unit. It smelled like piss.

"Defectors!" A soldier with ears too big for his body smashed his foot down on to Orange's head. Minho held his breath, waiting for the same to be done to him. Instead, another soldier stepped forward—with boots as outsized as the other's ears—and stomped on Orange's head even harder than the last soldier. Minho cringed, stopped himself from crying out. It was as if he'd felt the pain himself.

If his hands weren't combat-tied behind his back, he would have punched them all, no matter the consequences. Complaining would only make things worse. It killed him inside to not do anything, but he knew it was the only way he could help Orange even a little. Each of the four Orphan soldiers turned their attention to him, taking turns kicking his torso. Three targeted his ribs and when he rolled over one of them stabbed his kidney with a boot-toe. He let his body go limp to appear weak and defeated, but mostly to let part of his arm fall on top of Orange's to check the skin of her neck to make sure it still felt warm.

Orange didn't make a sound.

She was alive, but Minho didn't know for how much longer. But did it matter. As a traitor, the Remnant Nation would torture them both to death either way, so what if it came quickly or took weeks? His heart pinched with every breath; he prepared himself to slowly lose the use of his lungs with more cracked ribs.

Screams from outside the Berg stole Minho's attention.

A gunshot.

Then another.

Silence the enemy. Kill on sight. It was the Remnant Nation way. *Shoot then loot.*

He lifted his body off the ground just enough to vomit next to Orange. He tried to hold it in, but he couldn't. Not after the sound of those gunshots. Close range. Execution-style. He wished he'd never met Roxy and the islanders. His stomach and his eyes stung from it all. He regretted every second of his time with them, despite the deep love he'd felt, actually having what people called a family. But he regretted it all the more so.

Because if they'd never met him, the Orphan named Minho, every last one of them would still be alive.

2
ALEXANDRA

The Goddess hadn't made it very far into the woods before a small group of soldiers had grabbed her, then dragged her along the bumpy, brush-strewn ground like the Pilgrim she appeared to be. Everything inside of her wanted to shout at them to *get their hands off of her, didn't they know who she was*, but she kept her composure and stayed silent. She'd hide her identity until she could escape.

"This one stinks." The soldiers pushed her in line to stand with the others. If they thought she stank, it was because they had no idea what herbs and florals a Goddess could afford.

The sound of a body-sized splash into the unforgiving waters nearby made Alexandra's whole body weaken.

"You shot them!" Roxy cried.

The hood of Alexandra's cloak covered her head too tightly to see who the soldiers had shot and thrown into the waters. The Goddess waited to hear Sadina, *Dear Sadina*, somewhere beside or behind her, but the islanders went silent except for Roxy. Not even Trish's cries of panic or Dominic's mouth-breathing lingered within earshot.

"Keep quiet or we'll *make* you quiet." The soldier turned from the waters of Alaska. What a fool to not realize what he had done. The Evolution be damned. Alexandra recited the digits and the Flaring Discipline.

Soldiers pushed her forward again, stepped on her cloak. It pained her to not correct them, to demand they treat her with respect. But even she had survival instincts and the hidden humility to act on them. She kept her eyes pointed down, lowered her head, so that her hood covered as much of her face as possible. They didn't deserve a glimpse of the one true Goddess.

"Put them in the cage with the two defectors," an older man said; he wore a cloak similar to Mikhail's. No matter how many soldiers Mikhail sent, no matter how hard he'd tried to remove her from power, she remained the one and only Godhead. She would forever be the One, and she *would* usher in a new Evolution. It didn't matter how many orphans Mikhail and the Nation had trained—she would find a way to turn them all to her side.

In time, they would all be her Pilgrims.

CHAPTER SEVENTEEN

Piss and Ash

I
ISAAC

Isaac sat slumped, his head in his hands, leaning against the side of the Berg. The machine vibrated and hummed beneath him. He no longer cared on which island of Alaska Cian and Erros chose to drop him off, he'd never get back to *his* island, and everything about home felt further and further away.

Sorrowful, nostalgic thoughts filled his mind and heart with pain. Sadina trying to get him to hang out with the west-siders after his parents died. His constant refusal because he felt out of place. They were all so happy. Isaac would give anything for just one more invitation from Sadina to go out to the ocean together. He'd never thought he could lose so much, again, and again, and that the things he'd once hated were now something he longed for.

Ximena looked over at him and his body surged with anger. "I don't know how, but you knew about this fire—"

"Don't you get it?" she snapped. "How can you not understand that things happen the way they happen, no matter what? I'm just as tortured by my inner-knowing as you are!" She looked like she was about to cry, but Isaac couldn't bring himself to care. There wasn't anything *left* to care about.

"It's not her fault, Isaac." Jackie sat down next to him.

"Jackie . . ." He couldn't believe she was trying to defend Ximena. But then again Jackie still had family at home; she still had plenty of west-siders on the island to go back home to. *Isaac had nothing.*

Only Frypan could understand Isaac, now. "It's alright boy . . . just sit with it. It'll be alright." He tapped the floor of the Berg with his sharpened walking stick.

"It's not okay. She . . . cursed us, somehow!" He pointed at Ximena.

Ximena seemed genuinely hurt by his words. "I can't help knowing certain things. You think I wanted to know that my mom was dead before this one told me?" She flicked her wrist at Jackie. "You don't think I wanted to be able to stop that? I couldn't!" She held her hands up, clenched into fists, before slamming them down on her thighs.

Just hours ago, Isaac would have sacrificed himself and his future to protect Ximena from Cian and Erros finding out the truth—that she had lied about knowing the location of the Sequencers. But he just didn't care about protecting her anymore. Or anyone.

Isaac didn't care about anything.

2
MINHO

Castaways from birth.

Abandoned without concern.

Minho's entire life had prepared him to take beatings without a fight, but since he'd met Roxy and the others, things had changed. He wanted to fight back more and more. His breath quickened as he listened for another gunshot; there were only two. He probed his left ribs to see if any were broken or just badly bruised. The Orphan couldn't feel any cracks, but breathing each breath got harder. His lungs couldn't quite expand and it hurt like hell.

"Get 'em in here. We'll sort them out." This was a deep-voiced Grief Bearer, speaking from the outside. Minho wanted to puke again. Grief Bearers were just older and dumber versions of Orphans. Stupid enough to come back to the Nation after their cliff ceremony and forty days in the wilderness.

Soldiers marched in the captives, one by one. Minho didn't dare lift his head enough to show the Grief Bearers that he cared about the people they'd captured alongside him. But from the very corner of his eye, he saw Roxy and Sadina hoisted into the Berg and pushed in the direction of the cage. His relief almost made him forget the pain.

Orange still lay motionless, but her skin felt warm.

"Ever see one this old?" one soldier said to another as they tossed Roxy into the cage.

"Nah. Ever see one this fragile?" They threw Sadina in. She cried out as she landed on top of Roxy, but otherwise they appeared relatively unharmed.

"Come here," Roxy whispered to Sadina—who was crying, quietly. Minho knew that her cries could get her killed next. Remnants hated weakness and were scared of emotion—they'd shoot a weeping trespasser more quickly than a raging screamer. Anger, they understood. Fighting, they knew. But tears, they couldn't abide.

He whispered as softly as he could to Sadina. "Breath through your nose. Tongue on the roof of your mouth."

"It's okay . . ." Roxy whispered in a soothing voice. "We're together."

A loud thump against the Berg's loading ramp stole their attention. Minho turned to see who would be carried or pushed into the Berg next. Through his twice-punched blurry eye he could see a puke-yellow cloak stumble forward, Alexandra's worthless and godless body pushed in their direction. He'd been certain one of those bullets he'd heard would have been lodged into Alexandra's head already because of the Pilgrim's cloak she wore. But the so-called Goddess fell toward him. That left Dominic, Trish, and

Miyoko. Only one of them—at most—would be walking into the Berg, now.

Orphans didn't have a higher power.

Minho didn't believe in Gods.

But he wanted to pray, wanted to see at least one of them.

The Orphan looked to Roxy, questioning with his eyes. She just shook her head, the saddest thing he'd ever seen.

3
ALEXANDRA

The Goddess' shoulder hurt from the filthy Orphans throwing her against the inside of the cage. She would have walked in and sat down, had they merely asked. She fixed her cloak and tightened the hood around her face. She hadn't survived the war for this long just to have the Remnants recognize her silky garments underneath, or that her hair wasn't that of a feral Pilgrim. She huddled into the corner of the rusted metal cage, as far away from Minho and the others as possible. It smelled like the pits of Crank Palace. Like piss and ash. Crank Palace, where Alexandra first got her name—and her purpose—had a grip over her, as tightly as she gripped her Pilgrim's cloak.

Crank Palace had provided an end for many, but a beginning for her. And the piss and ash in the cage reminded her that she'd find a way out of this situation, too, no matter what. She rubbed the back of her neck and dug her fingers into the spot where her spine met her head. Her soul itched to separate from her body. The Evolution behind her eyes pounded, making the Goddess' vision shake.

"Are you alright?"

Sadina, concerned about her welfare, despite everything. Dearest Sadina.

"Always," the Goddess whispered back, relieved to see the girl's tear-stained face across from her. *Dear Sadina, descended from the family of Dear Newt. The Evolution would continue.*

"Stay quiet," Minho growled.

Alexandra had no plans of being loud. She could be of no help to the Evolution if she were dead. *Silence is power*, Nicholas would say. She placed her hand inside her cloak and guarded the *Book of Newt*. With her palm against its pages, she could feel her own heartbeat. She hadn't been this shrunken inside her own skin since that night back in Crank Palace—the night she met Nicholas. As the Goddess held tight to the *Book of Newt* and her Flaring Discipline, she curled into a ball against the corner of the cage.

34, 55, 89, 144 . . .

Eyes closed, Alexandra couldn't help but see the arrows of fire. She hadn't slept since the war started and the unprocessed events flashed across her mind. A hornless Mannus. The people running. Buildings crumbling. Flint's knees hitting the ground, staring up at her as he faced the horrors of death. Mikhail be damned. A false Great Master and certainly never a Godhead. She breathed in for three seconds, held it for three seconds, and exhaled.

The blood slowed in her body.

Her shoulders relaxed.

She entered the Infinite Glade.

4
MINHO

Soldiers needed to be stealthy.

Everything, including their emotions, needed to be well-hidden at all times. And Sadina's crying would get her killed. "Orange? Orange?" Sadina wailed even louder as she nudged Orange's limp body.

"Sadina...you've got to stay silent. Don't say anything." Despite whispering, he said it with as much conviction as possible. "Roxy... they'll..." He didn't want to say it.

"They already did." Roxy looked back at Minho with as much shock in her face as when he'd first asked to drive her truck along the coast. He felt an invisible punch so deep inside his gut that he almost threw up again. He'd left the Remnant Nation with every intention to *join* the Godhead. But now, sitting in a prison with the so-called Goddess, all he could think about were the different ways he could kill her.

For Orange.

For Skinny.

For poor, half-beaten Kit, who might be alive or might be dead.

Minho's fists tightened looking at Alexandra, with her eyes closed like the weak field rat she was. He imagined ending her life in two blows, one from each fist. Maybe two from each fist. But just as he agreed to follow his fate—the last Remnant soldiers entered the Berg and closed the hatch.

"Hurry up." Two older soldiers pulled Dominic by his shirt's collar, then quickly shoved him into the Berg and into the cage, right on top of Alexandra.

Minho relaxed his fists.

CHAPTER EIGHTEEN

Something Much Worse

I
XIMENA

Las desgracias nunca vienen solas.

Misfortunes never come alone, something Ximena knew well but wished she didn't have to learn from experience. She looked out the window of the Berg and shifted her weight below her. Within the next twelve hours, Carlos would likely arrive back at their Village in search of her, to yell at her for all of the damage she'd caused at the Villa and the risk she'd put her mother and Mariana in. But Carlos wouldn't find her hiding under one of Abuela's handmade blankets, and he'd still have no idea that his wife and the future he'd planned with her were already both dead. She cracked her knuckles thinking about how worried he'd make Abuela before she returned home, but she trusted her grandmother's inner-knowing wouldn't let Carlos spin her into unbearable sadness.

Ximena looked back at Isaac, leaning against the Berg in all his islander misery. She didn't have the luxury the islanders had to fall apart as their world crumbled. Her whole life had been one loss after another, but she didn't get to break down—she had to keep pushing forward, and from Ximena's inner ears all the way down to her big toes, the skin holding her body together tingled. She'd never had such a physical reaction to an inner-knowing or second-sight before.

Something worse was coming. *Algo mucho peor.*

Ximena pushed all of her fingertips together to try to calm her body, but nothing helped the feeling subside. She wished she could have asked her Abuela about this type of knowing, an inner-knowing that brought such an intense explosion of feeling, but she couldn't count on anyone right now. She closed her eyes as she walked up to Cian and Erros piloting the Berg and imagined what her grandmother might say to her if she were there.

When there is pain there is death.

And where there is death there is rebirth.

She looked out the pilot's window but could barely see the colors of the aurora. Cloud cover from the smoke of war hung in the sky. *The next island*, her inner-knowing shouted louder than she'd ever heard it. It didn't make any more sense than her earlier knowings, but it was the loudest knowing she'd ever felt in all her sixteen years.

"There. That one." She pointed to a small inlet ahead, barely visible through the smoke. "That next island right there."

"Huh?" Eros turned to her, but she didn't want to have to explain.

"There! We have to land there. Drop them off, and I'll take you to the Sequencers." She folded her arms in front of her heart as it pounded louder and louder.

"It's too dense with trees; we can't risk the damage," Erros said to Cian. "Remember the last time—"

"I know, I know," Cian said, continuing to steer over the island.

Ximena's head pounded with her own heartbeat—it felt like if they didn't land right there at that island, right then, that her intuition would somehow revolt from the inside out and cause her body to burst every last blood vessel. Her inner-knowing became so cantankerous and painful that if she didn't follow it, she feared the worst.

"It's vital to the Sequencers that we land there. Please." She didn't shout, and she didn't throw herself over the controls like poor Isaac had tried to do. She simply said it in her quiet, exhausted voice.

Cian looked over to his brother.

Erros swept the hair off his forehead. "Dammit, I actually kinda believe her."

Ximena's head pounded a little less.

"Fine, there's a landing spot south of here from the looks of it. And there seems to be at least some sort of shelter on this island." Cian pushed and pulled controls on the dashboard. "Wheels down. Prepare to land, and you all can make yourselves at home."

Ximena gave a sigh of relief as the tightness and tingling in her body calmed. Whatever was on that island must be important to the Sequencers somehow. She looked over her shoulder at Frypan and Jackie consoling Isaac. They'd be fine as long as they had each other. She, on the other hand, had no idea what came next. The islanders had ruined her mission to destroy the Villas one by one, and now she had to lie in order to get them to where they wanted to be, only to have them turn on her. She put her hand on her knife, the one for which her mother embroidered an eagle on the sheath for Kletter. A symbol of truth. Her inner-knowing became more and more frantic. But also clear.

The truth is a weapon.

The truth will remain buried.

The truth is a weapon.

Don't let the truth stay buried.

Cian piloted closer to the island and as he circled, looking for a spot to land, Ximena couldn't help but notice the shelter he'd mentioned looked unmistakingly marked with black-painted doors. "That's a Villa . . . ?" Ximena asked Erros.

The two brothers squinted to see what she'd seen below as they finally initiated landing in a clearing meant for a satellite Villa. "Could be . . ." Erros said to Cian. The others stood up, not realizing how lucky or unlucky they were about to be. Cian untied his red scarf from around his neck and wrapped it around his head for some reason.

Ximena rested her forehead against the window of the Berg. "It is. I'm telling you."

"Well . . ." Cian descended the Berg closer, then touched down. "We've never found this one before."

He looked over at his brother and smiled.

2
MINHO

Orphans think about death more than most.

The Orphan named Minho had always known one thing about his own death—that it *wouldn't* be quick.

In a Berg transformed into a prison, Minho planned on savoring every minute of the long flight to Nebraska before they reached the fortress and its lowest level, Hell. His lungs burned with each breath, but he knew much more pain awaited him once they landed. He'd enjoy this temporary pain as long as he could.

"Any plans?" Dominic whispered over the engines, just enough for Minho to hear.

Minho only ever had one plan. "Fight."

Dominic nodded. "I was afraid you'd say that."

"What's going to happen to us?" Sadina had too much panic in her eyes, and panic would only help to get her killed more slowly. The Remnant Nation liked to watch prisoners suffer like animals. Minho just shook his head to answer Sadina's question. He should have spent more time instructing the group, but he never imagined that in all the years the Remnant Nation trained Orphan soldiers to kill the Godhead that the Remnant Nation would actually and finally leave Nebraska and do it. For decades upon decades, the only time an Orphan soldier left the Remnant Nation was after a cliff ceremony. And even then, they always came back.

Except Minho.

He never wanted to go back. Which made their capture and flight to the Remnant Nation even more disappointing. The Orphan looked around at each person he had grown to care about. Dominic . . . they'd probably torture him by starvation. Sadina . . . she'd likely be killed first just for the crying. Roxy . . . she didn't deserve any of this. Orange . . . Minho felt the most sorry for her because the Remnant soldiers would keep her barely alive, on death's door—or as Minho called it, Hell's floor—for weeks until she begged them to kill her.

He'd overlooked Alexandra because she was slumped so far into the corner of the cage in her oversized wool cloak, she practically disappeared into the pile of fabric.

A wave of relief washed over Minho.

He *did* have a plan, after all.

He had the Godhead—or someone who claimed to be the Godhead—the one thing the Remnant Nation came to Alaska to destroy.

Two thumps from the bottom of the Berg startled him out of the thought. The only noise from the bottom of a Berg when flying is the release of landing gear.

"Orange." Minho tried to get her attention as the Berg decelerated. "We're not going to the fortress." But Orange's bruised face was still lifeless. Minho's heart sped up, his eyes darting to watch the soldiers as the Berg prepared to land. *Where were they headed if they weren't going back to the Remnant Nation?* He just assumed they'd go there, be taken to the lower floor called Hell, and tortured.

"This is it? We're landing?" Dominic looked at Minho, but the Orphan didn't have any clue what might happen next.

Minho knew the rules in Hell. He knew step-by-step what the Grief Bearers would do once they got there, what they would say, and every way he might possibly escape. But that would now do him no good. As the Berg landed quickly with a series of thuds, Minho could only tell the islanders and Roxy one thing. "Don't say a word. Not a whisper. Heads down." He looked at Sadina, right in her eyes to add, "and whatever happens *don't* scream. That's exactly what they want."

CHAPTER NINETEEN

Flare's Devil

I
ISAAC

Tall, pointed trees blanketed the island so heavily they had no choice but to land the Berg a mile south and walk north to the building Cian had seen from the air. They trudged along white snow that melted a little with every step.

"You sure it's this way?" Jackie asked. The air was cold, and Ximena walked with her hands wrapped around the bare skin where she'd ripped her shirt for Isaac's wound. He looked down at the material wrapped around his calf, all covered in blood.

"It should be just up here." Cian checked some sort of device in his pocket and pointed ahead. Darkness limited their sight but the moon and aurora lit their view enough to see one footstep in front of the other. Erros cleared tree limbs until his arm got stuck in some sort of fishing wire. "What is . . ."

The sound of cracking branches caused everyone to freeze and look up—everyone except Old Man Frypan, who took two steps back. The cracking sound reminded Isaac of the Griever coming down the steps of the Villa. With a thud into the snow, three axes came falling from above. “Watch out!” someone shouted too late. But no one was hit.

“Flare’s Devil!” Cian tightened the red scarf around his forehead.

“Nearly took my left hand!” Erros shouted. “That’s my favorite hand!” He looked left, right, and then above before taking a large step forward over the axes sticking out of the ground. “Come on, then? Can’t stop at every threat we receive now, can we?”

Isaac turned around to check with Frypan. “He’s right, they’ll see we’re innocent when we get closer. Maybe they’ll have some answers about how long that war’s been going on in Alaska.”

He stepped over the axes but then turned around. He may have given up on a lot of things, but he was still a blacksmith at heart and could see that the axes were well crafted. Small but sharp. He handed one to Old Man Frypan, just in case. One to Jackie. And kept the other for himself. He positioned it on his belt loop with the blade away from himself so that there was no risk of falling and slicing himself open again.

“You know. In case we see any Grievers here.” He tried to make it a joke, but in truth, he already trusted this Villa less than the last one. He wanted to be prepared for anything. Everything. Even Grievers.

2

The painted black door of the Villa hung wide open, and broken glass littered the entryway. There was no use walking around the front of the house and knocking politely.

“Something didn’t end well, here,” Isaac whispered to Jackie. Despite this being the only house on the island, the whole scene reminded him of the row of homes he and Jackie had stepped into before getting kidnapped—right before Kletter got her throat sliced open. If fear had a scent, Isaac could smell it in the doorway on top of the broken glass.

“More axes you think?” She peered up and around the house.

"No . . . something's off." He looked behind the group at Frypan as the old man caught up. "Does it smell weird to you?"

"Smells like . . ." Frypan took a big whiff. "Pine trees and smoke? Almost reminds me of back home."

Isaac knew they shouldn't go inside but then Ximena entered fearlessly right behind Cian and Erros. Jackie entered after her. And so Isaac carefully stepped on top of the broken glass.

Black curtains hung in every room. Some of them covered windows, and others covered equipment. Cian and Erros looked behind every single one.

"Who would put a Villa all the way out here?" Isaac stepped farther into the first room, not touching anything. An exact replica Villa from the one they'd just escaped from. "Crap." He turned around to stop Frypan from walking in through the open door and seeing all the vials and science equipment, but it was too late.

"Oh . . ." Frypan's face showed the exact amount of disappointment Isaac felt. This place couldn't have been more like the last. The only thing missing was a glass pod in the corner and a Griever dispensing medicine. *At least the Griever was missing.* But Isaac's ears stretched for any sounds of metal creaking and clanking in the distance. His whole body tensed, waiting to hear or see one of those crazy mechanical beasts.

"It's really a Villa." Jackie peeked under a cloth covering. "All this equipment just like at the last one. Up here in the middle of nowhere?"

Ximena kicked the broken shards of glass at her feet. "I guess someone already destroyed this one for us."

"Wonder how long it's been empty?" Cian traced the cabinets with his finger. "Not long enough to collect any ash from the fires."

"Surprised they didn't spark this up, too." Erros opened and shut cabinets.

"Anything?" Cian asked, doing the same. Erros shook his head.

Isaac didn't know if he should be happy or disappointed that they'd found the Villa empty. The dread in his gut about the fires and the others grew. He couldn't help but think that if Sadina were alive, she could be in yet another Villa, somewhere in Alaska, kept hostage and forced to eat terrible flour cakes and get stung by Grievers. He didn't know which was worse.

"So what do we do now?" he asked Frypan.

"Shhh . . ." Ximena held her finger over her lips. Even on his island it meant the same thing–*shut up, Isaac.*

He paused and listened for what she may have heard. The fear in his gut grew, and his imagination went wild. "It's probably just—"

"Isaac! Shhh!"

A scrape and a clank came from behind. Isaac pivoted to face what he hoped wouldn't be a Griever. Nothing there. "It's too dark in here to see anything . . ." His blood pumped faster, making it hard to hear anything but his own heartbeat; he spun around again to pinpoint the noise. He pulled up the small axe, gripped it in both hands. Even if a Griever appeared, he would fight metal with metal. He positioned himself in front of Frypan because the poor man didn't deserve any more Grievers. The lower cabinet to the left of Cian slowly opened and an arm reached out.

"Whoa!" Cian and Erros backed up, but Jackie ran to the cabinet.

"Oh my gosh!" Jackie practically screamed for all of Alaska to hear. "Miyoko!"

Isaac couldn't believe his eyes. "Miyoko?" He set his axe down and joined Jackie in hugging his east-side friend. The hopes he'd barricaded somewhere deep inside of him broke through, filling him up. "Where's everyone else hiding?"

"No . . . just me," Miyoko said before crying.

Isaac's heart sank as the others poured out questions.

"How did you get here?"

"Where's everyone else?"

"What happened?"

Miyoko slowly answered between sobs. "The others are still alive, just not here. We came here with the Godhead and then the Nation—what do they call it—where Minho and Orange are from?"

"The Remnant Nation," Frypan replied.

"Yeah, those people." Miyoko's nose dripped with snot from all the crying. "Minho and Orange shot some of them, but there were so many of those stupid Remnants." She cried so much while talking, it became harder and harder for Isaac to understand her. "Sadina and Trish screamed, and I panicked and hid . . . and then listened as they took everyone away." Her whole body shook. Jackie squeezed her tightly and wiped her nose clean.

"It's okay, you're okay now," Jackie whispered to her; Isaac imagined Cowan or Roxy doing the same if they'd been there.

Ximena kicked at a big metal cylindrical piece of equipment in the center of the floor; it started sputtering out pressured air.

"Careful." Frypan coughed. "There could be something tranquilizing in there."

Ximena had a real necessity to destroy things that were already doomed. Cian coughed and Erros covered his mouth as he bent over and tried to read the lettering on the tank. "It's just air. Must be for some of the machines that need pressure to transfer energy." He rolled the leaking cylinder to the furthest corner of the room. "But be careful, dammit!"

"Oh wow . . ." Miyoko dropped to the floor. "Kletter's . . ."

"Don't, there's glass everywhere!" Jackie warned.

She pulled Miyoko back but not before she'd picked up a small booklet. "It must have dropped from Minho's pocket when he fought them." She brushed debris off the notebook and handed it to Isaac.

"What is it?" He flipped through the pages quickly, but the lettering in the notebook looked like some kind of code. He recognized the letters but not the grouping of them. He gave it back to Miyoko.

"It's Kletter's. We found it on the *Maze Cutter* on our way up here."

"Let me see." Cian practically ripped the book out of Miyoko's hand.

She took a step back. "Dominic found it in between the boards of the lower deck, but none of us could read it. Only a few words here and there."

"A lot of good that does us." Isaac waited for Cian's face to reveal something about the journal, but his face remained blank.

"It's in Spanish," Cian said to Erros. "Kletter and her damn linguistics."

Erros motioned to Ximena. "You can read it." He stepped closer to her. "You can. I've heard you say a few things in that language, mostly under your breath." Ximena looked like she wanted nothing to do with any thing that had belonged to Kletter, but the look in Erros' eyes was almost threatening. "Read it," he said again, forcefully.

She took the small notebook and flipped through the pages as Isaac had done. He hoped Kletter wasn't dumb enough to log details for the day she'd killed Ximena's mom and the other crew members. Even though Ximena deserved to know what happened. But if Kletter did write about poisoning and shooting her mom, after everything Isaac had learned about Annie Kletter, he doubted her version of events could be trusted as accurate.

Erros and Cian both crowded behind Ximena's shoulders as she tried to read the log book. Her lips moved without sound and her eyes darted as she flipped pages.

Miyoko paced in a tight space. "We need to find where the Remnant Nation took Sadina, Trish, Dom . . . everyone."

"How would we even begin to find them?" Isaac asked. He had such mixed feelings—thrilled to know they were alive, but no closer to seeing them safe and sound. Further, perhaps.

Cian shook his head. "It doesn't matter *where* they took them. The Remnant Nation doesn't keep prisoners of war for very long."

"So, they'll let them go then?" Miyoko asked with such innocent hope that it was heartbreaking to hear.

Ximena exhaled in a way that prepared Isaac to hear yet again about *How the islanders were all naive.* But for the first time since meeting her, Isaac had to agree. She looked up at Isaac from the notebook with knowing eyes, and a simple glance confirmed it. *Ximena knew what Cian meant.*

"They'll just let them go?" Miyoko asked again.

Isaac turned to see the same look in Frypan's eyes. *He knew what Cian meant, too.* But Isaac couldn't betray his heart to say it out loud. *Sadina and the others were as good as dead.* He had lived through losing his entire family. But not Sadina. Please, not Sadina.

He couldn't lose her, too.

CHAPTER TWENTY

Senado de los Secuenciadores

I
MINHO

Orphans are born motherless. Penniless. Powerless.

The only way for an Orphan soldier to advance is to enter into the initiation of the Remnant as a Junior Grief Bearer, but even as a young soldier watching Griever Glane, Minho never wanted to be like any of them. They were seasoned losers. Weaker than even some of the youngest soldiers. Because while leaders like Griever Glane had power and handed out punishments, they grew lazy with that power.

Orphans were trained to fight. Protect the Nation. Kill the Godhead.

And it finally came time for Minho to do all three.

As the Remnant soldiers pushed him off the Berg, the relief Minho felt at realizing they weren't going to the depths of tortured Hell in the fortress were immediately replaced by the suffocating smell of sulfur and ash. It was another smell Minho knew well, and one he tried not to think about. The smell of burning flesh.

He lifted his head and tried to see through swollen eyes. The army of Remnants had set up hundreds of fires in makeshift camps that stretched for miles. Remnant snipers stood watch on top of any buildings still standing. The Nation had already set up posts and lookouts to protect the ruins of what used to be the City of Gods, and the Orphan soldiers were all too happy to drag Minho and a barely conscious Orange in front of the Grief Bearers to present them as the traitors they were.

Minho didn't bother twisting or kicking; the sounds of the Nation and the sheer quantity of soldiers around him well signaled his defeat. He only turned his head as best he could, past the soldiers who beat him and carried him forward, to see if they were separating him from Roxy, Dominic, and Sadina.

"Griever Ayers, Sir." The soldiers dropped Minho on to the ground with a thud and kicked his back to flip him forward-facing to the Bearers. They also kicked the back of Orange's knees to bend her body to a bow.

Minho looked at the Grief Bearer in front of him. He knew better than to look any Bearer in the eyes, but what were they going to do if he did—*kill him?* So he did. His jaw clenched as he stared deeply into Griever Ayers' dark, soulless eyes. An anxious spirit of rebellion rose inside him the exact same way it had the day of his cliff ceremony. But today would be different.

"There aren't any mountaintops to throw me from." Minho squinted.

The Grief Bearer rubbed his little hands together like a man that had waited his whole life to play with fire. "We'll shove you off the only cliff that matters." The Bearer showed his teeth, but it wasn't a smile. "The one in your mind."

Griever Ayers was right. More painful than the stabbing in Minho's chest, the Orphan admitted to himself that the cliff in his mind held the most danger. Orange had known that when she'd told him to *get off that wall in his mind* back on the *Maze Cutter.* He looked over at a lifeless Orange before realizing he shouldn't have. A kick to the back of her head confirmed it.

The Orphan named Minho knew his life would end at the hands of the Remnants, one way or another, and he wasn't going to waste his death. "You've destroyed this whole town, probably killed thousands," Minho said as he looked past Griever Ayers, "but what's really gotta chap your ass is the fact that the one person you came here to kill . . . you've barely managed to inconvenience."

He let out what sounded like a pathetic chuckle and then a sudden burst of air as a soldier kicked the back of his head then stomped on his kidney. But he wasn't done taunting them. Not yet. "In fact, you've led the Godhead to the *one thing* they were looking for, what they needed to complete their ridiculous Evolution." The Orphan let his pain and nerves escape him through another laugh, a sound the Grief Bearers hated most. Minho was pleased with himself—even the boot to his back felt damn good.

"What makes you say that?" Griever Ayers asked. "Speak, boy!"

Minho laughed even louder, because Grief Bearers never asked such weak questions. Certainly never questions they didn't know the answer to. Even if Minho died at that moment, he would consider it a victory. He outsmarted the Nation not once, but twice. He and Orange weren't traitors—they were rebels who held the most important information of the war. The location of the Godhead.

"Say what you meant by that." Another Grief Bearer stepped up and demanded Minho's attention, but he wouldn't give it to them. He already gave them enough.

"You're too dumb to figure it out?" Minho took two more swift kicks to the back and coughed up blood. He spit at the feet of the Bearers. "I guess that's why the Godhead is still alive . . ."

"Go. Now!" The Grief Bearer waved his arm. "Take them to the other captives!"

The soldiers behind Minho kicked him in the ribs one more time for good measure, then dragged him to his feet.

"Take them all to the Maze," Griever Ayers ordered.

2
ISAAC

Ximena stormed out of the Villa with Kletter's notebook.

"She won't get far. Grab what you can for our next stop." Cian spoke with Erros while packing items from the cabinets. "Stabilizer?" Cian held up a vial.

Erros nodded. "Bring it."

Old Man Frypan motioned for Isaac to follow Ximena. "Go on. We'll stay here."

He obeyed, hurrying out of the Villa, but couldn't see Ximena anywhere. Dead soldiers littered the lightly snow-covered ground, and Isaac walked around their bodies as carefully as he could. Tiptoeing around the bodies, he finally spotted Ximena, not far from the bank. Beyond her, farther down the ocean and almost out of view, the bright fires of the *Maze Cutter* flamed on and struck Isaac's heart. His world continued to burn in so many ways as sections of the ship crumbled, slowly breaking down and falling into the cold, dark ocean.

Ximena held the notebook by her side just looking at the burning ship. "There's probably something in this book that can help us . . ."

She turned around to face Isaac and shook her head. "Things that will help us . . . and things that will hurt us. Hurt *me* at least."

Isaac still couldn't quite figure her out. *She wanted the truth so badly, she was willing to threaten Erros with a crossbow to his throat, but now that she had Kletter's diary, she was afraid to read it?* "You seem so fearless . . . but you're . . . actually really scared."

"I'm not scared." Ximena sat on the bank of the island. "I'm angry."

He joined her on the ground and kicked out his injured leg. Maybe the cold ground could help numb the pain. Finding Miyoko had given Isaac hope again. He wasn't as mad at Ximena as he'd been back on the Berg. Maybe it was seeing her face her mother's death alone, but he understood her anger. "I'm scared, too, sometimes. I get it."

"No, you don't," Ximena snapped. "That ship is where Kletter killed my mom, and now I have to read about it from Annie's own selfish words like any other one of her absent-minded excuses. I have to look and see it in *her* handwriting." She waved the captain's log in the air. "There's not one thing or one person, alive or dead, who I could possibly hate more than Annie Kletter . . . and I sure as hell don't want to hear the truth from *her*."

Isaac thought for only a second before he had an idea. Maybe a stupid one, but maybe not. "I can read it out loud." He shrugged. "For you to translate."

"You don't speak Spanish." She looked at him like he was an idiot. He'd long since gotten used to those looks.

"I definitely don't. But I can sound out the words, close enough to something that sounds familiar to you, and that way . . . you won't have to hear it from Kletter. Better than nothing." He scooted closer to her and lifted the journal from her hands. He slowly opened it to the first page—filled with cross-hatch markings as if Kletter had measured or counted something.

"Okay. But whatever we find . . . don't . . ."

"Don't what?" Isaac asked. He wasn't sure there'd be anything Kletter wrote that could shake his world more than it had already been shaken. The *Maze Cutter* sat on the ocean, engulfed in flames only yards away. His best friend, Sadina, and all the others were as good as dead. There wasn't anything they could learn that would change any of that.

"Don't tell those two anything we find. Not yet," Ximena said.

"Cian and Erros? I know you don't trust them, but you don't trust me, either."

"I don't have a feeling about you," she said without emotion.

"Oh." Isaac's throat twitched with something like shame. For some reason, her words made him feel good about himself, as if he'd passed a magic test.

"Sorry. What I meant is . . . I have feelings when bad things are about to happen. Visions. I hear things. I don't know why it's mostly bad feelings, but right now I feel like we can't trust Cian and Erros with whatever's in here." She brushed her hair from her face. "Just not yet, okay?"

"Okay," Isaac agreed, then looked for words next to the cross-hatch marks on the first page. "Millas náuticas . . . "

"Nautical miles."

"So far there's just a lot of lines and numbers." If the first page of the notebook was an indicator of what went on inside Kletter's head, she could have been a half-Crank. Very erratic. He flipped to the next page. "And here . . ." Isaac pointed . . . "It's hard to tell if these are words or scribbles . . ." He tried to sound out what might have been something comprehensible. "Última oportunidad . . . ?" He looked at Ximena. "Is that something?"

"Yes, keep going." She nodded.

". . . Para el Senado de los Secuenciadores . . ." He tried to say that last squiggly word again, "Secuenciadores?"

She repeated the same word back but made a rolling sound with her throat at the end. "Secuenciadores . . ."

"So what's that mean?"

She lowered her head. "Last chance for the Sequencers, or last chance for the Senate of Sequencers . . ."

"Oh . . . so, what Cian and Erros were saying is true? About the Sequencers?"

"It's bullshit." Ximena got to her feet in a huff.

"But *true* bullshit," he said as she paced the bank of the island. "Right?" Dark water softly swished in small waves against the dirt leading up to where he sat.

"If it's all true, then my Village got wiped out, my mother killed, all for some separate under-earth society that may or may not want to rejoin the world? And you . . ." Isaac prepared himself for her to snap at him about being a naive islander. "How does that make *you* feel? Knowing you came here for some fake Cure and your friends are all dying for nothing?"

He peered down at Kletter's notebook. There weren't words for how he felt, at least not in his language. He looked back to the Villa where Jackie, Miyoko, and Frypan were all still alive inside, and he planned to keep it that way.

"I don't know how to honor my friends' lives and make their deaths have meaning, other than to try to find the truth." He paged through Kletter's journal. "Maybe we were lied to about the Cure, and yeah, maybe we came out here and it's not what we thought." He looked over to the still-burning remnants of the *Maze Cutter.* "But maybe . . ." He took a deep breath of cold Alaskan air. "Maybe we're the only ones who can unearth this."

Ximena dropped her shoulders and softened. "I do want the truth. The world deserves the truth." She held out her hand for the book from Isaac, and he was happy to give it to her. "I guess no one's been naive enough to think they could find it until now," she teased.

"Or crazy enough," he teased right back. "But after eighty years or so, it's been long enough." He slowly stood up. Ximena helped him balance. The cut in his right calf was starting to make his whole leg stiff. Isaac looked up at the sky. The stars looked the same as the ones on his island, but the auroras made everything so different, so ethereal. The greens and purples shone bright through the clouds of smoke that traveled overhead. "You ever see these colors in the sky before?" he asked, but she was staring at the water.

"Isaac . . ." Ximena slowly moved backward. "There's something out there." She pointed, but the water was too dark for Isaac to see anything, and the moonlight was shielded behind the clouds of smoke from the war.

"It's probably just debris from the *Maze Cutter*. The whole thing looks like it's falling apart. It'll be driftwood, washing up on the shore somewhere." He had a sudden pang in his gut, thinking about the driftwood necklace he'd helped Sadina make for Trish.

"It's not . . ." Ximena looked absolutely terrified. "It's not driftwood, Isaac. But I do think it might be from the *Maze Cutter.*"

He looked out to the ocean waters again. Nothing on the *Maze Cutter* was important enough to have her make this face she was making.

But then he saw it.

Splashing against the current, a body floated and moved back and forth near the bank.

"Oh." Isaac took a step back. The other dead bodies he'd walked over weren't moving, but this one did just that, shifting with the current, and it creeped him out. "It looks like a young soldier. An Orphan probably." He glanced back at the others behind him, dead on the cold snow. They all appeared to be around his age or even younger.

Ximena was shaking her head adamantly. "But the wrist . . ." She rubbed her own wrist.

Isaac stepped closer to the body, floating face down, and the arm at its side. His brain couldn't process what he was seeing. A braided palm bracelet wrapped around the floating wrist, just like the one Trish had made Jackie.

It couldn't be.

Letting out a sound, somewhere between a whimper and a scream, he tried to pull the body ashore. It was heavy, water-logged, slimy. Ximena came to help, pulling on the body. They finally succeeded in flipping it over, only to see the driftwood necklace that Isaac had helped Sadina make for her precious, loving, kind, funny, wonderful girlfriend.

The face removed all doubt. Swollen and purple, it was still all too familiar.

Trish.

Isaac released a wail from deep inside of him, a noise that pierced the night and shattered his heart.

3
XIMENA

Más remedio tiene un muerto.

The dead have no choice, but Abuela said that even the dead had something to hope for.

Frypan stabbed the sharpened end of his walking stick into the wet dirt next to the dead girl's bloated body. Isaac helped console Jackie and Miyoko as best he could, though he seemed to need it more than they did. Ximena stepped back and let the islanders mourn their friend, knowing the grief they held wasn't just for Trish but for their entire world as they knew it. Maybe they'd finally understand Ximena's anger now that every death the islanders experienced could be blamed on one person: Annie Kletter.

Ximena walked over to the open doorway of the Villa as Erros carried out two air canisters.

"We're packing up some stuff, then we'll be ready, okay?" he said as he walked by.

She looked over to the islanders and back at him before nodding. "Yeah. Okay."

"Hey, Cian, watch these Remnants. . . . They're everywhere and it's hard to see out here." Erros squinted in the dark, stepped over a dead soldier. "I'll meet you at the Berg."

Ximena wasn't ready to get back to the Berg yet. She needed more time to figure out where to direct Cian to fly to "find" the Sequencers —a group of people she hadn't heard a single whisper about until earlier that night.

Cian exited the Villa with an overflowing box of supplies. Something toppled out and he set the box down at his feet. She helped him reorganize the items so that they all fit. Such mundane activities after finding the body of a friend, bloated and dead.

"I told you there'd be stuff for the Sequencers," Cian said.

She actually had no idea why anyone would want the things he had packed: old plastic containers, glass vials, weird measuring tools. Nothing of value to Ximena, but sometimes her inner-knowings surprised even herself.

"Some of this, the Sequencers have never seen. *I've* never seen." He held up a tool and made a face before stuffing it into the box of supplies.

Jackie's and Miyoko's cries grew from the bank, hurting Ximena's heart. They were all so devastated. "We can't leave them here," she said to Cian, motioning to Isaac and the others. "Not after their friend got killed by the Remnant Nation and—"

"No. They stay here." Cian looked up at Ximena for only a second before his attention fell back down to the box. "That boy almost killed us."

"I could have killed your brother, too." She put her hand on her knife. "I still could if I wanted to." She tried to make her young voice sound threatening, menacing, but it came out as a pathetic, empty taunt. She was more exhausted from the day's events than she'd thought. It was all catching up with her.

Cian picked up the box of supplies, now looking more balanced but still very heavy. "No. Not even up for negotiation." He walked over the first dead Remnant. "See you at the Berg."

"Isaac has the captain's log, and there're things in there you should see. He'll share it if—"

An arm seemingly came out of nowhere and swept Cian's feet from under him; the box of Villa supplies flew out of his arms with a crash. Cian landed flat on his back, now held at knife point by a Remnant Soldier, still alive.

"Erros!" he cried. "Help!" His arms flailed as he tried to free himself; his feet kicked at the arms of the soldier. The Remnant appeared disoriented, stabbing at the air, the ground, and what he could of Cian's moving body.

Ximena pulled her own knife and went at the Orphan soldier. He was distracted enough that he didn't see her coming—she jumped on him, placed the tip of her blade on his bare neck. She blew the air and the fear out of her lungs, focused all her attention. She slid the knife into the Orphan's flesh, at least an inch or two, watching as his arms slowly stabbed at the air with less energy and movement. Cian still struggled beneath him, having at least one wound himself.

"Bring the islanders with us, and I'll end this." She could let the soldier stab Cian as many times as he wanted to, if the man wanted to be stubborn. Cian tried to regain his footing but the snowy earth gave way. He shook his head at Ximena, refusing despite his desperate situation.

"Fine," she said. "I'll give you the Cure if you let them come."

"You already said you would!" He wiggled his body around to face her.

"I said I'd take you to the Cure, but I wasn't going to give it to you." She scoffed. "Why would I?"

"You lied." He grunted and struggled.

"I'm telling you the truth, now. It's in my backpack, front pocket. Let them come with us to safety, and it's yours." She could easily let the Orphan soldier go, let him die a slow and painful death, bleeding out from gunshots and a stab wound in the cold. Or she could give him mercy, slit his throat like she had so many chickens back in her Village.

"Okay, alright!" Cian shouted as the soldier's blade neared his chest in a wild swing.

Ximena flicked her knife, choosing the way of mercy.

"They can come. And the body of their friend, too," she negotiated.

Cian sighed as he crawled to his feet. "Fine. Whatever. But you're in charge of that kid, and if he tries anything like that little stunt he did again—you're both getting thrown from midair without a parachute."

"Reasonable enough." Ximena pulled her knife, the one that used to be Kletter's knife, out of the dead Remnant's back. "If anyone has a right to visit the Sequencers, it should be them." She looked Cian up and down. "Unless *you're* the one lying. About Frypan's family being a part of it all, this whole under-earth thing?"

Cian just smiled. "I guess we'll find out, won't we?"

CHAPTER TWENTY-ONE

Sacred Ground

I
MINHO

Four soldiers pulled Minho's limbs in different directions as they descended into the depths of the earth, into what looked like another world. For being underground, everything looked so alive and green. The walls lining the Glade were larger than life, all stone and majesty and vines. Bigger than any wall Minho had ever kept soldier's watch upon.

The Glade. The Maze. He was actually there.

The greenery confused him. Back in the Remnant Nation, all the underground tunnels and bunkers were cold and lifeless, especially Hell itself, whose dirt floors were pounded in place by each and every soul who'd met their end there. But the site of the Maze gave Minho an overwhelming sense of awe, a sense of beauty, despite the ruined nature of its remains.

He saw the Remnants lining the Glade with small clusters of war prisoners, scattered in between the Orphan soldiers. Some of the prisoners were being beaten while others looked already dead. Had he really ever been a part of such a brutal, ruthless people? Was this who he was?

"Go." The soldier behind Minho kicked his left calf. "March to your death."

They pushed him and Orange, paraded them in front of the others. Minho tried to make eye contact with Orange but her eyes were just slits and her body hung limp in the soldier's grasp. She wasn't even walking on her own. The soldiers kicked her legs forward like the puppet of a corpse. Minho looked away. He could handle his own death just fine, bravely even, but it was the death of the ones he cared about that felt so impossible to bear.

"More prisoners from Griever Ayers' command." A soldier pushed Minho forward once again; he turned just enough to see Roxy and the others behind him. Their faces were full of fear, their lives no longer their own.

An older soldier that Minho recognized as someone whose cliff ceremony had been before his, walked behind him and pulled his combat ties so tight that his shoulder blades touched and his ribs ached. His head flung back in pain but he wouldn't scream or grimace; instead, he opened his eyes as much as he could to assess the Glade. Pain was always an opportunity to see more, and the Orphan named Minho noticed one thing missing: Grief Bearers. *Were they afraid of the sacred site of the Maze?* At least Minho wouldn't have to hear their commands before his death, their voices. He'd die at the hands of his former fellow soldiers.

The older soldier forced Minho stumbling ahead, toward open doors in the distance, impossibly big. "Go. Into the Maze." He commanded their fate. "Take the others to the Deadheads. We have room for more prisoners there."

Roxy reached out to Minho. "No! Please, don't take him. That's my son!" She pleaded for mercy, but she had no idea how her words would actually make his torture worse.

"Orphans have no mother!" The soldiers pushed and pulled Minho even harder, in the direction of the giant doors. The blood would soon run warm against him, but every extra lashing he got because Roxy had called him her son would be worth it. Because of her, he would die more human than soldier. More than an Orphan. He would die as someone's child.

"It's okay." He mouthed the words, along with his most convincing nod to Roxy before they yanked him by the neck.

"Go on!" The Remnant behind him drove his heel into Minho's calf. They dragged him and Orange to a makeshift prison that awaited them on the other side of those doors. One by one, the other Remnant soldiers along the way, busy beating and guarding prisoners, looked up at Minho and Orange as they came by. The soldiers stopped whatever they were doing to watch two of their own be dragged to torture and death. And they let it be known that they felt no sympathy.

"Traitors!"

"Death awaits!"

"Kill the Godhead. Kill the traitors!"

"Weakest of the Orphans!"

Walking to certain death, Minho looked at each and every soldier's face as he passed, just long enough to know that none of them were poor, half-beaten, Kit. That kid had probably died a painful death in the bowels of Hell. Minho's biggest regret was being too scared to even tell Kit his name at the time. Names had been forbidden, and he'd still been a coward in many ways back then. But he said it in his mind, now, said it with pride.

My name is Minho.

2
ISAAC

Jackie and Miyoko sat by the bank and wrapped Trish's body in a black curtain they'd pulled out of the Villa. They tied fresh pine branches around it to give her a proper send off. Isaac felt less and less hopeful about finding Sadina and the others alive, but he tried his best to focus on doing something about the Sequencers. It was the only thing within his control, the only thing that might make Trish's death —and perhaps the others'—mean something.

But deciphering Kletter's scribbled handwriting wasn't easy. Frypan, Ximena, Cian, and Erros all took their own turns flipping through the pages of the captain's log. The hash marks and scribbles on the first page always grabbed their attention.

Frypan pointed something out. "Those markings. Four lines, up and down, one across—we used a similar method in the Glade to count days."

Isaac looked closer at the hash marks. "Numbers." He counted them all. "Thirty-nine . . . does that mean anything to you?" he asked Cian and Erros.

Cian shook his head. Erros shrugged.

"Wait. These are separate. See the dots?" Ximena took the notebook from Isaac. "Six, then four with a dot. Then two, then eight, and two." She drew the numbers in the snow with her fingers. "One. Seven. Four, dot. Two, five. Two." They all stood around the sequence carved into the crust of the snow, but it looked like a jumbled mess of nothing. Just like Kletter's handwriting.

"What if . . ." Erros grabbed Old Man Frypan's walking stick and with the pointed end drew a line separating the numbers in half. "What if it's a *set* of numbers? What if she wrote the coordinates as hash marks? They've got to be!"

Ximena flipped back to the first page again. "Why not just write the digits?" She looked up at Isaac and rolled her eyes, "I forgot, it's Kletter we're talking about. Nothing she did ever made sense. Okay."

"Let me see," Erros asked, and everyone tried to get a look at the page.

"Here . . . this one and this one," Frypan pointed. "The last two marks, they look different. Not straight up and down, they're sort of leaning . . . those markings could be arrows."

Erros stepped back to the numbers in the snow, looking at them just like he'd stared at Isaac after he almost crashed the Berg.

"This first one points up. North. And this one. . . . Must be east." Frypan had to be right.

"They do look like they could be Kletter's attempt at arrows," Isaac chimed in.

"Those *are* coordinates," Cian exclaimed, then practically tackled Erros. "We've got coordinates!"

Jackie and Miyoko looked over in disgust at this outburst of emotion, but Isaac couldn't help from smiling at Ximena. They'd figured out something important. "Those are it, aren't they? The coordinates to the Senado de los Secuenciadores." He whispered it to Ximena. She could lead Cian and Erros to the Sequencers after all. She wasn't lying.

"You're pronouncing it wrong, but yes." She returned his smile. "The Senate of Sequencers." She looked back at the numbers then spoke up to the brothers.

"I could have directed you, but coordinates will be much easier to navigate."

They gave her a knowing grin.

A wave of peace settled into Isaac's bones, shadowed by the sorrow for Trish. It was the first time in a long time, other than finding Miyoko, that something finally went their way. And it wasn't just the coordinates to this Senate thing that made him feel this way. Because there were other markings, one in particular.

It had a phrase scribbled next to it, *Isla de los Immunes.* And Isaac didn't need Ximena to translate that one.

The Island of Immunes.

CHAPTER TWENTY-TWO

Deadheads

I
ALEXANDRA

Brute soldiers did their best to intimidate Alexandra by taunting her with the hallowed ground, but the Maze wasn't a punishment to the Goddess. No. It was her solace. Especially this place, where some of the original Gladers had been buried so long ago.

"They're going to kill him . . ." Dominic exhaled the words, barely above a whisper.

"No," Sadina said with her head in her hands.

"Shhh . . ." Roxy shushed the others through her teeth.

The Goddess observed them and the other Remnant soldiers and Pilgrims all around her. Seeing so many moving bodies in the Glade was very foreign to her eyes. And the sound of so many voices, foreign to her ears. Beatings. Screaming. Death. She tightened the hood of her cloak over her face. The entire Remnant Nation brought a madness born from Mikhail. A madness she didn't yet know the depths of.

"Where are we?" Dominic covered his mouth as he spoke. The

guard to their left was busy commanding others in the cemetery to get back.

"Is this the Glade?" Sadina asked Alexandra.

The Goddess nodded. *The Deadheads to be exact.* And Nicholas' dead head was buried around there somewhere, a hilarious detail for her at the time. Her fingers found moss below her and she clutched it and dug her knuckles into the dirt as deep as they would go. She had to stay in control of this situation. Alaska was her home. Her sacred ground. She wouldn't let any remnants of society take it from her. She looked around for a sense of what the soldiers would do to them and rubbed the back of her neck. She recited the digits and then used the tools of her mind.

She imagined releasing the Remnants' hold over her. With every digit she imagined herself escaping the Glade. *One.* The probability of her escaping the Glade doubled. Two. Then multiplied again. Two steps back for one step forward. *Three.* And again. *Five.* The Sequence empowered her vision. *Eight.* Escape was inevitable. *Thirteen.*

A shot echoed in the Glade and Alexandra jumped. A body under a Pilgrim's cloak fell to the ground with a thud. Remnants kicked the corpse. Another shot it again.

Sadina whimpered, but *she* wasn't the one wearing a Pilgrim's cloak. Alexandra tightened her hood around her again and watched as boots covered in ashes kicked the murdered body. That was her Pilgrim. And her ashes. Her sacred ground. Her city. Her Maze.

Enough with this already. She was the Goddess of this city, the Goddess of all. She stood up and lowered her cloak's hood, and walked away from the cries of Sadina.

"Hey, where are you going?"

Alexandra ignored the lowly soldier. She would walk right up to a man standing nearby, wearing a cloak similar to the one Mikhail had worn. She would tell this man something he didn't know. She would tell him something that no one knew—*who* the Master of the Golden Room was. Mikhail had given her one gift before he died, the greatest gift of all.

Knowledge.

Hell, maybe the man had planned it all from the very beginning.

2
XIMENA

Jackie and Miyoko sat in the Berg together, ready for takeoff with the dead body—decorated with pine-tree limbs—between them. Ximena's Village respected their dead and treated each burial with respect, and it was important to her that the islanders got to do the same. The tree branches around the body looked silly to her but at least it would keep the growing decay from smelling too bad, worse with every passing hour. Soon enough the sun would rise, the Berg would heat up, and that body would start to stink.

Really, Ximena. What a terrible thing to think.

At least she hadn't shared the thought out loud.

"How long will it take to get there?" Jackie asked. *The islanders had no patience.*

Cian had punched the coordinates into a fancy device on the dashboard of the Berg and now looked up, surprised. "Not long at all." He rubbed his forehead with the red scarf then turned his attention to his brother. "Makes sense it'd be close to the site of the first Mazes. Lots of giant caves and caverns around there."

"WICKED was nothing if not efficient." Erros fastened his seat belt, and Ximena braced for takeoff.

She sat near Isaac and Old Man Frypan, and after the launch, she opened Kletter's logbook. Most of the pages had unimportant notes, scribbled about the weather or wind speed. Some of the pages in the back held questions about the Cure. Questions Annie Kletter didn't have answers to. Ximena half-expected to find some big confession about all the worst things Annie did, but she hadn't found any pages like that yet. And by not finding anything remotely honest from Annie, it confirmed to Ximena that her Village's hero really was the absent-minded person she and her Abuela always thought she was. Ximena had sympathy for any Sequencers who thought Annie Kletter was their only hope.

"Why even bring the Sequencers back to the surface," she asked. "It sounds like they have everything for a perfect utopia. No Flare. No WICKED. No Experiments . . . for *them*." She scanned more pages with the word *secuenciadores*.

"*Perfect* is a perspective," Cian said.

That may be true, Ximena thought, but she couldn't stretch to imagine their lives being any tougher than the outside world she'd lived in her whole life.

Erros expounded on the matter. "They have their own hurdles, things that'll make them take one look at you and think *your* life is perfect." He acted as if he could read her frequency of confusion. "Your lungs for example." He paused. "Sequencers can't go even a few hours without smoking a coltsfoot cigar to help their respiratory system."

"I thought they had perfect genetics?" Isaac asked, his eyes still sad, filled with grief.

"A hundred years ago—they did." Cian looked over at Erros and shrugged. "What's your plan?"

Erros didn't look back. "No plan."

"That confident?" Cian scoffed.

Old Man Frypan and Ximena both noticed the exchange.

"Something's cooking, isn't it?" he whispered to her, and for a moment she felt as seen and as safe as she did with her Abuela.

"So what happened to their genes, then?" Isaac leaned forward but stayed seated—as promised to avoid Cian throwing him out like garbage.

"Mold spores. Ventilation systems failing. Humidity—plus the colder air makes breathing harder to begin with. Human genetics can adjust, and the Sequencers' lungs have grown larger to accommodate, but failing infrastructure puts a clock on things. They were never meant to live under-earth for this many generations."

"So why did they?" Ximena asked. "If they were the smartest people, the top scientists and everything, then wouldn't they realize they'd screwed up?"

Cian chuckled, either annoyed with all the questions or at the Sequencers themselves. "The Senate of Sequencers held on to the experiments of living within the earth that showed promise. The Senate only understood the negative effects of the solar storms. The damage. But that's like removing water from the surface of the Earth because of a flood that happened once."

Ximena looked at Frypan. His hands sat poised in his lap, his face relaxed. How could he not feel completely betrayed by his family, by WICKED, by the entire world?

He raised his eyebrows at her. "They should've had some of that second-sight you've got."

"You're so calm about this. How?" She wasn't sure what to think about the Sequencers, but if she were Frypan she'd probably feel pretty upset. "You have no righteous anger? It's kind of like a double whammy to you—your family hidden away, yourself sent to the Maze and the Trials."

"When you've lived long enough like me, and through enough bad stuff . . . you learn what's needed to survive." He held his hands up, palms open. Empty. Through the window, a beautiful sunrise grew on the horizon, just past his shoulder. Ximena didn't really understand what he might have been referring to.

"Peace," he answered her.

Peace? Sitting back and folding her hands wasn't going to save her Village or anyone else. "You're just accepting all of this?"

"*Observing*," he stressed. "I don't have the energy, inside or out, to fight against people and ideas like I used to. Peace is my only resistance to chaos now." Frypan stretched out his arm to Isaac. "But you kids . . . you're going to shake this up. I know you will."

Isaac didn't look sure of anything. "It's just been one big struggle after another. I can't imagine it ever ending. At least not in a good way."

Donde hay lucha, hay esperanza. Ximena always hated hearing Abuela say that when she grew angry at the way things were. It seemed like such a silly answer to the Village's biggest problems. *Where there is struggle, there is hope.* But Ximena hoped her anger in destroying the

Villa, taking the Cure, and finding the Sequencers might actually lead to something important. It wasn't what she'd envisioned her actions leading to, but she owed it to everyone in her Village, the living and the dead, to unearth the long-hidden truth.

She would accomplish this task, she told herself, and Death itself would just have to be patient and wait for her to finish.

3
MINHO

Soldiers could pin his hands behind his back, take away his ability to fight, but the Remnant Nation could never take away the Orphan's name.

My name is Minho.

Separated from the others, far from the sounds of Pilgrims shouting and soldiers stomping, a Junior Grief Bearer threw Minho into the shadowed depths of the Maze. At least the size of the structure would block out the noise from Roxy. He couldn't stand the thought of her hearing the sounds of pain as they escaped him. The Orphan had taken all his previous beatings and wounds in silence, but he knew what they were about to do to him would be different, animalistic. He himself dreaded hearing his own primal wails to come.

"Here." The Junior Grief Bearer pointed in a circular motion. "Hell awaits."

On his knees, Minho watched soldiers step forward in a line, standing only a few feet from him, and one-by-one assemble a makeshift Hell, far from the real one in Nebraska. A soldier dumped a bucket of ash in a circle. Another stepped up and threw an arm full of stones and debris. And another. The debris smelled of the fires of war, and the next soldier stepped forward with what smelled like gasoline. Which meant only one thing. Fire.

Someone lit a match, and flames whooshed up in front of Minho. A hellish fire pit formed, just big and bright enough for him to see Orange slumped over on the other side of the flaming debris.

"The Godhead . . ." Minho tried to speak up but broken ribs made it hard. "The Godhead is here . . ." He said it as loud as he could, but the Remnant soldiers in charge of torture couldn't care less about killing the Godhead. Their motto might have been *Kill the Godhead*, but most Orphan soldiers, who'd been robbed of every human emotion, only cared about the first part: *Kill. Kill. Kill.*

"Silent, now!" The Junior Bearer-in-training sprayed the remaining gasoline across Minho's face. His eyes stung and watered; he coughed and spit out what he could, his lungs already fighting to keep each breath moving in and out of his body. "These are traitors to the Nation! There can be no worse crime. Torture them as you will."

Blinded by the sting of gasoline and the earlier punches to his eyes, Minho listened for footsteps, trying to count how many soldiers gathered in line to beat the remaining life out of him. He knew most of them would lack the slightest creativity in their torture, stick with simple things they knew best— like stomping his head, or stabbing him between the ribs to separate the muscle away from his bone.

He coughed and coughed to clear his lungs, but if he'd spit up any blood, he couldn't taste it or see it anymore. He rubbed his eyes with his broken shoulder and tried to peek across the flames, but he could only see swirls of colors. "Orange . . ." he sputtered through a cough.

"Orange?" repeated a random soldier. He spit in Minho's face— such a childish, simpleton thing to do. "You'll be seeing *red*, traitor."

And then Minho received his first punch, right in the temple. It had begun.

CHAPTER TWENTY-THREE

Lake of Promise

I
ISAAC

"Read any more of that chicken scratch yet?" Isaac pointed to the captain's log that sat closed on Ximena's lap.

She shook her head. "Chicken scratch?"

"It's what we call things scattered all over the place like chicken feed. Kletter's scribbles." For the first time, *Isaac* had to explain something to *Ximena*, and not the other way around. Small victories. "You don't have chickens in your Village?"

"Of course we do. We feed them corn, not scratch." She sighed, but also allowed a small grin to appear. "Whatever that is."

Isaac almost smiled back. Almost. He'd run dry of such things for now. "Scratch is just broken pieces of corn, mixed with other grains and stuff."

"Don't let the boy confuse you—I've seen his handwriting and it's certified donkey scratch." Frypan chuckled at his own joke, pretty proud of himself, apparently. He tapped his walking stick on the bench of the Berg as he nudged Isaac. "You good?"

Isaac looked back at Jackie and Miyoko. Trish's body lay between them, wrapped in the black cloth of the Villa. Nothing felt *good* about any of it. "I'm good," he lied.

"Uh-huh." Frypan titled his head at Isaac, as if there was something more the old man expected of him.

"What else is there to say?" Isaac asked.

Frypan nodded. "What else is there to say . . ." he repeated, while certainly looking like he had something new to say. "Well, let's just speak frankly. Trish . . . that girl loved Sadina more than life, and the feeling was mutual. And with Sadina being your best friend, and Trish a close second, this is pure trauma for you. I've been there, son. I've been there. And I'm *here*, for you."

They sat in silence for a while, Isaac on the verge of tears. Finally, he found the strength to speak. "Trish wanted to have a big coop of roosters when she built her own yurt someday." He thought back to those brighter times on the island with Trish and Sadina. "I told her they'd all end up fighting each other, because that's what roosters do. But she swore up and down that she could make the roosters live happily together by giving them extra scratch. And when they had more than enough, she thought they'd be friends. Best friends. Simple, sweet. Dead wrong." He stared at the small, wrapped body at the back of the Berg and rubbed his shoulder, thinking of all the crazy ideas he'd never hear again from Trish. All the petty fights he'd never have to break up between her and . . .

Sadina.

"I can't think about losing Sadina, too." A few tears leaked out, dripped down his cheeks.

"Then don't," Ximena said, as if it were that easy. "Let's keep you busy, your mind occupied."

"Those two, Isaac and Sadina," Frypan said, raising his eyebrows at Ximena. "They've been best friends since they were old enough to eat sand."

Isaac tried to make light of it. "It's a joke, we didn't actually eat sand. Not on purpose, anyway."

"Thanks for clearing that up," Ximena responded, letting loose another grin. A tiny one.

Isaac thought of all the times that he, Trish, and Sadina did the dumbest antics they could think of, just to make each other laugh. Farting, burping, mooning, the whole lot. But what he'd miss the most were the sweet things Sadina did for Isaac. The things only she noticed about him. The way she'd saved him after his family died.

"Whenever Sadina thought I needed a hug, but thought it might embarrass me, she'd grab my hand. Just really quick with a little squeeze."

"She cared about you, lots and lots," Frypan agreed.

"And it seems like such a stupid thing to say, but when the world drained all the life out of me—you know, my family, the flood—she found a way to make life start flowing back into me." He felt like smiling and crying at the same time. "If she were here, right now, she'd tell me to quit being so sappy." He let out a slight approximation of a laugh. "And if Trish were alive, she'd say life is just a little wonky-bonky. So stupid." He looked down at the driftwood necklace they'd taken from Trish's body before wrapping her up.

"There's always more to say." Frypan patted Isaac on the back. "I'm glad you told us all that.

"Do you still . . ." Isaac wasn't sure if the question would upset Frypan or not, but he needed to know. "Do you still think WICKED is good? Or *good enough*, as you put it?"

The old man leaned back and exhaled. "I guess I don't know what I don't know." He squinted in the light of the rising sun. "I've seen people be evil and good in the very same life. Sometimes people change from one extreme to the other, but sometimes they're just . . . *both*, at the same time."

Isaac had too many thoughts at once, but the biggest question he needed an answer to was how the hell *Annie Kletter* got to be in charge of something so important like these Sequencer people.

"Hey Cian," he shouted up to the pilot seat. "How did Kletter get the coordinates to the Sequencers?"

The man answered without looking over his shoulder. "Only those who were a part of the foundation of WICKED knew the exact location, and each of them chose a successor to their secret, generation after generation. So she must be descended from someone all fancy and special-like."

Isaac looked out the window to see if they were still over the ocean, but land spanned out below them. So much more land than he had ever seen before—all trees and rocky hills and ravines, snow and ice and lakes and streams. Freshly lit and beautiful from the sun, well above the horizon now.

"How did all of this stay a secret for so long?" Ximena asked Cian.

"It didn't, not very well. Bits and pieces are heard here and there and those who hear it create their own story to fill in the blanks."

"Oh." Ximena looked like she had received some of those truths. "Like the Godhead in Alaska?"

Cian looked over his shoulder this time and nodded. "Exactly. The Godhead, the Nation of Remnants, everyone thinks *they* have the full story of what the Evolution truly means. But it's been a century plagued with lies."

"Even the Sequencers are wrong about their truth," Erros scoffed.

But how could they be wrong about their own history? Isaac thought.

"And you're going to be the one to tell them that?" Cian snapped at his brother.

"Hell, no." Erros ended the conversation right there.

They flew over some cliffs that reminded Isaac of Stone Point back home, miles and miles of black rock jutting up from the earth. The same cliffs he'd stood atop when he first saw the *Maze Cutter* floating toward shore. Maybe it was his own lame version of second-sight, but Isaac had a weird feeling looking down at those cliffs. He looked at Ximena but she didn't seem scared or deep in thought.

"Oh wow . . ." Frypan whispered as looked out the window of the now-descending Berg. "Just beautiful. Stunning."

As they lowered in altitude, the details of the cliffs became sharper, just like the rocks. The Berg turned just slightly to the right, readying itself to land, the gear already extended below. They went over a small rise in the land, revealing a large body of water nestled against the cliffs on the other side.

"There it is. The Lake of Promise," Cian said as he continued the Berg's descent, heading for a clearing by the water.

Isaac stared at the so-called *Lake of Promise*, more than a bit surprised that someone would choose such a name for what he saw below him.

The lake was filled with blood.

2
MINHO

Soldiers are trained to deliver pain. Strike with precision. And torture with pleasure.

Minho's thoughts began to float above his body. He no longer physically felt any of the traitorous blows he deserved. Instead, he became a witness to his own death. Sure, he could still feel the pressure of the punches—especially the ones that pushed his body further into the very ground the Maze was built upon. But he didn't feel any new pain. The stabbing ache in his ribs and the burning behind his eyes started to fade away. *This must be what it's like just before death*, the Orphan thought.

"Leave it," the Junior Grief Bearer commanded. "Save him for tonight."

Minho sensed impatience from the soldiers standing around him, and maybe some of his own disappointment. One more punch might have freed him from life.

"Is this one even alive?" a nearby soldier questioned. "She hasn't moved."

"Doesn't matter! Fifty lashes to the traitor's corpse. Now!"

Why her? Not him?

Minho witnessed Orange's beatings just as he had been out-of-body for his own. Eyes closed, he counted two, three, five lashes . . . before the soldiers suddenly stopped.

A sudden silence descended on the Maze and its broken walls.

The unexpected haze of quiet made way for a sound that he had trouble placing. But it jolted something, floating far away in his memory. *Wind through the sails of the Maze Cutter. Seagulls on the open ocean. Freedom. The sound of faint laughter on the ship's deck as Dominic sang about nothing and Orange hummed along.*

Humming.

The sound of beautiful, peaceful humming grew louder and louder until all the pain in Minho's body returned at once, as if his senses had awakened.

Orange.

Her melody grew stronger until Minho realized she'd had a soldier's plan all along. Playing dead . . . until she could throw the Remnants off the walls inside their own minds. He wanted to smile, but could only manage a cough. Orange added words, now, sang a beautiful song with emotion and strength that would have earned her fifty more lashes from any Grief Bearer had there been one. But it only distracted these stupid Orphans and worthless soldiers, all of them frozen in confusion as if she'd come back from the dead, maybe possessed by some evil they didn't understand.

Minho only wished she'd carried out the distraction sooner. Maybe then he could have stabbed a soldier or two . . . but with his hands tied behind his back and his body near its last breath, there wasn't much he could do but listen to her sing. She'd given him one final gift.

It sounded beautiful.

The Orphan named Minho had been born with nothing, but he'd die with so much.

Pain pulsed through every part of his body as he waited for the soldiers to snap out of it and end what they'd started with Orange. And with him. But her voice still danced and echoed between the stone walls of the Maze. She found some reserve of strength to sing even louder. He wanted to lie still, enjoy every second of it, but a shadow had darkened the space, obvious even with closed eyes.

He blinked them open, struggled to see anything through the swelling and the blood. There wasn't much there. Just the new shadow, a person of average size, squatting directly in front of the fire, leaning toward Minho. Then the shadow spoke.

"It's Kit. Remember me? I'm going to get you out of here, Minho."

CHAPTER TWENTY-FOUR

Delirious Daze

I
ISAAC

Isaac's brain almost broke itself right then and there as he stepped out of the Berg. The air smelled like rotten meat from a rotten animal who'd lived a rotten life. Next to a lake of blood, it was all just perfectly rotten.

"What the hell?" He turned to Old Man Frypan. "Is there a war going on here, too?" More than anything, he couldn't believe the color of the water.

"Never saw anything like that before." Frypan climbed off the Berg's ramp and steadied his walking stick while looking at the blood-filled crater.

Erros explained like it was no big deal. "The Lake of Promise. It's the mark of the Sequencers. Some kind of weird mineral or whatever makes it red. Who the hell knows." *It looked like a mark of death*, Isaac thought as Erros handed him a box of supplies to carry. "Can you handle this?"

"Yeah." He wasn't sure if Erros was referring to the heaviness of the box or the lake filled with blood, but the weight of everything together was starting to add up. Kletter. The dead bodies on the *Maze Cutter*. Being kidnapped by Letti and Timon. Lacey, Carson, Alvarez. Finding out about the Remnant Nation. Finding out the truth about the Godhead. Cowan in a coma. The Griever hunting her or helping her. Ximena's Village. Hollowers and half-Cranks. The sacred site of the Maze in flames. *Trish*. Isaac's arms weakened at the thought of Sadina being alive without Trish or worse—*being dead with her.* He shuffled the weight of the supplies and took a deep breath. "It's heavy but I think I got it."

Such a criminally simple thing to say when all the things of his life filled his mind.

"Thanks. Here." Erros handed more supplies from the Villa to his brother. "Careful. You know how precious they'll be about these."

"Why don't you carry them, then?" Cian replied. The man was incessantly annoyed.

Ximena stepped off the Berg last and avoided eye contact with anyone. Isaac waited for her to chime in with some know-it-all thing about the lake or her second-sight feelings, but she was unusually quiet. Jackie and Miyoko couldn't take their eyes off the red liquid. "Is there blood in it? What's going on?"

"Oh the color? It's always like that." Cian shrugged. "My doofus brother said mineral, but it's actually algae. Sometimes it's more pink, sometimes more red."

Erros tried handing a box to Jackie but she was too distracted by the lake. "Relax, the algae doesn't bite." He held the box in front of her until she finally looked at him and took it.

Isaac at least knew a little about something for once. "We have algae on our island back home, but it turns the water green. Never red." He took a breath and turned to Jackie. "You good?"

She shook her head. He knew it was a dumb question.

"Where are we going?" Miyoko asked. Erros skipped handing her anything to carry and instead gave the next box to Ximena.

"The cliffs," Cian said confidently. Isaac and Jackie both looked at Old Man Frypan, and he shrugged.

"Then what?" Jackie asked.

"Wait for the Senate to greet us." Shockingly, he seemed annoyed by Jackie just like everything else. But there were still a lot of unanswered questions and hers had been a good one.

Isaac thought about Sadina's mom and the Senate back home. How they never agreed at all on how to handle Kletter and what she'd wanted. It was the first issue he'd witnessed that divided the Senate so much.

"Frypan," Isaac said as he shifted the box in his hands, "how come you never joined the Senate back home?"

"Yeah, you're the smartest person we know and everyone respects you," Jackie added.

Frypan smiled. "Aw shuck, I don't know about all that, now."

"It's true," Miyoko agreed with a smile. "And you obviously very well know it. But what are we doing right now? There's no one here." She scanned the secluded land around the crimson lake, rocky and flat all the way to the cliffs. "Didn't you say we were meeting someone?"

Cian looked at Isaac disappointedly, as if he were actually supposed to have filled her in on things, somewhere between finding Kletter's logbook and finding Trish's body.

"They're supposedly underground," Isaac mumbled to Miyoko. The whole thing still seemed totally absurd and fantastical to him. "They were part of the original plans of WICKED, or before WICKED, something. I don't really know how to explain it. Mainly because I don't know what the hell is going on, either."

"My family, well . . ." Frypan looked at Jackie, "people who *might* be my family, are around here somewhere. Supposedly, like Isaac said."

"They're here, don't worry." Erros continued to organize supplies and button up the Berg. "And if not, then not much matters anymore, anyway. Maybe one of us should stay and watch the equipment."

"Bullshit, you're just scared." Cian smacked his brother playfully before lifting the air container and shoving it into Erros' chest. "Come on, then." He began to lead the way around the lake, heading toward the tall cliffs of granite. "No one's going to find us here."

"That's what I'm worried about," someone muttered.

Isaac didn't catch who.

2
MINHO

Orange's singing stopped all at once, as if it had never even happened. There were no lingering echoes. Death had to be playing tricks on him. Guilt and regret must have also overwhelmed his moments of peace because he was pretty sure the shadowy figure in front of him had just said his name was Kit. But it couldn't be. Impossible.

"Kit?" Minho coughed out. "Am I dead?"

"Roll on to your side and I'll cut your combat ties."

Only soldiers called them that. Minho rolled over and coughed some more until his arms fell freely to his side. "Kit . . ." He lifted his head. "Orange?" His vision was blurry but it looked like only the fire remained. No soldiers—none standing, anyway. Piles of them scattered the ground, however. What on earth had happened?

"Oh, you're worse than I thought." Orange. It was Orange! Best death-faker in history. Her voice came through clearly until she turned around to speak to someone else. "Gather what we can. Quick."

"Orange . . ." Minho had so much he wanted to say, but he could barely say her name. He rubbed his shoulder and somehow got himself to his knees, pain ripping through his every inch. "Kit . . . ?" He shook his head and tried to wipe the gasoline and blood out of his eyes, but he couldn't lift his arm well enough. His shoulder had broken in at least one place, maybe two. "What . . . ?"

"Just relax," Orange said. "Turns out a lot more Orphans were on our side than the Grief Bearers. Didn't take much to finally turn them. So relax. We have some time till others come into the Maze to find us."

Minho heard the clicking and stacking of weapons as Orange shuffled around to pick off the dead soldiers. Seemed like *didn't take much* hadn't been the most accurate of descriptions. A major understatement, in fact.

He coughed for the millionth time, his lungs fighting for their next breath. "What happened?" All he remembered was feeling like he was back on the *Maze Cutter*, in the open ocean, with Orange singing him to sleep. And then silence. "Did I black out . . . what happened?"

"Traitors got tortured, that's what happened." Orange clacked rounds of bullets into a gun. "And this kid was about to be next on their torture buffet for whatever he did." She snapped and clicked another weapon. "What *did* you do, kid?"

"It's *Kit*, not kid," the boy said, lifting the straps of weapons on to his shoulders.

Minho coughed until he laughed. "Kit, you really remember me? I stopped your beating in Hell, you were . . . you were . . ." He struggled to find the words after so many boots to his brain.

"Almost as beaten up as you are right now," Kit said, nodding his head. "Of course I remember you. I'll never forget. Good to see you, brother. It's an honor to know your name, now."

Minho, overwhelmed with emotions, could only say three words. "Orange . . . Kit's alive." He tried to stand but fell back into the wall of the Maze. Orange helped him situate his legs and feet under himself.

"Relax, you're coming out of it," she said, but Minho wasn't going through what soldiers called the *delirious daze*, from being beaten to a pulp. He was alive because *Kit was alive.*

"Kit . . . from Hell," Minho sputtered. "I'm . . ."

Kit beamed with an inner pride. "Yeah . . . escaping Hell is what got me arrested and brought here. I found a tunnel, stabbed some Grief Bearer in the sewer, and would have made it out if I could have killed him and worn his cloak. But that damn cloak was made out of something thicker than hog's hide." Kit gently wiped Minho's face with a rag so he could see better. "Couldn't get my knife all the way through. Lucky for me, they loaded up for war and brought me along."

"I think you mean unlucky for you, lucky for us," Orange replied, tightening her boots.

Minho took slow, shallow breaths and held his side, applying pressure—maybe he could snap them back into place. "The Great Master's cloak is like that. Some sort of rubber . . . cloth . . ." He coughed. "It's . . ."

"Take it easy, we need a plan," Orange said. "Save your breath. I'm going to put these on you, okay?" She hung the strap of a gun around Minho's broken shoulder; even the weight of it felt like heavy joy. From this point on, if he died—he'd die like a soldier, fighting.

"Your stab wound eventually killed the Great Master, Kit." Minho couldn't tell if it was laughter that escaped his lungs or just more broken-up coughs. "That man . . . I found him with the cloak you're talking about, stabbed. He's dead, now."

"I killed the Great Master?" Kit's voice cracked.

Minho nodded as best he could. "You're the best soldier I know." His face was too swollen to smile, but inside, Minho felt more pride and joy and love than he'd experienced in a long time. "Kit . . ." He tried to say the next phrase as loudly as he could, hoping the young soldier heard it clearly.

"I'm proud of you."

CHAPTER TWENTY-FIVE

Flaring Justice

I
XIMENA

Ximena had read about cave systems in the same military stories of the past where she first learned about grenades. But as she followed Cian and Erros toward the naturally carved-out section of cliffs, her feet slowed beneath her. The size of its entrance looked so much bigger than her imagination had previously provided. A crooked, jagged, gaping mouth of darkness, taller than any building she'd ever seen.

Someone bumped into her from behind.

"Sorry," Isaac said. "You good?"

"Watch it." Ximena traced her fingers all along her backpack to make sure nothing had fallen out. "Important stuff in here, you know." She couldn't care less if the Villa's Cure leaked out—she was more worried about the weapons she'd grabbed from the pile in the back of the Berg when no was looking. She'd also stolen a light-flare, now in her back pocket. Cian and Erros might be dumb enough to go into another's Village without weapons, but she certainly wasn't.

"I guess this is it," Isaac said sarcastically. He looked up at the massive entrance of stone—or lack of stone—probably thinking of Frypan's stories about the Maze, built inside of a giant cavern. "Looks a little creepy."

"Do we have to go in there?" Miyoko asked. "Maybe Jackie and I should stay out here, guard the Berg."

Frypan wasn't having any of that. "We'd better stick together—only way I know we'll all be safe." He held out his arm to Miyoko and she joined him, step for step. They entered the darkness of the opening. Erros lit up another one of his weird herb packets.

We can't let the truth stay buried, Ximena's inner-knowing shouted at her.

"Whatever that is, it stinks," Jackie said to Erros.

For the second time, Ximena agreed with her. "Yeah, ¿Qué es eso?"

"Coltsfoot and lavender, for the lungs. It's a different type of air down there, I'm telling you." A breeze swept the smoke of his cigar away from the group, but despite the cool air, Erros had what looked like sweat gathering on his forehead. He wiped it away once he noticed Ximena looking at it. "The families you're about to meet have lived for generations as if they were the only survivors of the solar flares and the virus that came afterward. About twenty years ago, someone got the bright idea to tell them that wasn't the case." He stopped to set the air tank down and get a better grip. "It didn't go well."

"That's an understatement," Cian said, turning back to the others. "We've been on the cusp of a war within the Sequencers. Typical civil-war stuff. History, basically."

Isaac shuffled the box in his hands—the glass containers clinked against each other. "Why lie to begin with? Why not just tell them the truth from the start?"

"Yeah, what was the point?" Jackie asked.

The islanders were so naive.

Cian fixed his red scarf around his neck and gave Isaac and Jackie a look like they'd just asked the dumbest question possible to humankind. "What do you think would have happened if everyone who worked at WICKED knew there was some great safe haven and they weren't invited?" Isaac and the others went quiet. "No one wants to be on the outside. That's what gives any society its power." He traded his box of supplies from the Villa for the second air tank Erros had trouble carrying. "Here."

He shouldn't have been lighting that coltsfoot cigar so close to an air tank, anyway. Everything from the Villa was flammable. Ximena was counting on it.

"You remembered the Cure, right?" Cian pointed at her.

She tightened the strap of her backpack. He didn't have to point at her; she remembered all too well what she had promised back at the Alaskan Villa. "Impossible to forget." Her life, even from before her birth, revolved around the small vial she carried. She'd stolen it to spite Professor Morgan, but also hoping to use it for leverage, somehow, somewhere, before destroying it. She was still convinced it should be.

"I have a plan," Cian said to his brother with a smile.

"Plan for what? I thought bringing them the Cure *was* the plan?" Ximena hated it when adults lied to her. *Maybe she shouldn't give it to them, after all.*

"It's not that easy," Cian said as he walked farther into the cave, where the light from outside was dwindling fast.

"A Cure never is." Erros scooped Ximena's backpack off her shoulder before she could react. He put it on to his own, picked up his box, then continued following Cian.

"Well, that's how you made it sound!" Ximena's body went rigid, head to toe, and she stopped walking into the tunnel. Not one more step into the darkness until she heard more.

Frypan stuck his walking stick's point into the soft earth of the cave. "What aren't you telling us? What exactly are we walking into?"

Cian turned around and rolled his eyes at Ximena. "Look, I didn't want to make it seem impossible, but the Sequencers . . ." he looked at his brother, but Erros wasn't any more forthcoming with explanations. "They don't exactly like visitors."

Everyone had stopped walking, now. They were spread out beneath the overhang of the mountain above them.

Even Isaac, who had a death wish and almost caused the Berg to drop out of the sky, set his box of supplies down. "This is why you said you needed a plan?"

"All those weapons back in the Berg and you handed us these boxes filled with crap?" Jackie let her box fall to the ground and something inside broke into pieces.

"Watch it!" Cian motioned to the noise from the box. "Don't be stupid! Weapons would have gotten us nowhere. The Sequencers *need* these supplies. Now, let's get in there!" Cian and Erros trudged ahead, deeper into the ever-growing darkness of the cave, but the islanders didn't budge. Ximena pulled the flare from her back pocket and struck it against the wall of rock in front of her.

"You want the truth?" She held the sparkling stick of light out to her side, away from her clothes so they wouldn't catch fire. It was a symbol, a slight show of power, if nothing else. She'd shown initiative, taken something that wasn't hers. "We're not going to find it standing here in the dark."

She moved forward, walking ahead of the islanders, lighting the way.

"Come on. Like he said, let's get in there."

2
ALEXANDRA

Remnant soldiers aimed their guns and pushed her back to the others. How quickly they brought her back down to earth.

"Okay. Okay." She returned to Roxy, Dominic, and Sadina as more soldiers hovered over their group. If they hadn't been surrounded in such a tight circle with weapons pointed directly at her, Alexandra might have felt protected by such an army presence. Mikhail had always refused Evolutionary Guards, and she'd never understood why, until now. All this time, he'd had an entire army at his disposal. If only the Orphan soldiers knew how manipulated they'd been, that they'd been led by a half-Crank. The pain in the back of her skull pulsed electrically. The Flaring Discipline be damned, the Godhead would not be defeated.

"We have to do something," she said to the others.

"And what exactly would that be?" Sadina whispered.

"Minho said to stay quiet," Roxy spoke through her teeth.

Alexandra needed a plan. Some sort of distraction to escape and get help from her faithful Pilgrims. Once the Pilgrims recognized her, they would protect her at all costs. She *could* find a way out of this mess. An idea popped into her mind.

"The Godhead," she said aloud, but the soldiers around them didn't hear her. She cleared her throat and lifted her head to the trio of soldiers who surrounded her, then spoke louder, directly to them. "You have in your presence the one and only Godhead." Her heart beat in sync with the digits, 2, 3, 5, 8. She now had the soldier's attention, all of them. It was a word they'd heard from the day of their birth.

"Huh?"

"The Godhead. She's here among you." She watched as Sadina's eyes widened.

Dominic shook his head. "What are you doing . . . ?" he whispered.

Alexandra stood up, stood tall, and pointed a finger. "The Godhead is the one they call Roxy." The one true Goddess exhaled as she looked at Roxy, who'd frozen still, completely.

"I won't protect your lies, not anymore!" Alexandra slapped the woman across the face. "She's here. The Godhead! This one! Right here!" She stepped back as soldiers swarmed in to grab Roxy. "That's her and I can prove it. Kill her. Kill the Godhead!" She pointed again to leave no doubt.

The soldiers yanked Roxy up, began dragging her away. She said nothing, didn't fight back. But her eyes glared, fiery with betrayal.

"No!" Sadina pulled at Alexandra's cloak, pleading. "Why would you do that?"

Sadina. *Dear Sadina*. She would forgive her in time.

"Oh, child." Alexandra rested her palm against the girl's face. "One of us must die in order to save the rest. There is no grander gesture in all the world. And I wasn't going to let it be you."

Sadina went as still as Roxy, her eyes dropping to the ground.

Just as she'd wanted, confusion and chaos reigned as the news spread. People were running this way and that, in every direction, no one quite sure what was happening. Rumors created more rumors. Her lie grew and blossomed, then grew some more.

It had worked. Of course, it had worked. She was a Goddess.

Alexandra slipped away from her group. She ran for the cover of the strange forest, still growing within the Glade after all these decades and decades, like a blight.

3
ISAAC

The darkness had a smell which reminded Isaac of the waterfalls inside the caves of the cliffs back home. Earthy. Unforgiving. He limped behind Jackie, Miyoko, and Ximena, who still held a hissing, sparkling light, through the tunnel beneath the mountain. He ran his hand along the side of the dark rock wall that rose and arched high above him. The echo of Cian and Erros talking ahead of the group made Isaac want to pick his words more carefully.

"Frypan," he whispered. "Two lefts and a right . . ." There weren't any markings in the rock, and he needed to make sure they could find their way out of the cave system.

"Way ahead of you." Frypan knocked his walking stick against the wall then gestured at the dirt beneath them. He'd been dragging the point of his stick into the earth, leaving a deep groove to guide them out.

Or guide anyone else in.

Isaac shivered at the thought, not knowing if it was good or bad.

4
ALEXANDRA

Alexandra heard the betrayal behind her as she fled.

Sadina was shouting at the soldiers taking Roxy away. "No, she's wrong! She's not the Godhead! Please, don't take her!" Sadina then screamed, but that only enhanced the distraction Alexandra needed to escape. 1, 2, 3, 5, 8, 13 . . .

Her Pilgrim cloak slowed her down, but shedding it would only show them her true garments. The Goddess ran from the commotion as fast as she could, waiting for gunshots or screams from behind, but there were none. She ran a path between pockets of Pilgrims and Remnants, distinguished so well by the colors of their clothing and the way they stood. Her Pilgrims looked defeated, slumped over and beaten, and the Remnants stood on the heels of a power Mikhail didn't deserve. Had never deserved.

Alexandra's hood slipped as she ran; she quickly pulled it back over her head.

"Goddess!" A Pilgrim reached out and grabbed her, spinning her to a stop. Tattoos covered his face, tattoos of names. *Thomas. Newt. Alby. Chuck.* "You . . ." He stared at her with a fanatical, almost evil smile. *Zart. Minho. Winston.* The names of Gladers of Old, staring back at her along with the face of the crazed Pilgrim.

The Goddess fought to get free from the desperate grip. "No, you're mistaken." She pulled her hood tighter with her other hand as she wiggled to break away. "Let me go." She dug her nails into the Pilgrim's arm. "Let go of me!" she demanded.

But he didn't budge or loosen his hold on her. His eyes widened with lunacy. "You . . . you tried to have me executed in front of the whole city for your *own* deceit. You killed Nicholas. . . . It was you, not me! The Godhead killed their own!" the tattooed Pilgrim shouted to the others behind him. "The Godhead lives!"

Another Pilgrim ripped at her cloak. "It's you . . . ?" she whispered. "It's really you. Here in the Maze to save us!"

"She's here for flaring justice!"

"Goddess!" Pilgrims flocked around her.

"Flaring justice! Flaring justice!"

"Calm yourselves!" Alexandra commanded, but without her podium, without her guards, without her song and dance and all the trimmings, she was nothing. The Pilgrims were out of control.

"Let go of me!" she screamed, growing desperate with panic. She never should have made her people so dependent on her. Remnant Guards were closing in, now. She'd drown a slow death in the pitiful Pilgrims' desperation.

"They're crazy," she said to the soldiers, shaking her head. "Absolutely mad."

"The Godhead lives!" The tattooed Pilgrim held up Alexandra's hand and a soldier released his grip from the Goddess.

"Thank you," Alexandra said. "They're crazy. Mad. Absolutely mad."

"Come with me." The soldier pulled her by the hood of her cloak, nearly choking her. He was joined by others, at least a dozen.

"No. You have to believe me—they're crazy! They're all crazy!"

The soldiers dragged her to the center of the Glade. It was all falling apart. All of it! The Evolution, all of it! She screamed, a thing so loud that surely the very stone walls of the Maze shook from its power. Her heart was melting inside her chest.

The tattooed Pilgrim chanted behind her.

"Flaring justice, flaring justice, flaring justice . . ."

CHAPTER TWENTY-SIX

Hissing and Haunting

I
XIMENA

The air got colder and colder as they walked deeper through the tunnel system, into the depths of the mountain. Ximena's flare had long burned out, but tiny lights had started to appear in the ceiling of rock, illuminating the way. Before long, things smoothed and refined, became more manufactured. In a slow transition, they went from rough-hewn rock to finished interiors with tile, wallboard, even carpet. Eventually, they reached a round lobby with multiple paths that came and went from a single entry point. An empty desk sat in the middle, not so much as a chair to accompany it.

Tiny shadows bounced across Cian's face as he entered the lobby. "Here we are." He set the air tank at his feet.

Ximena had been holding her extinguished flare; she dropped it in the tunnel through which they'd come—just in case they needed to remember how to get back out.

"Which way do we go, now?" Miyoko asked.

"Now, we wait," Erros replied.

"Where do all these lead?" Isaac walked around and looked into each open arch that led out. Five in total.

The tunnels were taller than most houses in Ximena's Village, houses that took a dozen men to build. She wondered how many men or machines it had taken to build all these underground tunnels. Not to mention the world of the Sequencers, the world of the Mazes. It was almost too much to contemplate.

"Why are there so many?" Jackie asked.

Cian answered proudly, as if he'd built the damn place himself. "Different levels for different Sequencers. It's all very organized. Look, none of that matters. The Senate's next vote is in a few months, and if we can get one or two of the Senators to come back with us. . . . Well, then we can get the others to vote to rejoin society above. We need them, and they need us."

Erros didn't sound so confident. "They aren't going to want to leave their homes, the only world they've known for generations." He rooted through the box in his hands. "So don't tell them about anything negative. Cranks, half-Cranks, Hollowings . . ."

"The war with the Godhead," Miyoko added, "or the Remnant Nation. Basically anything that's actually true."

"Definitely don't say anything about any wars or Nations," Erros snapped at Miyoko, completely missing her sarcasm.

Ximena took the opportunity of a distracted Erros to grab her backpack away from him. He pulled on it as if it were his, acting like a child. "We need this!"

"I'll give you the Cure, but the rest is mine." She zipped open the pocket where she'd tucked away the Cure, then pulled it out. The all-important, world-changing, blue-tinted vial. She held it in front of Erros and waited for him to take it. It certainly didn't feel like anything special to her. . . . It felt more like Kletter's knife: a weapon and nothing else.

"*That's* the Cure?" Jackie asked.

"What did you expect?" Ximena waited for Erros to take the stupid thing, but he only stared at the vial. The part of her that had spent years of her childhood inside a glass pod so the Villa could perfect their Cure wanted to squeeze the vial as tightly as she could. Squeeze until the glass broke in her hand and the liquid spilled on to the ground. "Take it already . . ."

But Erros backed up from her with a look of fear that had come out of nowhere. He tilted his head toward one of the pathways.

"What?" She lowered the vial, then heard the sounds. A familiar clicking and whirring noise echoed down one of the darkened tunnels, though it was hard to tell from where, exactly.

"Here they come," Cian said. "Now, listen. Don't be scared."

Ximena's body grew heavy. It couldn't be what she thought it was. Not here, not now.

She stuffed the Cure into the backpack, put it on her shoulders, then grabbed Isaac's hand, pulling him in front of Old Man Frypan.

"Hey," she whispered. "It sounds just like . . ."

The clicking and whirring and other machine-like noises grew louder. She didn't want to say it. Didn't need to. She didn't want it to be true. But nothing had ever burned deeper into her memory than these sounds of—

". . . A Griever." Old Man Frypan said as something in the distance of the tunnels rolled and whirled.

Clicking and clacking.

Hissing and haunting.

2
ALEXANDRA

The last living member of the Godhead joined a disgruntled Roxy at the center of the Glade.

"Some God, you are." Roxy spat at Alexandra's feet.

They'd fastened her wrists behind her back before she even knew what had happened. Now, they kicked the back of her legs and she fell to her knees. 1, 2, 3, 5, 8 . . .

Roxy was next, thumping down next to Alexandra.

"Worthless," Roxy said under her breath, full of venom.

13, 21, 34, 55, 89, 144 . . .

"How are those ridiculous numbers working out for you?" Roxy muttered.

Idiot. The digits were of infinite creation. Alexandra chided herself—she'd been a fool to think these low-minded Immunes could ever understand quantum entanglement and the power of the Flaring Discipline.

"Public torture is what they deserve!" a Pilgrim shouted.

Alexandra's vision flashed red.

"Which one's the real Godhead?" a soldier behind them asked.

"Kill them both!" another Pilgrim screamed.

233, 377, 610 . . .

An older soldier stepped in front of them, then faced the crowd to make an announcement. "We have very specific orders. All possible members of the Godhead will be taken alive and sent to the Bearers of Grief. They will decide their fate." The soldier glared down at them, as if he saw only a pile of rotting garbage, infested with rats. But Alexandra didn't care, her mind focused on what she'd just heard.

Taken alive.

The Goddess still had time to escape.

CHAPTER TWENTY-SEVEN

Doomed

I
ISAAC

The Griever sounds echoed down one of the tunnels. It scared Isaac so badly that he'd lost all feeling or thought, felt totally incapable of taking even a single step.

A low hum vibrated through the air, making it feel like the whole inside of the lobby was shaking. Suddenly the air around him got much colder than it had been a few seconds ago. He tried to snap himself out of his immobility.

"Why would Grievers be here?" Isaac asked Frypan. He shifted his weight to his good leg, but he didn't have faith in himself to run very fast. "Frypan?"

The old man didn't respond, just stared into the darkness of the tunnel ahead, and that only made Isaac even more frightened. "We've got to get out of here," he said, looking at the others, each in turn. "We've got to run! They tricked us!"

"No! Don't move!" Cian held his arms out. "Don't move or you'll make it worse! I swear on my mother's life!"

Isaac turned to Ximena, Jackie, and Miyoko. "We need to go that way." He pointed to the tunnel they'd come through earlier, but the three of them and Frypan just stood there as the clicking and whirring and hissing grew louder. It was as if the sounds of the Griever had put them in a trance. "Guys! We've got to go. Now!" He limped over and grabbed Jackie by the shoulders, shook her. "Jackie!"

"Running won't do us any good," she said sadly.

Erros kicked the desk. "The Senate couldn't wait for us to get down there and explain? They had to send these things? They just had to?"

"We can't just sit here." Isaac's leg hurt too much to run, and he couldn't leave Frypan, but Jackie and Miyoko were close to the exit tunnel. "You guys go!" he yelled half-heartedly.

"Stop! Just don't move!" Erros shouted back at Isaac.

The Griever stepped into view from the farthest tunnel. Slimy skin, a giant slug with metal legs. A walking terror. It cleared the tunnel's opening, whirring with its mechanical noises.

Ximena hurriedly opened her backpack then turned to Isaac. "Here. Take this." She shoved a gun into his chest. He also had the axe from earlier, still looped through his belt, but Isaac wasn't sure any weapon would help against the Griever.

"Just stay still and it won't hurt you!" Cian shouted. But Isaac couldn't forget what had happened to Cowan. Or how the Griever had attacked the glass pod holding Old Man Frypan, stabbing it with some hideous metal arm sticking from its flesh. It was still too fresh in his memory.

Isaac felt like they had nothing to lose, now. He steadied his feet below him and aimed the gun at the body of the Griever, clicking and whirling its body, closer and closer. When the Griever crawled close enough for Isaac not to miss, he pulled the trigger.

The bullet ricocheted off the beast and Isaac shot again. Ximena started firing as well.

Bullets flew, the sound of the gunfire echoing in the lobby of tunnels, but the Griever kept moving, now looming over Isaac and Frypan. Ximena walked backward toward Jackie and Miyoko.

"Stop!" Cian ran over, struggled to pull the gun out of Isaac's hands and a rogue bullet fired, hitting a tank of compressed air. There was a loud pop; the tank turned into a missile that launched toward Frypan and hit his walking stick, breaking the thing clean in half.

"Just stay still!" Cian yelled over the squeal of air rushing from the tank, the metal scrape as it dragged its last bit of life across the tile floor.

The Griever creaked and whirled closer. W*hy hadn't Cian and Erros said anything about these things being under the earth?* Isaac didn't have many hopes left, but one had been to never see one of these monsters again. Frypan had a look of lost wonder as the Griever mechanically lifted itself even closer to them. Isaac held his hands out protectively in front of Ximena and Frypan, as if that would do a damned thing.

"Maybe if we move slowly toward the exit . . ." he whispered.

"It's got . . ." Frypan looked at the Griever without blinking, without moving, obviously traumatized by his past. "It's got a mind of its own . . ."

The Griever screeched a tremendous and hideous noise at Erros, who had flattened himself against the wall of the lobby. The monster's top, slug-like parts formed into a head, lurching out to smell Erros before moving on to Isaac.

Jackie screamed his name.

The mechanical beast seemed to suck up every cubic inch of air in front of Isaac; he held his breath. Somehow he already knew what would happen next—the Griever lifted its metallic arm, pulled back, then shot forward and stabbed him in the neck with a thin needle.

Isaac yelped, flinched, fell to the ground—more in shock than from the quick and sharp pain. The machine clicked in rapid succession before moving several feet away from him. The pain stung, getting worse, like a burn from hot metal in the forge back home. He struggled to stand up, but worried that if he collapsed or moved too much, the Griever might attack him again for good measure.

Dizziness swept through his body. He fell to his knees, completely unaware that he'd ever actually made it to his feet.

"Isaac . . ." Ximena pulled on his arm to help him up. "Isaac, come on. Please. You can do this. We've got to get out of here . . ."

"Glory to the Gladers of Old, forever and forever." The words fell from Old Man Frypan's lips like a prayer. Isaac's heart raced just as quickly as his spinning mind. Metal twisted and clanked from all around them, the whirring of machinery filled the air.

Five more Grievers walked out, one from each of the connecting tunnels.

Isaac blinked but he couldn't trust his eyes.

"Get up! We've got to go!" Ximena pulled him to his feet, then back toward Jackie and Miyoko. The five Grievers moved in some kind of horrific synchronicity, in a militant march toward the islanders.

Isaac knew they'd never outrun these things. Pure fear paralyzed him, swallowed his will to survive. The others seemed to have given up as well. Isaac could only stare as one Griever's arms and legs rolled and tumbled forward, stabbing Cian and Erros in their necks as it moved.

Then its hideous, bulbous, slimy head turned its attention on Frypan.

The Griever moved toward him. All of them did.

2
ALEXANDRA

"Yes, the Godhead sits among you, but so does the Great Master!" Alexandra was stretching now, thinking of anything and everything she could say to save her skin. "It's me."

"The Great Master?" Roxy muttered, but the soldiers behind her fell still.

They had probably never, not once, ever heard something so blasphemous to their ears.

Alexandra had them right where she wanted them. They would be under her power, soon—falling in line and taking orders within a matter of moments. She could make Mikhail's entire army her Evolutionary Guard. *Brilliance. The Evolution would always provide the way, the path, for her.*

"The Great Master has no face," an Orphan soldier spoke up, his face almost comically stern.

"And that is the very reason I never showed my face in the Golden Room of Grief." Alexandra paused, proud of the immense training she had poured into her voice. *But had she said it correctly? Golden Room of . . . something.* "Because your eyes betray your training. You look at me, now, and think that I can't possibly be the one ruling the Nation?" She glared at the soldier to his left. "What should I do with this denier?"

The soldier appeared wary as she looked Alexandra up and down. "The Great Master would never wear a Pilgrim's cloak."

"What better way to know the enemy than to blend in with them?" Alexandra stared deep into the young orphan's eyes. 21, 34, 55, 89 . . . "If you lift my cloak and check my wrists you'll see the Remnant symbol tattooed there. The exact symbol that's etched into the walls of the Remnant Nation and the Golden Room." She waited while the soldier hesitated. She finally loosed the tie on Alexandra's wrist and pulled her sleeve up.

"There's nothing there." The orphan flushed, worried that *she* had screwed up somehow. It was working, indeed.

"The other one."

The soldier looked at that wrist. Alexandra waited impatiently for her to say something but there was no reaction. None. *Had Minho lied to her about the Godhead's symbol being on the walls of his buildings?* "You see now?" she asked. No response. *Mindless soldiers.* Her patience thinned to nothing. "If you untie my hands, I'll show you properly."

A cloaked Grief Bearer entered the Glade from the corridors of the Maze, itself—where they'd taken any Orphan traitors—with a soldier on either side of them. Someone must have told him what was going on. Alexandra's heart sank a little.

"The Great Master does have that tattoo." The cloaked man spoke slowly and chopped almost all his words in half. "But so does the

Godhead." The Grief Bearer slowly raised his right arm and pointed straight at Alexandra. "She wears the cloak of a Pilgrim, but there stands the one and only remaining member of the Godhead." A very long pause, then a silence settling over the Glade that would've seemed impossible a minute earlier. "And she killed the Great Master."

Panic now bounced within Alexandra's body, throttling her spirit. *The digits escaped her.* The hood of her cloak tightened against her throat as the soldier behind her pulled her head back. A cold knife rested just above her collar bone. Her skull pounded at the top of her spine. The Evolution was doomed. *How*, she thought with terror. *How had it all fallen apart?*

"No. NO!" She had no time to think. "It's true, I killed Mikhail, but . . . but doesn't that make *me* your master now? Isn't that how it works? Who better to lead you than the one who's defeated the greatest?" Someone pushed her down; she landed with a thump, temporarily lost her breath. She struggled against the ground—the ground of this hallowed Glade. "And Nicholas, his head is here, here in the Maze!" She could show them. She could convince them all. *She could—*

The Grief Bearer spoke one last time. "The Great Master has no face and no name." He turned away, as if condemning her by the action, and then it seemed as if everyone in the Glade shouted at once.

"It's time for her to die!"

"Kill the Godhead!"

"Kill the Godhead!"

"Kill the Godhead!" The chant grew from there, grew until even the most faithful of Pilgrims watching nearby began to mouth the words, themselves. *Kill the Godhead.*

All had been lost. Alexandra struggled pitifully against her restraints, writhed in the dirt. The movement made her hood fall from her head, and Pilgrims and Remnants alike stared at her beauty.

"It's really her . . . Alexandra Romanov!" a Pilgrim screamed with bloodlust in her eyes.

"She admitted to killing Mikhail and Nicholas. Traitor!" More chaotic shouts and screams, words, countless words, filling the air like toxic fumes. But eventually they bled together, came fully in sync. And the chant rose like a prayer to the stone heaven above.

Kill the Godhead. Kill the Godhead. Kill the Godhead.

3
XIMENA

Groggy and confused on the floor of the cave, Ximena rubbed her neck where the Griever had stabbed her. She checked for blood. None. Her mind raced even while her entire body relaxed. The half-animal, half-machine hovered over her with its arms and legs planted around her. A cage she couldn't escape. She could *think* about moving away from the mechanical beast, but her body wouldn't move. The Griever tilted its bulbous, head-like thing as if to question Ximena, then scuttled away to rejoin the other monsters.

The islanders were just as stunned as she was.

She breathed deeply, forced her body to catch up with her mind. "What did those things do to us?"

"The Grievers . . ." Old Man Frypan rubbed his hip and sat up. "Alby . . . Zart. . . . What they did in the Villa with Cowan. The Grievers in the Maze always had some other plan, like a mind of their own. Some hidden purpose."

"Yeah. Exactly." Erros rubbed his arm—where the Griever had stabbed *him*—but didn't say any more.

"What was in the sting?" Isaac yelled, grabbing his leg, where apparently the knife wound still hurt him more than the needle had.

"A basic anxiolytic," Cian pronounced, as if every human walking the earth learned the word while still in cloth diapers. He climbed back to his feet, seemingly unafraid of the machines still hovering in the far corner of the lobby. "It's merely a calming agent." He picked up his box of supplies, while Ximena could barely hold her own head up.

"More like a tranquilizer," Erros said.

"Why . . ." was all Ximena could ask.

An unknown voice answered her.

"The Sequencers don't let anyone into their levels without testing them first." A tall man with dark hair, dressed in blue, walked out of the farthest tunnel. The Grievers clustered together, then assembled one-by-one into a line. "And treating them."

"Senator Tove." Cian lowered his head.

"Cian. Erros. So glad you two could find your way home, but you know the rules . . ." The man held an instrumental pad in front of him, just like the one Professor Morgan had at the Villa.

"These aren't other-worlders, sir. They're part of the Sequence." Cian rushed the box of supplies to the Senator and motioned to the islanders, but Tove held his hand up.

"Stop. Don't embarrass yourself. Wait until the processing is done." The blue-suited man wouldn't even look at Cian, as if the man and his brother were beneath him.

Erros walked over to Ximena, his eyes expectant. She didn't know what he wanted until he lifted her hand into his. Her thoughts were so dazed she'd forgotten she still had the Cure. She found her backpack, unzipped it, reached inside, hoping she hadn't crushed the vial while trying to escape the Grievers. The machines clicked and whirred to themselves as they bunched more tightly against the far wall of the carved-out tunnels.

"Where is it?" Erros whispered impatiently.

Ximena pulled her hand from the backpack, relieved to have a vial that wasn't broken.

"Here," she muttered to Erros. She'd kinda grown attached to the thing.

"What are you testing us for?" Jackie asked, rubbing her head.

"That thing stabbed me twice but guess I can't complain." Miyoko leaned against the wall, looking very calm. "I had a killer headache from all the crying but it's gone. Completely gone."

Frypan stood tall without his walking stick; he tapped his hip. "I could've used a shot like that years ago. What is it?"

The Senator spoke like a senator, all fancy and high-minded. "It's likely you all received different doses of different sequences. If you were dispersed an agent, then it was the one you needed. Diagnostics don't lie." The man peered down at his tablet as if it held all the answers to all the secrets in the world. Ximena didn't like him.

"Cowan . . . at the Villa." Isaac looked at Ximena like she might know something, but Cowan had looked closer to death when they left the Villa than when she'd arrived. Nothing like the islanders looked, now. Taller, happier, healthy.

Ximena shrugged. "I just feel confused and groggy. Doesn't seem all that great to me.

"Oh." Erros laughed quietly into his shoulder. "Anger is an emotional toxin that the Sequencers treat with all sorts of different stuff. I guess they read you right."

"A toxin?" Ximena moved to her hands and knees and then got to her feet.

"Stress. Anger. It's all frequency. They gave you a relaxant. You'll balance out to a happy medium, but you'll probably feel pretty tired in the meantime." As conspicuously as possible, he handed the Cure vial to his brother, almost bowing afterward like a buffoon.

"Senator Tove, we did it!" Cian said it loud enough to echo through the adjoining tunnels. He held the vial up high.

"Did what?" The man tapped his tablet in frustration. "These are inconclusive for transient markers. All of them but one?" He lifted his head and looked at Cian in anger. "They'll need to test again." With a push of the tablet the Grievers all came back to life, churning with noise and movement. A strong thrumming vibrated the ground beneath them.

Ximena groaned.

"No!" Cian lost his mind. He ran at the Senator and pulled the tablet from the man's hands; he tossed it across the lobby where it landed with a loud crack. "Look, they're missing transient markers because they're not part of the otherworld. They're Immunes. From the original Sequence! Can't you listen to a damned word we say?"

The Senator was nonplussed, as if this very scenario happened to him every day. "That can't be," was all he said in response, showing no anger whatsoever.

"It's true." Frypan stepped forward. "I was one of the original Gladers. Test me all you want to know I ain't lying."

"They've come to meet the Senate," Cian said.

The man in blue stood there, unmoving, without emotion, without blinking.

"Please," Erros begged. "Let them be interviewed by the Levels and the Senate before your next vote. The Sequencers deserve to know the truth. All of it."

Ximena stood in the silence, waiting for some verdict she didn't even understand. She stared at the line of Grievers and the man in blue, who apparently could change the fate of the Sequencers, maybe the world, with a single wave of his hand.

After what seemed like an hour, he finally spoke. "The third level, then, but *only* to meet the Senate. Then you must vacate immediately."

Cian whooped with joy, then picked up his brother, swinging him in a circle while they hugged.

Ximena stared at them, baffled beyond measure. *What weirdos*. But she had to admit, she was starting to feel pretty good inside. What *had* that Griever stung her with?

CHAPTER TWENTY-EIGHT

Deadheads Redux

I
MINHO

Orange stood in a soldier's stance on Minho's right, and on his left, Kit held two guns, each one pointed at a soldier behind Roxy. Adrenaline had rushed through Minho's body, just enough to walk to the center of the Glade. His wounds and face were covered by the Junior Grief Bearer's cloak. The Remnants would never tell the difference. All he could taste and smell was the gasoline deep in his throat. But with Orange on one side of him and Kit on the other, he could die happy, now.

The chanting had slowed, then stopped. Silence returned. Despite all that talk about killing the Godhead, no one had rushed forward to actually do it. Minho spoke into the quiet, cool air.

"You once called me a traitor, for leaving after my cliff ceremony. But I returned. And when I did, I brought to you what even the Grief Bearers above couldn't see. The one true Godhead, the one ultimate thing we've been taught to destroy. Well, there she is. You can call me whatever you want, but I'm still one of you." He lowered the hood of his cloak with his right hand; his left arm hugged the gun under his cloak. Just in case.

An Orphan soldier—the one with ears too big for his face—held Alexandra by her long, luxurious hair. Or what had been. Now it was filthy and tangled.

Minho pointed at her. "She's the Godhead. All that's left of it, anyway. You have the honor to kill her if you'd like." He knew every soldier there would have fought to be the one chosen to kill the Godhead. But if he could get Ears to do it, the one who'd led the charge against Minho and Orange as traitors, then he could get the rest of them to see the truth, too. But no one moved.

Minho sighed, as loudly as he could manage. "We've waited our whole lives to kill the Godhead, and now you want to wait? Sit here and wait for the Grief Bearers to tell you what to do?" He held in his immense urge to cough and pushed his lungs to speak louder. "You're good soldiers. Sharp. Disciplined. Smart." He looked as many in the face as possible, his vision still a bit blurry. "You've lost the ability to think for yourselves. You've killed thousands in the search for the Godhead, but now that she's right in front of you . . . nothing. You can't do it. Why?"

"He's right . . ." a soldier nearby murmured.

Orange threw the last spark into the kindling. "We've fought for this moment. Kill the Godhead and we'd be free. Well, here we are." Her voice boomed, echoed throughout the Glade. "Kill the Godhead!" She raised her weapon high above her head in a war cry. "Kill the Godhead!"

Others joined in. The chant returned. Confidence returned to the faces of the soldiers. Minho knew that this time around, they'd actually do it. They'd actually end Alexandra once and for all.

"Kill the Godhead!" All the soldiers chanted it as loudly as they could.

Minho simply nodded, setting the precedence of his command.

The soldiers swarmed like ants.

2
ALEXANDRA

The Goddess Romanov couldn't move as the blade—the first of many—slowly sank into her skin, cutting layer by layer. But she moved her eyes toward Roxy, who looked away. If Alexandra's arms hadn't been tied behind her, she might have reached for Sadina in the distance. Might have called her name. Might have said so many things that needed to be said.

Her vision buzzed into a static red, and then a bright flash of crimson light. A color so bright it looked like a sun flare, exploding in the sky, blinding her. Another knife stabbed her, the blade in her throat, piercing deep. All her muscles fell loose.

She pondered the Evolution amongst the pain and the light. The Flare virus, mutated and expanded within her mind, had almost changed the universe forever. Almost. Almost. She pondered an infinity of thought and knowledge; she pondered it all. And when it vanished, when her mind emptied, there was only peace.

The sacred site of the Maze, such a fitting place for a Goddess to die.

She had only one regret: dying in a lowly Pilgrim's cloak. On some level, beyond the light and the darkness that waited, the pettiness of the regret brought her a final and wondrous joy.

She became weightless, a strange view of the Glade suddenly filling her vision, as if seen through a thick glass. The center of the Glade spun around her, the Maze in the background, all of it spinning and spinning and spinning. The world was a blur, a haunted smear of color.

She blinked three times, then entered the Infinite Glade of Death.

3
MINHO

Soldiers were bred to fulfill orders, and the war against the Godhead had been won.

But the war to take control of the Remnant Nation had just begun.

Minho had once heard a rumor that decapitated heads could still hear, think, and feel for up to twenty seconds after being cut from their body. The odds were slim, yeah. But everyone knew about the proverbial chicken with its head cut off. Just in case, Minho placed his boot right in front of the Goddess' head, just in case Alexandra's brain still had firing neurons and synapses. He shouted to the surrounding soldiers, building his case for leadership with every single action and word. "May the Godhead's death be long, and her name never mentioned again, for the Evolution . . . is ours now!"

He swore he saw one of Alexandra's eyes blink before a Remnant lifted her decapitated head high in victory. He swung it around for all to see. Cheers erupted from both Remnants and Pilgrims, alike.

"We did it, Minho," Orange whispered to him, placing her hand on his shoulder gently.

"*You* did it, Orange." He owed her his life. "You definitely did it." He took in the celebration going on all around him.

"I thought you were dead!" Roxy cried from below, still kneeling next to the bottom half of Alexandra's body.

"Me too . . ." he replied, wishing so badly that she hadn't experienced the Remnants' heinous acts of war. Embarrassment for who he really was rushed to his face, but Roxy looked at Minho and gave him a loving smile.

"My boy, come here so I can hug you."

For the first time in his life, Minho wanted to cry. She had watched him instigate a brutal murder, right in front of her eyes. She'd seen him bloodied and uglied by war, doing the evil means to reach an end he could just barely conceive—a new Nation of Remnants, under his control. All of this, and she still cared for him as much as ever. He cut her combat ties and gave her the longest hug of his life. An overwhelming sense of warmth rushed through his body, along with an overwhelming amount of pain.

He saw Kit nearby and hailed him to come over.

"Roxy . . . this is Kit, the strongest, bravest soldier in the whole Nation. My little brother, Kit."

"Oh!" Roxy pulled Kit into another long hug. She looked at Minho like he'd just given her the gift of life. He'd taken more lives than he could count as a soldier, but introducing Kit to Roxy felt like he'd given them both something that no one could ever take away from either of them. Another son for a mother; a mother for another orphan.

Kit smiled shyly, but had no words.

"Roxy makes the best stew, Kit," Orange said, adjusting her gun strap to a relaxed position. "She's a real good mom to all of us."

Dominic pushed through the crowd of Remnants to get to Minho.

"What the hell?" the boy asked, and Minho understood it to be one of those questions that wasn't meant to have any real answer. He probably looked like a monster in more ways than one to Dominic.

"I'm sorry," Minho said, not completely sure why.

"I'm just glad you're okay." Dom hugged him without warning, and Minho was too proud to tell him how much it hurt.

Orange slapped the boy's shoulder. "Careful, Dom. He's got some broken bones." She looked around the Glade. "We've got to get you to a combat medic . . . but I don't see one . . ." Any medic on this war mission was likely gathered close to the Bearers of Grief, the weakest people of the Nation.

"They're probably back with Griever Ayes." Minho winced at the thought of facing them again.

Orange's face grew fierce. "We'll take you. We'll all take you there and kill every last one of the Grief Bearers if we have to." She hoisted Minho up straight.

"Hold on, there's something I need to do first." Minho coughed as he bent over to lift Alexandra's blood-soaked Pilgrim's cloak. He shook the cloak out until the *Book of Newt* fell from within its folds. He grabbed it carefully, sure not to get any of his own blood on it.

"Where's Sadina?" he asked Dominic. His ribs screamed and burned with every twist and turn of his body.

"Here I am . . ." a soft voice whispered from behind.

Minho turned around to see a terrified Sadina. "I'm sorry about the Godhead. I'm sorry for everything you had to see. I really think she brainwashed . . . she did it to all of us." He wanted to apologize for so much more. He handed her the book along with his sympathy.

Sadina took the *Book of Newt* and folded her arms around it. "Thank you." She looked at Kit and Roxy, Dominic and Orange. "I'm sorry, too. I really let her suck me in. From what I overheard the Pilgrims say, she was a horrible person." She tilted her head at Minho. "I know that you were just trying to protect me. All this time. Thank you." She cried as she gave Minho a gentle hug.

"Can we get you to a combat med now?" Orange asked over the many sounds of Pilgrims and Remnants mixing in the Glade.

"No. Not yet." This was far too great of an opportunity to plant more seeds. A Revolution of Evolution had begun, and he couldn't leave without telling the Nation what awaited them.

"Soldiers . . ." His voice faltered. It seemed like he'd already exhausted his last bits of energy.

"Hey, listen up!" Dominic shouted to get the people's attention.

Minho lifted his gun in the air with Dom's help, fired a single shot. The Glade quieted to complete silence. "Soldiers! The Remnant Nation was built to destroy this city . . . and now that their mission is complete, what do you think they'll do with you afterward? They'll destroy you, too. Just like they always have." He cleared his throat, willed his lungs to draw strength as soldiers around him murmured. "They entertain themselves with destruction. If you want to continue to fight, then fight the real enemy—the Grief Bearers above who've placed you in the living prison you've always been trapped in."

Most soldiers raised their weapons in agreement, but a few others looked unsure of what they were hearing.

He continued. "There's freedom out there. There's a whole world of people, places, and sounds you've never even been allowed to make or hear . . . like laughter and singing. There's feelings that you've never felt and sensations you've never touched—like the sand under your bare feet on the coast of the ocean and the water cooling your legs. I'll take you, I'll show you. And I promise you it's better than all your rules and regulations, or any level named Hell you leave behind." He watched as the tide of support turned ever more in his favor.

"What about the City of Gods?" one doubting Remnant asked.

"It's ours, now! Why would we leave!" another shouted. Orange shifted to a soldier's stance. But the naysayers were already the minority, by a long shot.

"Let these Pilgrims keep their history." Minho looked around. The Maze and the Glade deserved to stay sacred to those people. They'd been through enough. "We can, and we will, create our own story. One of courage and creation instead of constant, incessant destruction!" His lungs burned and his chest felt splintered into pieces. He wasn't sure what else to say to convince these fellow soldiers to change their fate. To be something more than orphans who owned nothing. It was up to them, now.

Orange raised her gun, but this time, in place of *Kill the Godhead*, she shouted, "Free the Remnants!" And just like that, all at once, the Orphans from all corners of the Glade had their new mission. They raised their guns and chanted along with her in unison. *Free the Remnants. Free the Remnants. Free the Remnants.*

Dominic joined in. Roxy and Kit cheered. Sadina raised the *Book of Newt* like a beacon.

Minho's entire family chanted as one.

"Free the Remnants!"

Everything was coming together. So well, in fact, that he thought maybe they had time to take a little ride in that Berg he'd found.

Some unfinished business . . .

CHAPTER TWENTY-NINE

Subject A3

2
ISAAC

They walked down one of the long corridor tunnels adjoined to the others, lugging the supplies for the Sequencers in silence until finally Frypan broke it. "I'm telling you, those Grievers have a mind of their own, just like in the Glade . . ." Isaac watched as Frypan's eyes looked like they went to another place, far away. "They killed so many . . ."

They kept following Cian down the dimly lit cave that smelled like ocean spray against wet rocks. He spoke to them over his shoulder.

"The first Grievers weren't calibrated—they truly did have minds of their own. The early Sequencers dealt with many deaths from them, too."

"No one hates them more than me." Erros turned to Isaac, who doubted anyone could hate Grievers more than Old Man Frypan. Glader of Old.

"This is bonkers," Miyoko said, shaking her head. "No one will believe us."

But Cian's optimism had not waned in the least. "Yeah. Imagine how hard it's been for *us* to convince the Sequencers. There's so much disbelief that accompanies the truth. Having you here to tell the Senate about the outside world will do more than any Cure ever could. We can't thank you enough." He held the box in front of him as if it were a prayer.

"And if they don't believe a single thing we say?" Jackie asked.

"What if they take us someplace we can't . . ." Isaac whispered to Ximena.

"Get out?" she finished.

He nodded. He'd already lost track of how many turns they'd made and Frypan didn't have his stick to drag in the dirt. Not to mention he seemed lost in his own world, right now.

"We won't stay long, trust me." Erros took the heavy box of supplies from Isaac's grasp. "Just remember, don't say anything negative about the outside world."

"No wars, no Cranks, no death," Jackie said, the sarcasm thick. "Nothing bad ever happens. Got it."

"They're not going to take Frypan for tests or anything, are they?" Ximena asked.

Cian and Erros exchanged a look. Erros let out a slight, crooked smile. "Tests?" He shook his head. "No . . . but his *patience* might be tested. He's the first Subject A to ever come home."

Home wasn't a word Isaac expected Cian to use. "What do you mean?"

"Subject A3." Cian pointed at his own neck. "You know, Frypan's tattoo. Group A. He was a part of the very first Sequence. . . . This guy's as good as royalty here." He walked them farther into the tunnel, and now there was much more light, its source not clear.

Old Man Frypan shuffled his feet forward—in the absence of his walking stick, he'd put his arm around Jackie. Isaac didn't expect to see such bright light in a cave far underground, but they were soon walking under a filtered sunlight that held all the colors of the rainbow.

The City of the Sequencers was very close, now.

2
XIMENA

La belleza perece en la vida, pero es inmortal en el arte.

Beauty perishes in life, but is immortal in art.

Ximena couldn't keep her eyes fully open. Between the beauty before her and the relaxant injected by the Griever, it all felt like a dream. Like she might be back home, under one of Abuela's blankets.

"It's so bright . . ." Jackie covered her eyes.

When Cian and Erros had first mentioned the Sequencers living under-earth, Ximena had imagined people living in a cave system would have to be blind, like burrow animals in her Village. Those born in darkness had no need to see . . . but it was clear to her in that moment that the Sequencers were so much more. She squinted her eyes after walking so long through the cold and dark tunnels. All of them used their hands to shadow their faces as they gawked at the city of Sequencers.

"What are these materials?" Jackie asked. Unique arches and ornate molding with statues of lions and countless other things adorned the corners.

"Earth minerals," Cian answered without elaborating.

"Minerals?" Isaac looked at Frypan as Cian led the group through gold-lined walls, then out to a terrace that overlooked a city filled with more vegetation than stone, from which most of the beautiful buildings had been carved. A false sun shone down from the roof of the cavern—far, far above them. People milled about here and there in the vast city of low structures and parks.

"Wow . . ." Ximena couldn't find any other words. "This is . . ." She turned to Isaac and Frypan, but they just stood there, frozen in wonder.

"It's unbelievable," Isaac finally replied.

Ximena leaned over the decorative molding along the arched terrace and slowly felt more like herself. "This is . . . at least a century old?" she asked.

Cian beamed with pride, again acting like he'd actually had something to do with all this. "It's something special, isn't it?"

But it was more than special. *It felt unreal.*

Ximena couldn't help but think as she watched Frypan process the buildings and plants below them that everything he saw was a life he *could* have lived. If only his parents, WICKED—or whoever—hadn't decided to trade his childhood and future to the Trials, to the effects of the Flare.

"No wonder they don't want to leave," Jackie mumbled. "It's so beautiful."

"I just got here and I don't even want to leave," Miyoko said.

Cian led the group farther on to a terrace balcony overlooking the city. "The Senator allowed us on this floor only, to observe. We're not supposed to interact with anyone but the Senate, and the Senators will have questions in the Hall of Congress. Just remember—"

"We know, we know, nothing negative," Jackie said. "How many times do you have to remind us?"

"It's not just about scaring them," Cian said as he turned to Jackie. "Each Senator has their own agenda that they'll try to push, and they'll turn anything negative to their benefit. Try to focus on sharing the *good* truth."

The truth will remain buried.

Don't let the truth stay buried.

After seeing the beauty of this place, she no longer saw Cian and Erros as complete whackos. A part of her even wanted to follow Cian's rules. But she couldn't stop the overwhelming resistance she felt within her to speak up.

"You say you don't want us to tell them anything negative—but the truth is . . . a lot of bad things have happened and are still happening."

She looked at the others before looking back at Cian. "How can you say you want the truth to come out but keep trying to *hide* the real truth from the Sequencers? Those are polar opposites!"

"Yeah," Jackie agreed. "Make it make sense."

"She's got you there, brother." Erros shrugged.

Cian's shoulders slumped. "I don't want you to lie . . . I just think if they saw the truth themselves, then they'd see it's not as scary as it might sound." He stepped back from the terrace. "Just like this place . . . if I would have told you anything more you would have either not believed me or been scared in some way, right?"

"Maybe." Jackie looked around. "But maybe not. Let them decide."

Ximena nodded in agreement with her.

"These two are right," Old Man Frypan said, finally snapping out of his self-reflection of a hard life, long-lived. "We ought to tell the truth and let them decide. Otherwise, they'll feel like they were lied to."

Cian rubbed his forehead. "I'll think about it."

"Hey, what was that all about back there?" Isaac motioned to Erros, "When he said *welcome home*? You didn't tell us you were a part of this whole group."

"Because this hasn't been our home for years." Erros glanced below, at teenagers tossing some kind of ball around. "Once we left, we couldn't find our way back." He had a longing look in his eyes. "It's been almost twenty years. So much has changed."

"And some things have stayed the same." Cian pointed to some younger children playing hopscotch with numbers 3, 5, 8, 13, 21, 34, 55. "I bet I can still beat you in Sequence Scotch," he teased his brother before walking farther down the long terrace. The others followed. "When news first came of the above, only a handful of us were brave enough—"

"Or stupid enough," Erros interjected.

"—to leave," Cian finished. "And the Senate forbade anyone who left from coming back. They thought we'd bring the diseases back that they'd worked so hard to keep out for the last hundred years."

"But you brought them a Cure . . ." Ximena could see the sadness in Cian's face.

"So you need the Cure, too?" Miyoko asked.

Cian shook his head and leaned against the molding. "I don't think anyone really *needs* the Cure, but it will help some people's confidence on reentry into the above. They need to know that there's people in the other-world that care about them, people who deserve the truth about everything that happened in history." He straightened and continued walking to a large golden door at the end of the terrace. "Erros and I spent our first few years in the above sick as hell. It wasn't great, but we eventually adjusted. The Cure will help for a smoother transition, hopefully." He looked at Erros. "Well, his lungs are still shit when he gets stressed."

He led them all to the large, ornate, golden door. Jackie reached out her fingers and touched it; Ximena couldn't help but smack the islander's hand away.

"What? I wanted to feel it," Jackie said.

"They're worried we have germs and you're touching things," Ximena whispered.

"It's alright, you can touch it." Cian pulled on a round door knocker. Ximena wanted to feel it, too, but hesitated. "Really, it's okay. It's made of Ionic Gold, has antimicrobial properties. Go ahead, touch it."

Jackie touched the door again, along with Miyoko and Isaac. The islanders didn't waste a second smudging the door up with fingerprints, but Ximena joined in more slowly, felt the smoothness of the mineral. It was colder than she expected. The door opened with a rush of air. Ximena jumped back and Jackie let out a noise of surprise.

The man in the blue suit greeted them.

"Cian. Erros." Senator Tove held the door open and nodded at each of them. "I've gathered the other heads of Levels and the Senate. We'd like to take your testimonies. Please, come in and have a seat." He held his arm out to the room behind him—bigger than any room at any Villa. Benches, carved from beautiful black stone, lined the room in a semi-circle, with a table of heavy white stone facing them. The shelves along the walls held more books than Ximena knew existed in the world. There were a dozen or so people seated here and there along the benches.

"Wow . . . hi." Isaac walked into the room looking up and down, all around, taking it all in.

"This place is amazing," Miyoko said, pulling Jackie along to show her some of the intricacies.

Ximena couldn't even pretend she wasn't blown away. She tried to remember every little detail of what she saw, to tell Abuela about it when she returned.

Tove addressed them. "I've shared the diagnostics with the full Senate, and I've also let them know we have a Glader in our presence." The Senator bowed toward Old Man Frypan. The others in the room did a strange hand movement—one palm twisting on top of the other—and bowed as well. "We're honored to host you in this chamber of congress."

"Thank you," Frypan said, his eyes a little teary.

Cian motioned for everyone to sit down on a long bench, more decorative than comfortable. "Here. Before we start. Erros?" His brother set the Cure vial on the center of the table. "And yes, it's exactly what you think it is."

The Senate grew quiet.

Cian continued. "Advanced immunity for the world above. Our visitors have agreed to share testimonies with the Senate for as long as you'd like, but we have just one request in return for these gracious gifts."

The Senators shuffled and mumbled at each other. Senator Tove asked on behalf of them, "And what is that request?"

"Whatever it is, we'd have to vote on it," one woman grumbled.

Erros looked at his brother before speaking. Cian nodded. "We request two or more families to rejoin us on the surface, to experience the other-world and learn the truths firsthand. They can collect information for the Sequencers' next generation."

A bald Senator crossed his hands in front of his chest. "No. We can't banish anyone just to collect documents."

"How else will the truth of history be recorded?" Erros slapped his palms against the table. "The real truth!" He pulled his hands back at the collective gasp of the Senate. "You call it banishment, but some of those kids out there in the middle levels"—he pointed at the golden door that was now closed for privacy—"They might call it freedom!"

"No," the bald one said. "We don't even need to vote—the answer is no."

A Senator, with her long brown hair in a braid, spoke up. "A resounding *NO* to sending our children out there."

"Denied," another said.

"Then *you* go!" Cian shouted at the group of leaders. His face turned just a few shades less red than his scarf. "You *all* need to experience the surface before your next vote. Otherwise, you have no right to deny others the life that you know nothing about! See for yourselves and let *them* choose!" He couldn't stop his rant. "You can't choose the future out of fear! That's what destroyed the . . . the . . ." The man got emotional. "Fear and lies destroyed everything."

"We'll discuss." Senator Tove held up his hand.

"I think if we asked the people," Erros said as he stepped up to the table again, but this time much more calmly, "they'd want to have the option to explore themselves and—"

"I said we'd discuss." Senator Tove tapped a small bell-looking thing, but the sound of the chime vibrated much louder than Ximena expected. It was as if the chime cleared all tension out of the room. "Now, are there any other questions for the Senate before we begin transcribing?"

Erros looked at Cian. Cian nodded and turned to Old Man Frypan. "Yes, Senator. We ask that Frypan be granted viewable access to the library of all participants and all lineages of the Subjects from Group A." He clasped his red scarf between his hands. "It's the least we can do for his sacrifice all those decades ago."

"The least we can do." Erros echoed his brother.

One by one, the heads of Levels and the Senators looked away from Cian and the rest of the group, and then down at their own hands. Although none of these people had been alive when Frypan was taken for the Trials, separated from his family, even Ximena knew it was time to right a long-forgotten wrong.

Senator Tove finally nodded. Another Senator jumped to his feet and went over to the library of thick, black books on the farthest shelf. She pulled out a large, leather-bound book, and then sat it down with a thump in front of Frypan.

"You may review this for as long as you like," she said. "We only ask that when you're finished, you bring it back. Here, to the Lineage Library."

Frypan looked down at the closed book, "Group A Trials" etched into the cover. He traced the text with his hand. "Thank you. I appreciate it."

Ximena squinted at the shelf from which the woman had grabbed the book and counted how many more there were. Over twenty. WICKED was truly wicked.

"Well?" Isaac looked at Frypan.

"Open it!" Jackie squeezed the Glader's arm lovingly and Jackie, Miyoko, and Isaac crowded over his shoulders as he opened the book of Group A's true history. Ximena couldn't help but peek over at the sacred artifact, too. The first page contained photos of teenage boys with numbers written under each of them. Old Man Frypan ran his hand along the grid of pictures while the faces of each Subject A stared back at him. His aged fingers then lingered atop the photographed face of his younger self.

3
MINHO

Remnant soldiers continued to chant for freedom as they rushed to the surface of Alaska's City of Gods. They wanted to find the Grief Bearers who'd held them down, kept them enslaved since their births. Minho trusted they would get the last of the war-itch out of their systems before he introduced them to the peace that awaited. Well, relative peace. They deserved the future of freedom they fought for, all of them.

He'd used every last bit of energy he could conjure up to lead the soldiers to their destiny, and he needed a minute. He wasn't yet ready to trade the safety of the Glade for the war-torn world above them. He was exhausted, utterly, and every breath became more difficult than the one right before it.

Orange knelt beside him in the grass. "Hang tight. Kit's getting a med pack, and he'll even bring the medic down if he can." He nodded, trying to say thank you with his eyes.

Dominic plopped down on his other side. "Hold on, buddy. We've still got a lot of stuff to do—you're gonna get better."

"Lots of stuff," Roxy agreed; she scooted closer to Minho.

Sadina sighed. "How are we supposed to do anything when the *Maze Cutter* is in flames and we're stuck here?"

Dom suddenly shouted, "Oh! That Berg in the woods!"

The kid finally remembered, Minho thought with a hidden smile.

"Berg in the woods?" Roxy asked, rubbing her wrists.

"Minho found it when he followed Alexandra." Dominic didn't seem bothered by the Pilgrims right behind him, worshipping every inch of the Maze with their own odd rituals.

Sadina looked hopefully at Minho. "So, you can take us to find my mom, my friends?"

He nodded. He knew Isaac would be waiting for him at the spot along the coast where they'd said their goodbyes and split up into groups. Isaac had made Minho promise that if things went south they'd meet back there, and in that moment and every moment since, Minho knew it would come to be. Not quite everything had gone south, but they'd meet there, anyway.

"A promise is a promise." Minho coughed up a bit of blood and closed his eyes. "Sadina?"

"Yeah?"

"Can you read me something from your book . . ."

"Absolutely. I know just the thing."

She cleared her throat and flipped to a certain page in the *Book of Newt*. She read aloud her favorite passage:

Even as the darkness whispers across my mind, beckoning with smoky tendrils of blackness and rot, even as I breathe in the stench of a dying world, even as the blood within my veins turns purple and hot, I feel the peace of a certain knowledge. I have had friends, and they have had me.

And that is the thing.

That is the only thing.

EPILOGUE

From the Sea to the Sky

I
ISAAC

Isaac walked to the tree line of the beach; he surveyed the damage from a recent storm until he found the fallen tree where he'd once carved a symbol for Sadina. He sat down and cleaned out the carved grooves with the knife that Minho had given him.

Ximena was nearby and walked over. "What's this mean?" She rubbed her finger over the roughly carved wood and sat down beside him.

"*From the sea to the sky*. Sadina and I used to say it when we were little, whenever we promised each other something." Isaac looked out at the ocean. Both the blue of the sea and the blue of the sky went on forever. Separately, but together. Considering Sadina left on the *Maze Cutter* and Isaac flew back to this spot in a Berg, he considered it a promise well kept. He knew she'd be returning to this beach soon. Very soon. He knew it.

Ximena looked out at the ocean as well. "I always wished growing up that we had lived near the coast."

"Yeah?" Isaac waited for her to say something profound, preferably in a different language. But she just stared at the ocean with a peaceful look in her eyes. "No second-sight?"

She shook her head.

"Nothing?" Jackie chimed in; she was gathering palm leaves and firewood.

"Stop. I just think it's nice here, the waves coming in and out like the lungs of the earth breathing. I think the Sequencers will like it here."

Jackie smirked at Isaac. "So, you *do* have an inner-knowing."

She shrugged. "I have hope that the truth won't stay hidden." After a few seconds that seemed a lifetime, she continued. "I've talked about my Abuela many times. But what I've never said is... Well, she was in the original Maze Trials. Group B."

No one responded. A hush that was almost sacred settled upon them, only broken by the crash and splash of the waves. Finally, finally, someone broke the reverence.

"Who was it?" Jackie asked.

Another pause. Isaac, as shocked as he was, wanted to tell her to hurry up and say it.

Tears came to Ximena's eyes. "She never told anyone her name after the new generation came along. She didn't want to be famous, always talked about. She... she's the greatest person I've ever known." More tears came, and Jackie hugged her, then the others. It was one of the sweetest moments Isaac could ever remember.

After a few more minutes of silence, he stood up and walked closer to the water. He stood in the same spot where he had said goodbye to Sadina and the others, and he felt the weight of everything he wanted to tell his friend. He felt the pain of all the death. He felt so much. Too much. Everything.

The waves crashed in. It would take time for the Sequencers to process the truth of their world and the world outside of theirs. That it was never about the Cure or even about the Flare. It was always about what those in control did to *remain* in control.

Ximena brushed against his hand and squeezed it just once. He looked at her and nodded. “Thanks.”

“It’ll be okay.” She looked over her shoulder and shouted, “Right, Frypan?”

“What’s that?” Old Man Frypan poked his head out from foraging.

“You think they’ll make the right decision?”

Erros added his two cents before Frypan could answer. “You gave the best testimonies you could. It’s up to the Senate and their vote now.” He smoked a coltsfoot cigar. “If they have any questions, we’ll answer them. All’s well that ends well.”

Old Man Frypan finally spoke his piece. “You never know. Some questions just don’t have answers.” He loaded the fire on the beach with the wood he’d foraged. “And some endings don’t make a lick of sense.” He pulled a long stick out of the flames before it could burn, then sat down to sharpen the end of it. “In fact, most endings don’t.”

2

Isaac stood in the sand. A Berg had just landed, and he had no doubt as to who was on the inside of it. There was a bang and a clank and a squeal. Then the ramp lowered from the bottom of the ship, hydraulics hissing, metal groaning. It took forever. An interminable amount of time. Seven or eight lifetimes. His patience had never been tested like this, despite all the crap he’d been through.

After what felt like forty-thousand years later, the ramp’s bottom edge finally thumped on to the ground. Someone was already halfway down it, sprinting at full speed. Isaac felt her body slam into his, felt her arms wrap around his neck, their momentum carrying them backward and backward, into the sand they toppled.

Isaac laughed.

End of Book Three

The #1 New York Times Bestselling Maze Runner Series From

JAMES DASHNER

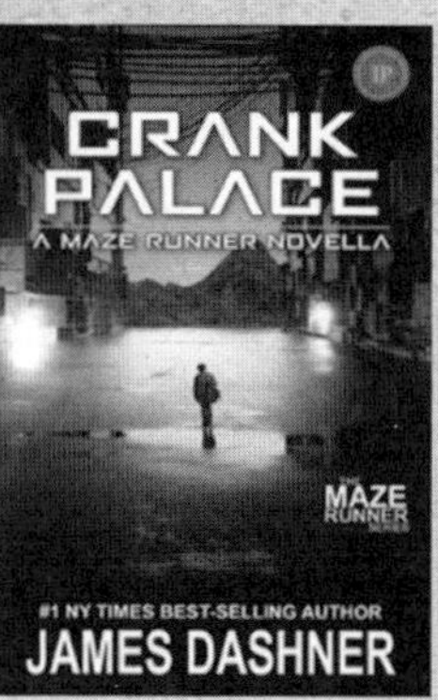

Published by Delacorte Press, an imprint of Random House Children's Books, and by Riverdale Avenue Books.

 **@JamesDashner**

 **@DashnerJames**

JamesDashner.com

ABOUT THE AUTHOR

James Dashner is the author of the #1 *New York Times* Bestselling *Maze Runner* series (movies by Fox/Disney) including *The Maze Runner*, *The Scorch Trials*, *The Death Cure*, *The Kill Order*, and *The Fever Code*, and the bestselling *Mortality Doctrine* series (*The Eye of Minds*, *The Rule of Thoughts*, and *The Game of Lives).* Dashner was born and raised in Georgia, but now lives and writes in the Rocky Mountains with his wife and their four children.

Join the #DashnerArmy for exclusive content and giveaways at JamesDashner.com